LASER-STROKE!

There came shrieking out of the darkness an LS 4 that leveled out above the highway, skimming meters above the people who began running and screaming with terror under the sudden blaze from the landing lights. Darenga turned abruptly and began running again down the center of the roadway that was cleared of people for these few minutes. She slowed as a pain struck her side, but she still pushed herself forward, head down, breath coming in noisy gasps as she turned off the highway onto the road that led up the long hill to the settlement. Now she slowed to a walk, knowing that she couldn't keep up her pace along that distance and stay conscious. And it was then that she heard the LS 4 seeping back. And she knew that this time they were using laser-stroke!

FRANCINE MEZO

NO EARTHLY SHORE

AVON
PUBLISHERS OF BARD, CAMELOT AND DISCUS BOOKS

NO EARTHLY SHORE is an original publication of Avon Books. This work has never before appeared in book form.

AVON BOOKS
A division of
The Hearst Corporation
959 Eighth Avenue
New York, New York 10019

First Avon Printing, March, 1981

Bind us in time, O Seasons clear, and awe.
O minstrel galleons of Carib fire,
Bequeath us to no earthly shore until
Is answered in the vortex of our grave
The seal's wide spindrift gaze toward paradise.

HART CRANE, "Voyages II"

Chapter 1

The door opened, and the dull light from the outer room fell across the bed and the man who lay sprawled, half-naked, on the cover.

"Lord Andor," the man in the doorway called softly. Receiving no answer, he left the door open and came up to the figure on the bed. The air in the room was heavy and cloying with hanj. The aide glanced at the empty pods on the bed table, then bent over and touched the bare shoulder. "I'm sorry to disturb you—"

Now the man on the bed turned his head and pulled his long hair away from his mouth. "What is it, Jacques?"

"The stations have picked up a Galaxy-class ship outside the Spinandre Fold."

The man on the bed pressed the heel of his hand against his eye, then hard down his cheek. "Spinandre Fold? Spinandre Fold?" he asked, his muffled voice stupidly repeating the words. "What are you talking about?"

"They think it's the 231."

"The 231 . . . ? Are they crazy? Tell them to check their damn computers." But he raised his head, groped forward to the stand beside his bed, knocked over a goblet half-filled with liquid onto the heavy polished top. "Clumsy . . . get the light, Jacques, will you, please?"

He sat up and watched as his aide mopped at the hanj pooling in the soft glow from the lamp. "That's all right. Don't worry about it." He raked his fingers into his hair and pressed his forehead into his palms.

"Would you like me to send for some stimulant?" Jacques asked.

The ends of the man's hair swung free of his shoulders as he slowly moved his head back and forth. "No, I'll be fine. What makes them think it's the 231? Have they communicated with it?"

"No. There's something wrong with the onboard equipment. The ship's deep-space communication system isn't working."

Andor Seldoldon looked up at his aide who stood quietly beyond the lamp with his face in shadow. "Then what the hell are they basing their opinion on?"

"Enough of the automatic ID code has come through to rule out Claufe's ship, and all the rest are accounted for."

"Even our Arcustan and Arkdikh pirates?"

"Yes, Lord Andor."

"Let me think a minute," Seldoldon told him. He stared into space. "How many people know about this?"

"The operator, the aide on duty, myself, and you."

"Then if we can't contact them, we can't take any chances: it could be Claufe."

"That could be a possibility."

"Everything's so shaky now . . . even a chance that Claufe is still alive could unite the factions against us."

His speech was thick and slurred, but Jacques saw that his mind had grasped the problem and was trying to deal with it. He moved out of the shadow of the lamp.

Seldoldon bowed his head back into his hands and sighed heavily. "I want absolute secrecy, Jacques, until we find out who's aboard. Arrange for a rotating watch in communications with our most trusted people. Has their course been plotted?"

"They're set toward the Triad."

He looked up. "Arrival time?"

"Thirty-eight days, twelve hours."

"Thirty-eight days." He came unsteadily to his feet, stood looking down at his aide expressionlessly. Then he turned his face away. "Eight years. What's happening?"

Jacques took a step forward and stopped, held by propriety.

"I've got to clear my head." Seldoldon moved away from him. "Notify DHO's advisors that I'll be at his quarters within the hour. And make it seem like a routine visit, will you?"

"I will. Shall I have breakfast sent up to you?"

"I'll go down to the dining hall later," he called from the bathroom.

He stripped, and then stood, swaying, against the open shower door. An arm reached past him, waved up the release. The water fogged out and the arm swiftly withdrew.

"Thanks," he murmured, and stepped down into the steam.

The ancestral home of Andor Seldoldon, known as the Gemainshaf Hall, housed the government of the planet Ronadjoun, first planet in the solar system of three named the Triad. It was also headquarters of the Systems' Alliance. The entire east wing of the massive stone building had been given over to the Alliance, and one section of that wing had been constructed as a life-support area for those members who were not oxygen breathers, or who required other mediums to exist.

The high ambassador of the Systems' Alliance, his hair still damp and hanging in a loose glossy wave to his shoulders, sauntered down one of the corridors of this section, a dark figure in traditional Ronadjounian brocade, the brown relieved only by the gold threads down the left side of his chest.

He entered a narrow passageway through a heavy door, and came to a glass-enclosed chamber with a sealed hatch. He pressed a bar and a Baaranic guard appeared in the darkness beyond the opposite side of the chamber. Two other guards entered with a box and set it into an alcove designed to receive it. They attached a thin net from a wall compartment to the exposed surface of the box, and then withdrew from the chamber, closing the seal on the door after them.

Seldoldon waited. Several minutes later, the captain of the guard signaled him; he nodded, and the door in front of him slid aside. He stepped into the chamber, into the swift fresh circulation of oxygen.

"May the gods rest in you, Andor."

"And in you, DHO."

There had been a scintillation along the network stretched over the box, which had sung in Seldoldon's skull like a woodwind, electrical impulses translated by the Implanted Translation Unit in his brain into sound.

"There was a sense of urgency in Jacques's message," the voice said.

"I'm not sure of the urgency. I have come for your advice."

"Whatever knowledge I have is at your disposal."

"I appreciate that. At the moment, DHO, this is the situation: the automatic deep-space stations have picked up what my people downstairs believe is the Galaxy 231 coming out of the Spinandre Fold area. Apparently the INGALCOM aboard the ship isn't operational, so we have no idea who's aboard. And we won't know for . . . well, the earliest would be nineteen days, if we intercepted them."

"Their course is for Ronadjoun, then?"

"The Triad, affirmed; presumably Ronadjoun."

"But Andor, you were a witness to the Fold collapsing on the 231 and on Claufe's ship. From your own account, and the recording devices of the Galaxy you were on, both ships were absorbed into the matrix."

"That *is* what I saw and the instruments recorded. I don't know how they could have escaped. The only reasonable, sane explanation we could arrive at downstairs was that the data were distorted by the matrix itself as it collapsed, and the one ship, anyway, stayed just ahead of it until they were clear and into the Spinandre Quincunx."

"And how did they get back on this side? Is there an explanation for that?"

"A new weir is forming; they managed to navigate it."

"I see." A brief silence, and then the voice inside his skull, "The possible danger is if Claufe's force somehow gained control of the 231."

"Exactly."

"I agree with your desire for secrecy. For the time being, at least. The conjecture alone that Claufe is alive could trigger dangerous confidence in some members of the Council. Another thing, if you are seriously considering sending out an intercepting force, I would ask you to think about the speculation that might create in the Council. The problems you already face might well be multiplied."

"It was a point I had some hesitancy about myself; thank you."

"Now what if Claufe has not survived, and this is the original crew?"

"We'd have to have solid proof of it. You know how Klote and Leend will reason. They'll take the possibility and explode it into a certainty, so they can convince everyone who floats around their camp that Claufe is still alive. It would be the rallying point that would draw in the more cautious of the faction, the ones who are preventing a complete rupture of the Alliance now. No, we'll have to wait until the ship is close enough for us to determine who is aboard. And take action accordingly."

"So, in either case, secrecy is primary for as long as it can be maintained."

The high ambassador sighed without meaning to, an exhalation of fatigue and strain. "Precisely, DHO."

There was an evaluative pause from the box, a pause during which Seldoldon dropped to a wall bench and sat with his forearms across his thighs, his hands clasped loosely between his knees as he stared at the floor.

"Do you have a list of the 231 personnel, Andor?"

"Yes, there's a list."

"There were two Maintainers aboard—two clones: Captain Darenga, of course, and a clone from the Beta House, if memory serves—"

"Bendi Felix."

"Yes, that's right, Bendi Felix, astronomer *par excellence*. Two rather vital components to successfully bringing a ship through the delicate maneuvers required in such a passage. But—" he went on as Seldoldon raised his head to speak "—the clones have a dependency on Longlife, and treatment cycles of ten years. Was the date of their next treatment on the records?"

"Yes. Bendi Felix had just completed a treatment." He looked down at his hands. "Captain Darenga was due for treatment in four years when they went into the Fold."

5

"So there is every possibility that Bendi Felix, barring accident or disease, is alive."

"Yes."

"But we must conclude Captain Darenga is dead."

"Yes."

"Who do you suppose was commanding the ship, Andor, in that incredibly delicate situation? Who of the 231's crew could have accomplished it? Or who—if we must consider the worst—of Claufe's crew would have the skill and experience of a Lambda clone?"

"These are questions I've been asking myself. I don't have any answers." He pressed his hands slowly together, staring at them, not seeing them.

"One of the Circle members with him, perhaps?"

As the Tremanic ambassador waited, Seldoldon gradually became aware of the silence, and that a response was expected. "I apologize; I didn't hear your question. What was it again?"

"Could one of the Circle members have piloted this ship?"

"No, none of them, as far as I know, could have commanded a space craft. They didn't have to; they had the Lambda clones for that."

"Yes, they did." A musing silence. "Original concepts can be noble," DHO began again. "And before their final corruption, the Circle had brought into existence a remarkable system that benefited many worlds."

"A system that required an army of clones to keep it from disintegrating. It wasn't noble; it was a horror."

"You accomplished a great deal through them, Andor."

"In spite of them. There was no freedom under the Maintainers. You forget that. Every movement we made was tracked by pattern control. Every cell in our bodies was monitored, analyzed, and recorded, and the information stored to ease their paranoia about treason."

"How do you define freedom, Andor? Unencumbered movement? Uncensored thought and speech? Both, perhaps?"

"Both, of course." Seldoldon gazed thoughtfully at the box which held a creature made up of the elements of its world, who, in its natural state, was linked with its fellow creatures and borne on the winds in chains hundreds of miles long. They gently filtered through their net the thoughts and experiences of the other beings of their world, filtered into their seine of knowledge every physical detail of their environment—these beings whose thoughts were guided by their leaders, yet who could freely add their own definitions, their individuality, to the reticulum of general knowledge.

And DHO, having seen the benefit of an alliance of worlds, had been unable to resist the lure of what was unknown and beautiful in a universe which was suddenly opened to him. He had disconnected himself forever from his species, to be confined, except for brief periods in the life-support section, to a box of one cubic foot. Seldoldon had often wondered if he ever regretted what he had done —this voluntary severance from everything familiar, everything cherished. Would DHO consider that act and its consequences "freedom"?

"I don't think we can arrive at a definition that would be satisfactory to all rational beings," Seldoldon replied.

"If we can speak to each other and understand, we can agree on definitions."

"Can we another time, DHO?"

A pulse of laughter. "Of course another time. Sometimes I fear the composition of my elements is changing."

"I grow old, too," Seldoldon replied, standing up. "I grow old."

"Your voice doesn't betray it. Only there is a great weariness."

"I am tired, DHO." The air blew fresh against his hair, the quiet circulation of air so vital to him, so deadly for the entity in the box.

"A weariness of body or spirit?"

It was a moment before Seldoldon answered. "Of spirit. And mind."

DHO replied slowly, there in the intimacy of Seldoldon's brain, "I feel acutely helpless at times, because in my world to alleviate is to engage. I wish to understand the source of your anguish, but, to my sorrow, you and I who are sentient and reaching toward each other, for us to physically contact would be for us to die. So we continue to grope in this mechanical way toward mutual understanding, toward . . . unity."

Seldoldon moved impulsively toward the box, stopped. "You've . . . been a good friend, DHO."

"We have been friends a long time." The brilliant little network synchronized in a thoughtful pattern. "May one who knows you well, and whom you consider a friend, speak to you directly?"

"Of course."

"There are certain members of the Council who have been speaking among themselves about the need for alcohol you seem less able to control these past few months. I perceive it as a minatory boldness, Andor, which will grow if it is fed."

"I know who they are, and their reasons. Need for alcohol! I have a little hanj—wine, sometimes. When has that interfered with alliance matters, or in the governance of my own planet? They have no legitimate complaints against me. They're trying to tie up soenderbiests with hairs, and no one's going to listen to them beyond their own little group. What I do in my own quarters is no one's business but my own."

"I respect your right to your own sorrows, but, as your friend, I must warn you that they are quite seriously looking for an opportunity to sever you from the alliance. Don't give it to them."

"I appreciate your warning." In the darkened glass of the far door, Seldoldon looked up to see himself, and turned away from the image. "Do . . . you want me to call the guard for you?"

"No, I can call them when you have cleared the chamber. We will be meeting again this morning in Council, won't we?"

"At nine." Seldoldon looked across at the box. "They're marshaling against us, DHO. I think Klote is going to be able to persuade the Council that Arcus is the best site for the freighter assembly."

"Unfortunately, I must agree. And, you must admit, it

is, logically, the most feasible location, if we don't consider the possible consequences. If we forget the vessels they have pirated and still have at their disposal."

"Yes, damn it. Democracy has a way of tightening the cord around its own neck."

"We've won concessions in the past. If it keeps the general peace, we have to lose sometimes as well."

"There may still be a chance. The memory of Claufe's war can't be that dim." He glanced toward the door he had entered. "I'd better go, or we'll start a rumor we'll be weeks trying to squelch."

"Good judgment and knowledge be your companions," DHO said in the way of Tremanic farewell that chooses the first part of the phrase to emphasize what the speaker wishes the listener to remember.

"They have always found me receptive," Seldoldon answered, and let himself out the door, carefully sealing it after him, looking back into the chamber at the metal box, that glittered randomly, now that he had left the room. In a moment the guards appeared, and Seldoldon went back up the hallway.

Chapter 2

Nearly all the members of the Systems' Alliance were in their places along the great semicircle that faced the rows of seats and the specially constructed perceiving stations for citizen-guests who required particular environments or sensing devices. The audience, for this session, was composed of a majority of Arcustans and Arkdikhs.

A packed house, Seldoldon thought grimly. He was in full regalia: umber brocade, a gold chain looping down from his left shoulder. He sat in the center position in a high broad-backed chair, and had just brought the Council to order.

"Today we'll be hearing testimony on the selection of a manufacturing location for the SOL 14. You should all have in front of you information units containing proposed sites with a full breakdown on costs, accessibility to all worlds and, specifically, numbers of systems that would be involved in material supply to each proposed location. You should also have a summary of all this information. Is there anyone who hasn't received these units?"

In the moment he waited to get a response, Jacques came to the side of his chair and, leaning down, whispered, "Nothing further, Lord Andor."

Seldoldon nodded, turned his attention back to the Council. "There has been exhaustive work done by the committee on this project, and I want to express my appreciation to them for finishing it with alacrity and thoroughness."

He waited for the murmurs of approval and agreement to die, and then said. "We'll now open for debate on the choice of site. Please, in the interest of expediency, confine your remarks to this purpose. Ambassador Klote. . . ."

The Arcustan ambassador's oval head dipped slightly on

her long neck, and then she spoke, in the clacking language of the Arcustans, from the opening at the base of her throat.

"Mr. High Ambassador, Members of the Council, the leaders of my planet are unanimously agreed to provide the entire Plain of Aukak as the location for this freighter assembly complex.

"Our planet already has numbers of skilled workers available who will not have to be retrained, since Arcus was one of the assembly points for shuttle craft when the Maintainers were still in power. There is a major city nearby—Klandt—with all the technological and cultural benefits that a metropolitan area provides. At this proposed location, there is an abundance of water for manufacturing purposes.

"The figures are there in your information units, Members. Arcus is in a central position for all the planets who have raw materials usable in this project. Consider that the total involvement for the Alliance will be twelve—*twelve* systems, which means over half the Alliance members will directly profit from a site used on Arcus. Consider also, Members, the time. From the moment of decision locating manufacture of the SOL 14 on my planet, we can guarantee a finished and fully operational craft in two years, much sooner than would be possible at any other site. I, and members of my staff, will answer any questions about these plans, and we have information units we will make available to any of you who want them."

"Mr. High Ambassador!"

Seldoldon looked down the curving row to his left. "Ambassador Oah."

"Two years! *Plonian* years, perhaps?"

There was a little ripple of appreciation along the crescent around him.

"Ah, what would Ambassador Klote have us believe? That an industrial complex of eight square miles is going to be erected, furnished, staffed, put into operation, and spuut! the finished product squirted from its doors in two years? I can understand her desire to have the complex in her system—don't we all feel the same?—but we can hardly proceed to an equitable decision, Mr. High Ambassador, if a member is going to misrepresent the ability to deliver."

Klote rose slowly from her chair, turning toward the Juangese ambassador. Her thousand-fiber digitals rippled where she held them just above the gleaming table surface. "Does he call me a liar?"

"I'm calling your statistics into question," the Juangese ambassador retorted. Behind him, his aides were rising from their places, watching the hands of the Arcustan, the deadly fibers that, if she were aroused to anger—always close to the surface in the Arcustan personality—would be flooded with poison.

"Sit down, Ambassador Klote," Seldoldon said calmly. "Ambassador Oah, if you're going to comment on the Arcustan statistics, you'll need their information unit first." He glanced at one of his aides. "See that the member receives a unit from the Arcustan ambassador, please."

Klote had lowered herself back into her seat, her eyes still on Oah. But when the aide approached her, she slid a unit toward him from the stack in front of her.

"Mr. High Ambassador, may I say something here? May I, if you please, say a word in *defense?*"

"By all means, Ambassador Arguns," Seldoldon answered. "Go right ahead."

"Thank you."

Arguns rose, looked all down the semicircle. His two silver breathing coils flashed solemnly in the light as he surveyed the Council. Liquid gurgled softly in the tubes.

"In defense, a few words. We all understand the necessity of the freighters. For centuries the Maintainers, laboring under the illusion that they were the only judges of what was right for all of us—although the few who are left have certainly earned our confidence and gratitude for the services they have performed for us under the guidance of Ambassador Seldoldon—" he bowed elegantly to Seldoldon, whose only response was complete impassivity "—for centuries the Maintainers controlled all space and all craft. Their primary transport at speeds that were practical was the Galaxy-class vessel. And, having inherited this means of transportation, so to speak, we have found that this ship is too large, too cumbersome for our needs—that is, for simple transport of material between planets and between systems."

Arguns made a slow rolling motion, first to one side and then to the other, a thoughtful pacing movement. Everyone watched and listened closely, even though they all knew completely the information he was going over.

"What we needed was an SOL capability craft with the moderate size necessary to land on a planet, pick up a reasonable load, and depart. A craft that would not require the added step of transporting from surface to orbit to ship. And so we designed our freighter—" he interrupted himself as Seldoldon turned to give him a long look "—I will be brief, Mr. High Ambassador. Brief. My point is that we are *all* eager, *eager* to see a fair solution. But our reason should prevail.

"Certainly the Juangese ambassador heard the member from Arcus say that her planet had been an assembly point during the Maintainer era; and hearing that, perhaps it skipped his mind that the enormous plant and all its machinery, all the equipment, the computers, the *extremely* specialized knowledge of the personnel engaged at that facility, all are still available there. The months—nay, the *years* involved in setting up a new plant would be many! Perhaps two years was a *small* exaggeration; still, the time wasted in construction at any other site would be cut in half on Arcus, cut two-thirds, if I may. All this is in the information unit of the committee on SOL site location and, as I see you're viewing now, Ambassador Oah, the Arcustan package."

Arguns leaned back from his orator's posture with a thick congenial murmur through his pipes, as he looked with great deliberation on the Juangese ambassador, who had been forced by both Seldoldon and Arguns to make a show of looking at it.

"We all want what is best for all our peoples," Arguns began again, with a delicate and solemn drizzle of liquid through the elaborate breathing apparatus, a mannerism

14

which sent Seldoldon shuffling through the papers in front of him to hide the laughter he was trying to suppress.

The beings of all the Alliance had been part of his life for all his life, and the peculiarities of each, like the peculiarities of homo sapiens, had been accepted by him for what they were—differences. But Arguns had always affected him this way because the natural behavior of the Laotanarians was, bizarrely, a parody of every human characteristic that evoked humor. He had to remind himself over and over that Arguns was far from being a fool, that he was one of the most influential members of the Alliance, commanded respect from every member, and had a probing and resourceful intelligence. Still, Seldoldon was powerless to react to him in any other way.

The argument went on all day, divided, as Seldoldon had expected it would be, between the planets Juang and Arcus. Late in the afternoon, just before Seldoldon adjourned for the day, Jacques came up to his chair again and quietly informed him, "Roenay of Mont Clair would like to speak with you before going up to visit our abbey. Assuming your approval, I had him taken to your quarters."

Seldoldon nodded. "Did he give you any indication of what he wants to see me about?"

"He has been to Amper to see the Bishop."

"I see. Same old complaint. Well, nothing's going to be settled here today. Tell him I'll be along in fifteen minutes or so."

When Seldoldon entered his quarters, the Abbot of Mont Clair and two accompanying monks rose to greet him.

"It's good to see you again, Father. Sorry I took so long to get down here. Leaving a Council meeting is almost as hard as getting one together."

"No matter, we enjoy looking over your collection." He made a gesture that included the floor-to-ceiling bookcases that filled the walls.

"You know you're welcome to any of them."

"You've said so before, and I've taken advantage of it and will again."

"Anytime. Please—sit down." Seldoldon included the two monks in his invitation, and dropped into one of the big chairs near the windows as Roenay nodded to the monks and then seated himself.

"I understand you're on your way back from Amper, Father."

"Yes, I had a meeting with the bishop."

Seldoldon nodded politely. "How is he? I haven't seen him in some months."

"He is well. But concerned with the problems a big city fosters."

"Oh? Have there been some unusual problems?"

"Where there are beings of different worlds brought together in a human environment, yes, you might say the problems are unusual. And there are humans in Amper who have profited from the propensities of these beings."

"I think the city officials have tried to deal with that problem, Father."

"But not with any great enthusiasm. I suspect it brings money into the city. But I find the problem invading my own district."

"In Canigou?"

"We're a small, provincial area, Lord Andor, and we have no intention of allowing the kind of relationships between species that goes on in the back alleys of Amper. And we are particularly sure we are not going to have it between humans and aliens."

"Are you talking about a specific incident?"

"Yes. A group of Arcustan females came into Canigou last week and made their approaches to one or two of our townsmen. They were rejected, of course, but not without an unpleasant scene."

"Were they Arcustans attached to the Hall, or visitors?"

"I have no way of knowing that."

"The aides carry identification. But go on, tell me what happened." Nothing serious, Seldoldon understood, but he shuddered inwardly at the potential danger had the Arcustan temper been aroused.

"They were asked to leave, which they did, but not without threatening gestures. Lord Andor, our community

16

will not tolerate this kind of behavior, and the majority of citizens on this planet deplore the desire of aliens to have this kind of intimacy with humans. It is against nature, and it is against God."

"Well," Seldoldon said after a pause, "I'm sorry there was this incident in Canigou. I'll find out what I can about it, and inform Ambassador Klote's office. I'll pass along what information I get to you." He sat back in his chair and crossed his legs. "These incidents are rare, Father, extremely rare on a world that is headquarters for twenty-two solar systems."

"And we fully intend to keep it that way, Lord Andor, with all respect to you. I'm not the only one on the planet concerned; with a few exceptions, every abbot in the districts feels the same. Since before the Time of Exile, this question was debated and prayerfully considered, and the ruling was that there was to be no intimacy between humans and beings of other worlds. And we will continue to honor that ruling, Lord Andor, all of us—from the Bishop to the last parishioner."

"I understand that, Father. And, as I said, I will look into it."

"Thank you," the abbot replied, rising.

Seldoldon came to his feet with the monks.

"We must go, I'm afraid."

"Jacques told me you'll be staying on the hill," Seldoldon said as they walked to the door.

"Don't bother seeing us out," Roenay told him quickly, raising his hand. "Yes, we'll stay at the abbey overnight, and leave for Canigou early tomorrow morning."

"Well, have a pleasant trip," Seldoldon replied, and, with a vague feeling of frustration, watched them to the end of the hallway, and then turned back to his rooms.

Chapter 3

The evening rain had passed over the Hall, leaving only the diminishing fall of water from the deep casements of the windows. Seldoldon poured the last of the hanj from the pod on the side table and rose, glass in hand, from the chair he had been slumped in for the past two hours, and walked over to the windows to look out.

The shrubs and flowers and grass were all lit from the glowing windows of the Hall, and shimmered in the slight and steady breeze off the ocean. Far down the hill, and intermittently visible through the distant moving leaves, lay the Gemainshaf village. Seeing those lights, Seldoldon suddenly turned and went into his bedroom.

He changed from his brocade into a pair of dark, loose-fitting trousers and a white, opened-necked shirt with broad sleeves. He dropped his chain of office into a cushioned box and slid on a bracelet of carved and intricately linked gold, which he absently ran around and around his wrist as he gazed toward the windows.

When he had finished off the glass he had left on the table, he summoned Jacques.

"I'm going down to the village," Seldoldon told him, anxious now to get away. "I'll be there for a few hours. Anything new downstairs?"

"No," Jacques answered, disturbed at Seldoldon's manner and dress. "They've increased their speed slightly, but the difference is less than an hour earlier than the time I quoted you."

Seldoldon nodded. "I'll either be at the Little Farmyard or at Alain Vachon's place."

"Are you walking?"

"Yes," Seldoldon answered cheerfully, ignoring the strain in his aide's voice. "Nice evening for it, don't you think?"

"My lord—"

He turned to look at Jacques, his expression mild, his dark eyebrows slightly raised.

Jacques retreated. "The rain did freshen the air."

"Maybe it will do the same for me."

"Yes sir," Jacques replied.

Seldoldon came out onto the portico and stood for a moment at the top of the wide stone stairs, breathing the oncoming night as he looked down toward the village. Then he set out, taking the steps quickly and lightly and leaving a dull silver trail across the beaded lawns. He walked the road below the hill with his arms swinging freely, buoyed up, lifted by the clearness of the night, his mind suddenly released.

At the intersection of the Hall road and Abbey Hill, he turned away to the lower fork, moving more slowly as he followed the bend in the road around the copse of talfa that obscured the backward view. Still, by the time he had reached the clutch of buildings that announced the village, his earlier depression had lifted, in some measure caused by the lights of the Little Farmyard and the quick glassy chime of the tympanon.

"Qui dit non quand je dis oui?" he began singing as he neared the door. *"Qui dit oui quand je ne pourrai plus?"*

"Hey!" came a shout from inside.

"Alain Vachon!" Seldoldon called out as he came through the door. "I always know where the hell to find you!"

Three men were rising from a table against the wall. One, a stocky man with a chest like a bull, came over to where Seldoldon had paused at the bar. "Give them whatever it is they're drinking," Seldoldon told the grinning tavern keeper. "I'll have a bottle of Renaud Cabernet."

"On my mother's life, we were just talking about you," Vachon said.

"Complaints or credits? Here, I'll take it," he told the keeper as he started to put the bottle of wine on a tray. Seldoldon pulled over three beakers of wine the tavern keeper had poured. "Alain, give me a hand with these."

"I will!" Vachon locked his thick fingers through the

handles and came alongside Seldoldon as he headed for the table. "You walk down here?"

"Yes, I walked."

"Ehh!" Vachon grunted. "Are we going to make a night of it?"

"On your mother's life, Alain. That's why I'm here."

Seldoldon sat with his back against the timbered corner of the booth, listening to Serge Robitaille.

"So in all of Brouage, who was there to bring the flatboat down the Wyamette? Robitaille, that's who. So I did it, là! là!"

"Eh, what a liar," said Pierre Dorlat, closing one eye as he labored to focus the other. "The whole world knows the flatboat caught the current and brought itself in."

Robitaille's handsome face lit up with an expression of surprise. "What? Are you saying I wasn't heroic?" He grinned at Seldoldon. "Tell him whose idea it was to take the grain down the Wyamette when the roads were impassable. Tell old thubes and knicks who kept bread on the Gemainshaf tables when the waters were floating beans through his windows." Robitaille laughed and knocked Dorlat's hand out from under his chin.

Seldoldon made a quick grab to pull the wine beaker out of the way as Dorlat's head came down. "He's got you, Pierre. It was his idea."

"Don't take my wine away, my sweet lord," Dorlat said, reaching out for the beaker. "It's all that keeps me from puking."

"Why? Because I'm a hero? You should feel privileged to have me as a friend."

Vachon, who had been listening quietly, set his beaker down and crossed his thick, hairy arms on the table as he leaned forward. "Robitaille, you got out in the middle of the stream and lost the goddamn tiller. For three miles, you were hanging onto the splinters at the bottom of the boat while the thing went around like a carousel. You were so goddamn sick, when the boat hit the bank at Lac l'Orange, they had to carry you off."

Seldoldon tilted his head back against the booth and laughed uproariously.

"I wasn't that sick," Robitaille replied with a frown, and then with a white flash of teeth, grinned as they sat laughing at him. "Well, they didn't need a litter, anyway, là! là!"

He looked around at the glasses. "Whose turn is it to buy?"

"Yours!" they all said together.

Robitaille drew back, flinging up his hands. "I'm such a good fellow," he said, and got up and went over to the bar.

"Good fellow!" Dorlat snorted and put his glass to his mouth. He gave it a puzzled look and sighed. "Every time I pick up this glass it's empty."

Seldoldon looked over at Vachon. "What are you planting in that section south of your sheds?"

"I'm trying hemn grass. They had some good results with it at the experimental station at Pier."

"I'd think the rainfall would be a little high here for hemn grass. Pier's about four inches drier than we are."

"I don't know. They asked me if I'd grow some on shares, and I told them sure, I'll give it a try. If it works, we'll have some good fiber." He glanced up as Robitaille set four beakers on the table.

"What the hell is this?" Seldoldon asked, looking down into the glass.

"Try it."

"What's Bernard pushing off on you?" Vachon said dourly, staring into the liquid.

Dorlat drew the beaker over and smelled it noisily. "He probably got it at half-price."

"Go ahead, Lord Andor," Robitaille said with a disgusted look at Dorlat. "See if you recognize it."

"If I'm going to put the lining of my stomach in jeopardy, I want it worth my while," he answered. He lay his left arm over his knee where he had it drawn up on the bench, and rested the fingertips of his right hand lightly against the glass, as if he were sensing the vibrations in the liquid.

"Eh!" Vachon sat up. "Dump out your pockets, Robitaille. What have you got to put up against Lord Andor's palate?"

"You're betting you can guess?" Robitaille asked, straddling the bench and leaning toward Seldoldon.

"It wouldn't be a guess."

"Oh, ho! Well, let's see. What have you got to bet?"

"You mean, how many pièces?"

"I don't know. Wait a minute, là! là!" He stood up and dug into his pockets, searched through his wallet. "Thirty pièces?"

Dorlat snorted. "You're so goddamn cheap."

"What else have you got?" Seldoldon asked.

"My chronometer." He pulled it out and looked down at it. "It has a barometer readout."

"What do you have around your neck?"

"A Saint Anne of Quebec."

"Is it blessed?"

"Of course!"

"Want to put it up?"

"With the thirty pièces?"

"No, just the medal."

Robitaille considered. "All right. Sure. Wait a minute. What's your ante in this?" He took off the necklace, set it on the table and covered it with his hand. "My medal is worth—fifty pièces in money, much more in sentimental value."

"How much more?"

"Come on, Robitaille, put a price on it," Vachon told him.

"Hundred and fifty."

"My ass!" said Dorlat.

"That's all right. I'll accept that," Seldoldon said. He slipped his bracelet off his wrist and swayed it in the air briefly for Robitaille to see, then let it fall in a pile of gold next to the silver chain and medal.

Robitaille's eyes went wide. "This is theft, là! là!" he breathed.

"Not if I win," Seldoldon told him, with a glitter in his eyes that he was too slow subduing.

Robitaille gave him a suspicious look. "Did you see Bernard pouring from the bottle?"

Seldoldon held up both his hands. "On my honor."

"What's the matter, Robitaille?" Dorlat laughed. "Afraid of losing your very expensive Saint Anne?"

Robitaille glanced at him and back at Seldoldon. "All right, but let's agree on the terms."

"Name them."

"You're too damn agreeable."

Seldoldon laughed. "Quit stalling. Name your terms."

"I'm not stalling, là! là! All right. You have to identify it: the variety of grape, what winery, what year."

"And name all the little toes that crushed the grapes," Vachon said drily.

Seldoldon's head went down on his arms, his hair covering the sleeves. "Alain—" he shook his head "—would you let us get on with this?"

"Robitaille doesn't believe in hedging a bet."

"I'm not hedging it. Well, do you agree?"

"Fine with me," agreed Seldoldon. "Do you want to add any more terms?"

"Now I know you're bluffing."

"You think I'm bluffing?"

"Let's see you name it. Go on, identify. The name, the grape, the winery, the year."

Seldoldon smiled, lifted the glass, held it to the light, swirled it gently beneath his nose. His eyes met Robitaille's over the glass. "Tokay," he said.

"Tokay!" yelped Dorlat. "Are you trying to poison us!"

"Give him credit," Seldoldon said calmly. "It's good wine. In fact," he swirled the liquid with a delicate motion, "it is the Pont Rouge variety—"

"You haven't tasted it!"

"Oh? Was that in the terms? If you insist." He took a sip and, with great deliberation, let it flow over the surface of his tongue, touch the roof of his mouth. He swallowed gracefully. "Manseau Winery at Trudeau, year . . . 3037."

"Bravo!" cried Bernard from the bar and, reaching below the counter, held up the bottle for everyone to see.

Seldoldon gave him a gracious nod, and then sat smiling at Robitaille.

"How did you do that?"

"Just because you can't tell the difference between port

and lemonade. . . ." Dorlat said. He took a dainty sip from his beaker, and then a long swallow. He grimaced. "Too damn sweet. Unnh!"

Seldoldon slipped his bracelet back over his wrist, picked up the silver medal and held it in his palm. "For about five years, when I was a lot younger, I spent my summers in the vineyards at Renaud. You learn more than how to pick grapes when you work at a winery."

"Well, I guess you did, that's for certain. Go on, it's yours," Robitaille told him. "It was a fair bet. Wear it in good health. The Bishop of Amper blessed it himself."

Seldoldon sat with it in his hand for a minute, then reached out to grasp Robitaille's wrist. He dropped the medal into his hand. "I wouldn't want to be the cause of you falling into sinful ways, Robitaille," he said with a grin. "I'm the one who told Bernard to stock that wine."

"What? What?" cried Robitaille, ignoring the laugh from the bar.

Vachon and Dorlat groaned.

Dorlat said, "You had us going, **Lord Andor.**"

"I believed him," Vachon said.

Both men started laughing.

"Eh!" exclaimed Vachon. "Robitaille, you'd better pray to Saint Anne for humility. She's not going to be so quick to intercede for you anymore."

"But wait! But wait! The bet's still good, là! là! Didn't he as much as say he couldn't have met the terms if he hadn't known ahead of time?"

"Come on, greedy *cochon*," Dorlat said. "He was playing a joke on you."

"No, he's right," Seldoldon said. He took off the bracelet, and when Robitaille hesitated, he dropped it into his beaker of wine. "That will give you time to think about it," he said cheerfully. "Just don't swallow it."

"There's a reason for you to drain your cup," Vachon said.

"Take your thirty pièces now, and buy us something we can drink," Dorlat said to Robitaille. "This *merde*'s too sweet."

"Never mind, this one's on me," said Seldoldon.

Chapter 4

The tympanon had been playing steadily for some time, and a crowd had gradually filled the tables. Seldoldon, numbed and mellow, sat leaning against the booth, his foot tapping lightly on the bench as he tried to follow the conversation of Robitaille who, for some inexplicable reason, had let his sentence trail off. Seldoldon brought his eyes back into focus and found Robitaille staring beyond his shoulder. Vachon and Dorlat were staring in the same direction.

Seldoldon laid his head back and looked up at the dark smoky timbers of the ceiling. "What does she look like?" he asked. "Describe her."

"Ahhh," replied Robitaille.

Seldoldon looked over at him. "You can do better than that."

"Hair like ripe barley in the late afternoon sun."

"Ripe barley! A poet here!"

"Skin like milk."

"Cliché, cliché."

"She's alone."

"Know her?"

Robitaille shook his head. "She's not from around here. Look at her clothes, là! là!"

"Amper," Dorlat pronounced. "Pretty women are always from Amper."

Seldoldon turned casually around, saw the woman sitting quietly at a table, looking dreamily ahead, her pale blonde hair floating around her head in soft coils; skin, indeed, like milk. "Earth," he said, and resumed his position against the timber.

"What?"

"She's from Earth—Northern Hemisphere, probably Scandian Province."

"Excuse me," said Robitaille.

"Of course," Seldoldon replied. After a moment or two had passed, he asked, "How's he doing?"

"The sucker's sitting at her table," Dorlat said, and sighed.

Seldoldon looked up from his glass. He had been talking with Vachon, who had curiously faded away, and who was now approaching from the direction of the bar. Dorlat sat with his elbows spread on the table, his head wobbling as he blinked at a point somewhere in the middle of Seldoldon's chest, and Seldoldon wondered if he was waiting for him to say something, or if Dorlat was the one who was supposed to be speaking.

Seldoldon blew air from his cheeks. "I'm going outside," he told Vachon, who had reappeared at the table. He stood up. "I need to go outside."

"Fresh air helps," Vachon replied. He put his arm across Dorlat's shoulder. "Poor ol' Pierre needs air, too." He grinned. "Some air for Pierre."

"Right. He can't go to sleep in here. Wake him up."

"Wake up, Pierre. We're going to get some air. Air for Pierre. Pierre will have some air."

And, chanting this, Vachon and Seldoldon hauled Dorlat, grumbling, to his feet, and managed to get him out the door.

"I'd better take him home," Vachon said. "He's drunk."

Seldoldon looked down at the man dangling between them. "That's reasonable," he said.

"I'm going to take him to my place. His wife will be madder than hell if he comes in this way." He giggled. "She'll be madder than hell at me, too; I went out there and got him this evening."

"But Alain, what's she going to say if he doesn't come home at all?"

They stood there, considering this.

"Why don't you go with me?" Vachon said brightly. "She won't pop off at you."

"Oh, wouldn't she? No, you're not getting me into this. You brought him out here, Alain, you take him back."

Vachon grunted. "I don't think much of it, but I guess I'd better do it."

"That's the idea."

"Come on, Pierre." Vachon heaved a noisy sigh. "Come on, walk; I can't carry you all the damn way."

Seldoldon chuckled to himself as they reeled away, and then he turned back toward the tavern, swaying, trying to hold the light from the doorway and windows steady. But they kept crawling across his field of vision. "Time to go home," he told himself. He took a few steps, veered off down the road.

He made his way slowly along, glancing up now and then at the dim sky shining above the wheeling branches of the trees, as he tried to keep his bearings on the dark road. When the trees began to thin out, he halted abruptly and stared up at the stars. "Eight years," he said. "And who's left? Who's out there? Dear God!" he cried out, *"I want to know!"*

He reached the road bordering the sloping lawns of the Hall, where he took a narrow pathway that led up and around the hill and along the rear of the great building, passing around the wings to the north side, and a stairway that curved up to the third floor.

He climbed to the balcony landing and fumbled with the handles of the glass doors. "Locked," he muttered. "Damn thing's locked."

He negotiated the stairs again, and with difficulty made his way around the side of the building and up onto the portico. For a moment he stood swaying in the shadow of a pillar, frowning at the light that streamed out from the wide portal, then he straightened, breathed deeply once or twice, and, in the momentary clarity, walked forward into the Hall. And, once having started across the stones, was committed to his course and could not retreat when he saw the party advancing on him. And so Klote, Arguns, and Tren met Seldoldon in the middle of the room.

"So Jacques did find you," Klote said.

"Was he looking for me?"

"We're trying to call an emergency session," Tren said brusquely, sizing up the situation immediately. "The 26 has encountered one of the pirate vessels near Vrega. It appears disabled. Captain Tendrow wants permission to capture."

"Well, we'll need to call an emergency meeting," Seldoldon said, trying to follow him.

"Yes, that's what he told you." Klote's head swayed on her long neck as she scrutinized him.

Seldoldon heard someone running up the portico steps, and he thought *That's Jacques.* To Klote, whose steady hard gaze annoyed him, he said, "Imagine that—a disabled pirate ship. Tell me, Ambassador, how are you going to vote?"

Klote's head became suddenly still. Her voice was a hard clatter. "Just what are you saying, Lord Andor?"

Jacques had come up swiftly next to Seldoldon, and now stood staring at the Arcustan ambassador.

"What am I saying? I'm saying I want to know who the traitors are—the ones who supported Claufe, the ones who caused the war. They all have names, and I want to know them—"

There was an immediate heavy silence. Then Jacques moved forward at the same time Tren cantered ahead, both of them repositioning themselves between Seldoldon and Klote. Her arms shot up, the fibered digitals held directly in front of her. Jacques shrank inward but held his place, his eyes on her digitals. A shiver rippled over the heavy muscles in Tren's body, and his hooves raised nervously, but he remained in front of Seldoldon.

"Stand away!" Seldoldon commanded, angry now.

"I don't think we want this." Arguns moved up beside Klote, where she could see him but where he would be a safe distance from her.

Klote said nothing. Her small eyes stayed rooted on Seldoldon's face.

"We have more important affairs to attend to, Ambassador Klote," Tren said, his body motionless.

No one dared move but Seldoldon, who, under the long-burning anger released now by the alcohol and these circumstances, started to go around Tren, but was pinned back by Jacques, who turned to grab him. "Please, Lord Andor."

Klote made a sudden rasping sound in her throat and lowered her arms. "Let him go," she told Jacques as she swung away. "There's no honor in victory over a person who is not in control of his senses."

Tren danced sideways into Seldoldon as he pulled free of Jacques and started after Klote, shouting, "I know Claufe's supporters!"

"Get yourself together, Andor," Tren ordered in a grating tone, as Klote moved toward the far door, where two Arkdikh aides and some members of the Dendom group stood watching, a small crowd at their backs.

"I'm all right," Seldoldon answered, pulling down the cuffs of his wide sleeves, straightening himself. "Everything's all right."

"For once, Andor," Tren replied, turning his large and bristling muzzle toward the slowly dispersing figures, "you are very wrong."

Chapter 5

Seldoldon had awakened horrified that he could have been so out of control as to have said what he had to Klote, and in the presence of half the Council. Jacques was at his door even before he was out of bed, with the intelligence that the Executive Council was meeting to consider censure proceedings against him.

"They're not wasting any time," Seldoldon said. And it had all been for nothing, because while they had been standing in the entrance hall the disabled ship had made its recovery and gotten away. "Who gets to play this scene?" he asked Jacques. "Klote? Leend?"

Jacques glanced briefly away and then back to Seldoldon's face. "Ambassador DHO."

Seldoldon was in his office when the official notification was brought to him by the commanding officer of the Baaranic Guard, an indication not only of his position in the Alliance, but of the gravity of the charge.

He accepted it with dignity and then sat white-faced in his chair after the officer had left. *They're going to do it,* he thought, stunned. *They're really going to do it.*

He had thought about it for several days, what he was going to say, and found he could not assemble any defense. And now he sat in his office, his chair turned toward the window, his head bowed, when Jacques entered.

"Lord Andor," he said, coming around to the side of the desk, "we've just received a communication from Captain Wiley. She suggests that you give her permission to reactivate pattern control, so the personnel aboard the Galaxy 231 can be identified."

Seldoldon stared at him in utter amazement.

33

It had never occurred to him. In his anxiety and apprehension and the wild hope he had choked down inside him, it had never crossed his mind that he held the instrument that could answer his questions. Pattern control had been so long a symbol of tyranny, and so long in disuse, he had never even thought of it. Now he was frantic to have it put into operation.

"The discs are in the vault in a small box behind the Gemainshaf Chronicles. Get one up to her, for god's sake!"

He had lain awake all night, had heard the distant offices of the monastery being rung, and the bells begin their announcement of prime when Jacques finally came to his door. Seldoldon let him in and watched as he pulled a long tape and a sheet of paper from his pocket case.

"Here's the pattern control readout, and the final boarding list."

"Let's see it," Seldoldon told him.

Jacques gave him the tape and the paper, and then quietly moved to the window and stood looking out at the lawns that lay bright and steaming in the early morning sunlight. Behind him, Jacques could hear the tape sliding through Seldoldon's fingers. The sound stopped.

"M'dians?"

Jacques looked back at him. "Three hundred eleven. Their names are also on the list."

"All from Ilanu, it seems. None from any other town. This is . . . puzzling."

Jacques turned again to the window, but was intent on the sound behind him. And then there was no sound, only a deep and lengthy silence. Jacques looked down to where his fingertips balanced on the wide and spotless window sill.

Seldoldon's low voice came to him. "Well, we know it's not Claufe."

Jacques composed his features, turned around to face him. "No, thank god for that."

Another silence while Seldoldon stared at the tape. "Is . . . there any explanation for this unidentified person?"

"Only that it's human. What Captain Wiley was able to

34

read of the pattern." His own voice now was brisk, informative, as if he would draw Seldoldon up with its vitality. "It was incomplete."

"Why?"

"She doesn't know, except that it's not a malfunction in the equipment."

Seldoldon stared at the thick rug at his feet. The tape rested between his fingers. "The days have run together, Jacques, what's their arrival time now?"

"Ten days."

Seldoldon exhaled slowly. "At least we'll have the censure proceedings out of the way by that time. Then the opposition can start all over again."

At the end of three days, Seldoldon came before the full Council.

There was a sudden hush as Seldoldon came down the long aisle toward the semicircle of ambassadors and stopped. He stood waiting for acknowledgment from the glittering box mounted to the left of the vacant center chair. His aides fell back, but only a few paces: the instinctive desire to defend.

The random light tracings began a pattern that translated itself in Seldoldon's brain, as it was being translated to every being in the room.

"Members of the Council," DHO began. "It is said that it is easier to forgive a common citizen a felony than to excuse a great man a simple breach of etiquette. And what, at first, seems grossly overbalanced and unfairly demanded, upon examination is shown to be not only proper, but necessary for the survival of society, for while the bad act of a common citizen is against the moral and spiritual laws of his society, it is an act that affects a small circle of his fellow creatures; the bad act of a great man affects his time.

"To accept the title of leader is to take vows as solemn as any vow made by a religious. It is a dread responsibility, and in taking it, we relinquish all claims we may have had on the seclusion and anonymity that the ordinary citizen enjoys. If we have difficulties in our private lives, they must be suppressed. If there are appetites that would overtake us, they must be severely checked. If there are weaknesses of any kind, they must be overcome so we may protect and preserve the quality of our leadership for the beings who have given us their charge and, indeed, entrusted the safety of their lives to our ability and our clear judgment.

"When any one of our number seems to have failed in this trust, then we are obligated to bring that one to an accounting, no matter what his position. Therefore, today the Council has called Andor Seldoldon before it to censure him for improper and discreditable conduct."

In spite of his self-control, when Seldoldon heard this tears sprang into his eyes. He brought his head up, continued to look at DHO.

There was an uncomfortable silence, then DHO's voice again. "If you would like to address this body, please do so."

Unable to stop the trembling of his mouth, Seldoldon lowered his head for a moment and then looked up. "Thank you, yes," he quietly replied.

He had had a lifetime in the practice of effective rhetoric, in the proper balance of the rational, the emotional, the ethical appeals, but apart from the trained voice, the instinct for the proper words and phrases, he was unrehearsed and unprepared.

"Ambassador DHO, members of the council, I accept and understand the reasons for your disapproval of my conduct. I wish to make an apology now to Ambassador Klote for my reprehensible behavior to her, and to express my gratitude for her restraint in the face of my unprovoked remarks. I am sorry."

He remained quietly standing, waiting to be dismissed, having said all there was for him to say.

"Let the censure of Andor Quij Seldoldon be recorded in the proceedings of the Council," said DHO. "You are released."

Seldoldon turned, his body erect, his step measured. His aides grouped about him instantly, their faces grim, as they accompanied him to the door and out past a long line of the curious, who drew apart as he came through.

They continued through the east wing and down the deserted corridor that led to his rooms. He had no other thought than to reach his door and the safety beyond it, and was relieved that his aides slowed halfway down the hallway to leave him free to enter his quarters alone.

He made it into his bedroom and fell across the bed sweating, cold, numb. It was several minutes before he slowly turned over on his back and raised his arms to shield his eyes from the light from the windows.

He carried on his duties with the Alliance as he had before. No one mentioned the censure proceedings; the universal discretion of sentient beings. But there was an undercurrent, an attitude that was a witness to his growing ineffectuality, so he performed mechanically, automatically, and with a deadness inside him that expanded hour by hour. He avoided everyone, beyond the contact necessitated by his office.

The decision for the disposition and explanation of the spaceship, that had now entered the Triad, he placed on DHO; he was indifferent now. No, not indifferent—without energy, without will to even begin to approach the problem. There seemed nothing left, no resources to draw on.

He had gambled his life on a secret acceptance of Long-life treatment, in order to guide the Alliance through the difficulties he had foreseen. Gambled and gained forty years in the prime of his life, the irony being his resistance to the treatments. He would die at the end of his normal lifespan, but not gracefully or with dignity, but in pain and insanity. He had thought the price was worth it. But he had anticipated nothing of what happened in the intervening years, least of all his own fallibility. That least of all.

Chapter 6

The Council room was in an uproar. Seldoldon had expected a disagreeable response to the sudden appearance of the 231, but the magnitude of it surprised him. However, it was hardly a surprise that the members already hostile to him would immediately and illogically link the secrecy he had imposed on the Galaxy return to his recent censure. The references to it were oblique, but they were there. Even those members who were generally sympathetic, who always were at least objective about his ideas and proposals, were silent. They did not join the others led by Leend, Klote, and Arguns, but they did not speak on his behalf, either. And he realized that he had seriously miscalculated, that he had taken too much for granted, that he had relied too heavily on his ability to persuade. This time it was not going to work. He was particularly disturbed that, of all the members who should have been excited, Klote was calm and quiet-voiced, and he knew it was because she sensed a victory. It made him uneasy. He would rather have dealt with her anger.

But there was more than enough dissatisfaction and indignation, and he and DHO found themselves struggling to hold some kind of order until Tren could get the conofficer, the bridge crew, and Bendi Felix to the Hall.

It was Arguns who, as usual, brought to everyone's attention a crucial side issue of the whole confrontation. "May I suggest, with all respect to the high ambassador, that we consider a joint responsibility for management of the deep space communications center? We realize Ambassador Seldoldon had only the best intentions in delaying giving this information to us, but perhaps it wouldn't be out of order to remind the high ambassador that not long ago the same purity of intention prevailed in the Maintainers. . . ."

Seldoldon's quick protest was drowned out in the sudden outburst, and it took the polite sweep of the Baaranic guards, pressing the order call bar at each ambassador's place, to bring the noise level down to where Seldoldon could be heard again.

But in that brief delay Seldoldon decided that it would be folly to allow Arguns to center attention on the management of the deep space center. That issue was secure for the moment. The wealth of his family and of the Gemainshaf had been poured into the communications network, and it would take more than an impassioned few minutes in an excited Council to dislodge the Seldoldons and the Gemainshaf from their rightful claim on its directorship.

"I'd like to remind the Laotanarian Ambassador that if he wants to bring this issue before the Council it must be introduced through proper channels. Once he's done that, it will be fully heard. However, the issue we have before us now has priority, so unless you have remarks on the arrival of the Galaxy 231, Mr. Ambassador, please take your seat."

"I have a few remarks to make, with your permission."

"If you'll confine them to the subject."

"Most certainly, most certainly. According to Ambassador DHO, we are to expect the arrival shortly of the crew of the 231, who will be able to explain—we certainly hope!—how it is they have made this truly miraculous return to the Triad. Once these testimonies have been recorded, it would be my dearest, fondest hope that we meet to have the high ambassador, Ambassador DHO, and Ambassador Tren explain, in a more leisurely atmosphere, just why they felt it was necessary to keep the approach of the 231 a secret! A secret for over a month! How extraordinary the reasons must be. I am fully prepared to listen with great attention to their explanation."

"I agree with Ambassador Arguns," said Leend of

Arkdikh, rising up in a slowly unfolding sequence of calcareous plates, until he stood thin and erect within his cabinet. His voice was as thin as his body, but mellow, like an oboe. "We can wait," he said.

But the Mandobites from the Dendom system, and the faction they influenced, were not so easily satisfied. "Mr. High Ambassador, why should there be a delay? We oppose a delay. These are simple questions: the forthright answers should be simple enough to bring before this body *now*. Why, sir, did you withhold the information that the 231 had emerged intact from the Spinandre Fold and was set on a course to the Triad? A simple question. It should take hardly more than a minute to answer."

"A minute, Ambassador Rka?" Seldoldon answered with a slow smile. "You're being generous this afternoon."

"I know you are a man of honesty, and brevity when the occasion calls for it. And don't you agree this is an occasion for quick truth, not dead rhetoric?"

"As long as the truth is recognized for what it is, and the listener's mind isn't closed to it."

"My mind is open, Ambassador Seldoldon," interjected Klote. "Please illuminate it."

They were hemming him in, bringing him to the edge. All it would take would be for form to be given to the unspoken current that ran hotly under the comments.

The truth was, of course, that the three of them—Seldoldon, DHO, and Tren, trusted no one else. Glaring, blatant, with unpredictable consequences, that truth was waiting to be voiced. No one dared do it just yet. They weren't collectively sure yet. And Seldoldon was maneuvering to delay that coagulation of thought. Then, as DHO began a smooth distraction, the chamber doors suddenly slid back and a Baaranic guard came in, followed by Tren moving in a slow and dignified canter as he led forward the crew of the 231.

There were others with them, four M'dians—one, wearing a white robe and bronze-colored hood, and towering above the rest, Seldoldon recognized immediately as M'landan, the priest of Ilanu. Around the edges of the group were people of the Gemainshaf, come up to the Hall to see what was going on.

Seldoldon saw Bendi Felix walking side by side with Conofficer Randley, and, behind them, other members of the bridge crew whose faces he recalled, but whose names he had forgotten. All wore the bright blue uniforms of the Galaxy personnel, even Bendi Felix, although he had only been an advisor on that last mission.

He stood up, affected by their appearance, these ghosts. "Please, come forward, up here, yes. . . . Conofficer Randley—it's good to see you again . . . Bendi Felix—" He reached across the table to grasp the scientist's wrist. He stood back then, looked around the council chamber and back at the crew.

"On behalf of the Council and the Alliance, and especially for myself, let me welcome you back. None of us, I think, ever thought we would see this day. . . ."

As he was speaking, he found himself addressing the priest, looking into the massive eyes whose brilliance was masked now by the nictating membrane which had closed over them as protection against the bright lights of the room. Of course M'landan would have come with his people, and he wouldn't have been detected because of his unique cellular structure that pattern control couldn't penetrate. M'landan, unique in many things.

Seldoldon included them all in his welcome, and explained that they would not be kept long—he had made up his mind to that: they would not be questioned beyond what would satisfy Leend, Klote, and Arguns that Claufe or the treacherous Circle members could not have survived. Beyond that information they would have to wait until he saw them all comfortable and accounted for in the Hall.

"The one question that we all would like to have answered," Seldoldon said to Conofficer Randley, "is what happened inside the Fold, and how you were able to escape."

The conofficer's short, blond hair gleamed as he came

forward under the lights. He held his helmet under one arm, and a sealed box under his other arm.

"Sir," he said, approaching the wide table, "I've brought the recording unit from the Galaxy for the period of time from just before our entrance into the Spinandre Fold until several months after Captain Darenga left the ship—"

"Pardon me," Seldoldon interrupted. "You say Captain Darenga *left the ship?*"

"Yes, sir. She had been very seriously wounded during the Solar Force attack. It was her decision, in light of her injuries and the unavailability of a Maintainer Treatment facility, that she spend the remainder of her life on M'dia."

So she had died on M'dia. Seldoldon sat slowly back in his chair. He looked again at the priest. Yes, he would have seen that she was taken care of, that she was as comfortable as it would have been possible for her to be in those last months of Life'send. He would have to talk with him . . . later.

"Please continue," he said.

"Well, here's the recorder, sir." Randley stepped forward to set the heavy metal box on the table.

Without touching it, Seldoldon, in a quick decision, turned to his aide and told him, "Give the box to Ambassador Klote," and, seeing it delivered to her, focused his attention once again on Randley. It had been the right move. He sensed it in the reaction of the members all along the semicircle. *Good*, he thought, *we need whatever leverage we can get*.

"I could relate the details of the events inside the Fold, sir, but since I wasn't at the controls, perhaps Captain Darenga could give you a more accurate account," and he turned back toward the group behind him while Seldoldon sat stunned and silent as one of the M'dians came forward —not a M'dian at all, he suddenly realized, too short for a M'dian, even though the figure was well over six feet tall— came slowly forward to the table.

It was DHO who finally said, "It was our understanding you had died, Captain Darenga. We rejoice that we were in error."

43

She lay back the bronze-banded hood of her robe, and her thick copper hair flared out against the somber shades of the council room.

"Thank you, Ambassador DHO." The husky Lambda voice, the voice that had been one of scores of copies and yet so individual. "I'll give you any information you want on the events inside the Spinandre Fold."

They're going to ask me why I'm alive, M'landan. I don't want to tell them. I don't want them to ask about you. I'm not under their authority anymore. I'm not part of their system, and I want nothing to do with them.

If they ask questions, my Chaeya, then you must answer. What harm do you imagine they can do to me? If their purpose is to discover the truth, then we have no right to withhold it.

He had touched her palms with his long uncoiling tongue and laid his arm across her body. *Who is there for me to fear but the gods?* he had asked, and she had pulled his face down against hers to quiet her uneasiness.

"Tell us what happened when the ship under Doctor Claufe's command entered the Fold," Seldoldon told her, every nerve in his body sending alarms. He felt immobilized, submerged to his neck in confusion. He wondered that he was able to speak at all as he looked into her face, into the calm green gaze he had known all his life, and loved these past long years.

"I ordered a retreat into the weir to block Claufe's passage, because it seemed his intention to proceed through into the Spinandre Quincunx. We knew that he was en route to M'dia for the plant that he would be able to process into a substitute for Longlife. That couldn't be allowed. As you know, that plant is the only source of food for the M'dian people. Claufe would have taken all they had, and left them to starve.

"When he was far enough into the weir for me to judge his determination to pass us—let me say that at that time the Fold was so erratic I felt we had only moments until it closed completely—then I ordered the ship into a position near the lower matrix, expecting they would try to pass overhead. They did. I brought the ship up under theirs and elevated it into the upper matrix. There was, as I recall, about ten meters of it remaining on our hull when we accelerated SOL to escape the matrix ourselves. The remainder, of course, was absorbed as the weir came down."

There was a silence. Then Klote, in clacking stops: "You mean to say, Captain Darenga, that you are prepared to swear that all members of the Solar Force ship were killed?"

"I say, Ambassador Klote, that there is no possible way they could have survived. We barely escaped, ourselves."

"Are all of the crew willing to swear this before the Council?"

There was a hesitation, a shuffling, as the crew of the 231 glanced toward Darenga. She didn't turn around, but said, "If we seem reluctant, it is because we wonder why we should be required to swear to an event that happened over eight years ago, and which is fully documented in the unit that is sitting before you right now. But we will all swear to what we've witnessed, if that's what you want."

She turned back to Seldoldon. "Mr. Ambassador, this has been a difficult journey for all of us. As you are aware, we have with us over 300 M'dians, who are homeless and disoriented; we would like to see them settled in their quarters so they can be fed and allowed to adjust to their surroundings. And, Mr. Ambassador, in regard to their food supply, we would also like to ask the Council to consider that they are restricted to a diet of L'M'dia. If it is strictly rationed, they have about a year's supply left. We appeal to you to help us find a substitute. I'm sure that if the resources of the Systems' Alliance are concentrated on this urgent need, a solution could be found within the year, and we respectfully urge that you consider this problem."

Seldoldon answered, so formally, "We will take the problem of the M'dian food supply under advisement, Captain Darenga, and I don't think there would be any objections to our making it a priority item."

He glanced along the crescent. "I think," he said to the members, "the crew of the 231 has indicated their willingness to give us any information we request, and have shown they have no objections to their statements being made part of the permanent record of this body. If it is agreeable to everyone, I would like to allow them to go to their quarters."

He turned to his right. "Ambassador Klote?"

"Let them go," she replied, averting her face, the Arcustan gesture of agreement.

"Ambassador Leend, do you have any questions?"

"I have no questions."

Seldoldon looked back at the robed figure standing before him, and found her gaze resting on him. "We understand the difficulties you have all undergone," he told her, "not only in the past few weeks, but in the eight years you have been gone. We will review what the recording unit has, and call those of you again whose testimony may add to that information. Thank you all for coming before the Council, and we will be getting in touch with some of you later."

"Can we have an understanding that, until the unit can be reviewed, all crew members, including Captain Darenga and Bendi Felix, will remain in the Hall?"

Seldoldon turned to Klote. "If you insist, Ambassador Klote. I'm sure they'll agree." He looked back at Darenga. "Yes, of course."

"This meeting is adjourned," Seldoldon said, and stood up as Darenga revolved away and walked back to the crew, moving out with them as M'landan and the other two M'dians joined her.

Seldoldon's impulse was to follow her, take her aside, ask her the thousand questions that would cover all the barren years—God!—put his arms around her. But if he were to go running to her now, the interpretation would be all wrong. He could hardly risk that, not now.

He went over to Klote's place, where all the members were gathering, folded his arms across his chest, and leaned with his back against the table to hear and see with the rest what the recording unit had to reveal.

* * *

Darenga was tired. Exhausted. And in constant pain, a pain that she tried to conceal from M'landan. She didn't think she was successful. She never had been before.

She went through the rooms they had been assigned and drew the heavy draperies partially across the tall windows so the light was dimmed. When M'landan and his assistants Klayon and Tlaima returned from the evening prayers with their people they would be finally able to rest.

She lifted back the wall hanging of scarlet anemone and laimon vine with a hand that was crabbed and rigid, and passed through an opening into the connecting suite to adjust the light as she had in the other rooms. She came back through the concealed doorway and went into the bedroom and lay down on a bed heavily carved with the motifs of the Seldoldons: vines, windflowers, and the racing soenderbiest.

She closed her eyes, concentrated down into a narrow well of insensibility. Her sleep was fitful, the images erratic. But she heard M'landan return, and sat up slowly as he entered the bedroom.

His voice was lilting, clear, so melodic, and she felt the sudden lift she always felt when he was excited. "It is raining!"

She smiled. "Is it?"

She watched him go to the windows and draw aside the draperies with his gauntlet.

It was the evening shower drifting off the ocean to briefly drench a landscape tiered in flowers and interspersed with lawns and trees that glowed green against the gray sky. The rain slanted against the open windows, washed down the panes.

"There is so much," he said. "So much."

She came up beside him to pull the windows in as the first gust of wind billowed the heavy folds of the drapery material into the room.

"No, Chaeya, please. Leave it open." He moved his head slightly as the rain chimed on the glass.

Darenga left him at the window and struck off the fire that had been laid in the fireplace. She sat down on the

47

deep rug at the edge of the hearth, wrapped her arms around her knees, and stared into the flames, waiting for the sound of the burning talfa logs and their dry fragrance to catch his attention. But it wasn't until the rain began to slacken that he finally turned away from the window and came over to the fireplace.

"How beautiful it is! Does it rain often?"

"Every morning and afternoon, usually."

"And do people go out when it's raining?"

"If they want to."

"I would like very much to experience that. If it's permissible."

She looked up at him. "It will be when the Council is satisfied. I don't know how long that will take."

"Let's hope it will be soon. I want to see this planet. I want to talk with the people."

He was standing very close to her, and she lay her head against his heavy robe, against the legs that could move so swiftly yet rarely did because of the danger to his hollow, fragile bones. His gauntlet rested against the side of her head, the bronze material sparking over the brighter fire of her hair.

His face turned down toward her then, and he sang softly, "Chaeya, why do you try to hide your pain from me?"

It had been useless, of course, this attempt to dissemble. But she said nothing, only continued to stare into the fire. He came down beside her and sat quietly watching her as his gauntlet lightly balanced on the angle her arm formed as she clasped her knees.

"If I were to speak to Andor Seldoldon, he would understand the urgency and give his permission for you to go to the planet that holds your treatment facility. Let me speak to him now, this sunfall, please."

"No," she answered, still watching the flames, but so aware of him. "No, it's not a good time. We'll have to wait."

The priest was silent. And then he turned his face toward the firelight, and the flames blazed across the immense curved surfaces of his eyes, and touched with red-gold the rounded features, the broad nose and mouth that stretched over his face in a gentle, plaintive expression.

They sat in the darkening room with the flames slowly falling downward into coals, until only a rusty light thrown by the dying sift of logs illuminated their figures. Finally, the woman's head sank forward to her knees, and the only other movement in the room was the soft stroking of his gauntlet over her hair.

Chapter 7

Andor Seldoldon had forced himself to sit impassively through the first two viewings of the recording unit from the 231, but he couldn't stand to see it a third time. He didn't want to hear his own voice calling Darenga toward her console and placing her before the communications wall just as it exploded to bury her legs under flaming chunks of metal. He couldn't watch her again struggling with pain to clear her mind for the confrontation in the weir with Claufe's ship. And since he couldn't look down again into that small arena on the Council room floor and watch those events unfold another time, he got up from his chair and made his way around by the wall, skirting the projection in the semicircle as he moved toward the doors.

When he came out into the crowded corridor, Bendi Felix rose from one of the wall benches.

"Lord Andor—"

"Bendi Felix, I thought you'd gone to your quarters." And, still affected by what he had just seen, he said, "What a mess that was. A terrible experience for all of you."

"Areia suffered the most," Bendi Felix answered. "More than even those recordings show. I thought I'd wait for you to see if there were any . . . questions I might be able to answer for you." His eyes, the same bright blue as his uniform, held on Seldoldon's face.

The high ambassador glanced around, said, "Yes, there are some questions."

It would have to be public; there could be no suggestion that they were discussing anything but the most superficial matters. "Let's go to the cafeteria."

Bendi Felix nodded, immediately understanding.

They went through the corridor and an archway that opened into a wide dining area.

"They have catspaw," Seldoldon told him, handing him a tray.

"Ah," the scientist replied, and opened the spigot of the urn Seldoldon indicated to fill his cup with a frothy liquid.

"Bouillon, please," Seldoldon told the attendant. He set the cup on his tray and then led Bendi Felix through the contoured benches and pads, the cabinets and life-support devices, to a space, well into the traffic area, where there was a table and chairs. They sat down.

"You're looking well, Lord Andor," Bendi Felix said.

"So are you, considering the perils of the last eight years."

The scientist lifted his shoulders. "A little anxiety here and there, perhaps."

Seldoldon lowered his cup. "Areia seems to have recovered from her injuries."

"It was unexpected. Her legs are badly scarred, of course."

"Of course." Seldoldon looked away. "She had to have a Longlife treatment within four years, Bendi Felix; how did she survive all that time you were gone? How was it possible?"

His eyes were on some casual point across the room, his profile toward the man seated across from him, but the intensity of his question ran under the careful modulation of his voice.

"That's a question that requires a rather complex answer."

"I'd like to hear it," Seldoldon told him, leaning back in his chair. He held one hand loosely about the cup in front of him, his other hung casually over the backrest. With his eyes on Bendi Felix, he could still see who entered the cafeteria.

"How should I begin? She went down to the planet to die, and L'Hlaadin kept her alive."

"Who is L'Hlaadin?"

Bendi Felix stared at him, then nodded. "Of course, you would have known him as M'landan."

"M'landan. I see. How did he keep her alive?"

52

"His hand fluid—the laanva—had chemical properties that repressed Life'send."

"We knew it caused hallucinations." Seldoldon's mouth felt numb.

"Yes." It was unspoken, but Seldoldon understood; she had wanted the hallucinations.

"A lot has happened to them both in the last eight years."

"To us all," Seldoldon replied.

"Lord Andor, do you know who the Chaeya is?"

"Yes, the mate of the . . . priest. . . ."

There was a long silence. Seldoldon put his hands down around the cup of bouillon that had grown cold. Little circles of oil irridesced across the surface. He shook the cup slightly, scattering the droplets.

"Why did the M'dians come back with you?" Seldoldon finally asked. "Did his making her his Chaeya have anything to do with it?"

"Yes. When their relationship was discovered, his people's reaction was violent. The city was divided. The ones who came with us were the ones who had remained loyal to L'Hlaadin even after his exile."

"They exiled him?"

"It was a brutal and ugly time."

Seldoldon's eyes shifted then, and he leaned back again into his chair. Bendi Felix, taking this as a signal that someone was approaching, lifted the cup he was holding and took a drink.

It was an Arcustan aide. He came up to Seldoldon, turned his small, hard eyes briefly on the scientist, and clacked, "Excuse my interruption. Ambassador Klote wanted you to have this list of the 231 personnel who will be called before the Council tomorrow afternoon."

"Tomorrow afternoon," Seldoldon echoed genially, and took the scribe unit from the aide's digitals. "Please tell Ambassador Klote I appreciate her consideration in getting this unit to me."

The Arcustan swayed his head slightly in acknowledgment, and retreated.

Seldoldon slipped the small pack inside his tunic. "She's repaying me for handing the recording unit to her, and not Arguns or Leend; an Arcustan can't tolerate a debt."

"Can a human?" Bendi Felix asked quietly.

Seldoldon gave him a thoughtful look. "It would depend on the magnitude of the debt," he answered slowly.

"Yes," Bendi Felix replied. "But perhaps there are some debts that can never be repaid, although a lifetime may be spent in attempting to do so."

"It would be hard to imagine a debt that great," Seldoldon said.

The scientist's gentle blue eyes held Seldoldon's gaze. "Areia is starting into Life'send," he said quietly. "I'm sure of it, although she's said nothing to anyone, least of all L'Hlaadin. But she is in pain, I know it. She keeps her hands hidden in her sleeves, but I've seen them, and the joints are swollen. I don't know how much time she has until the acceleration becomes uncontrollable, but she must be given a treatment as soon as possible."

"I thought you said the laanva—"

"When the M'dians found out about Areia and L'Hlaadin," Bendi Felix told him in a low voice, "they cut off his hands."

"Good God!"

"It was a very sad thing; a terrible thing; one tragedy on another. Something must be done for her, Lord Andor. She will never speak for herself."

"I understand the urgency." But he knew that through his own folly his influence had been reduced, that everything he did now was viewed and scrutinized for motivation as it never had been before. If he were to bring this before the Council, there would be, in all probability, a fatal delay while they considered whether it was subterfuge for some darker reason. If he were to try and take her secretly to Tricreden—well, that was impossible. "I'll find a way," he said.

At M'landan's insistence, the door to the corridor had been left ajar: *Anyone who wishes to come through it is welcome here. To close a door is to close your heart.*

And Darenga had left it open, even though she reminded him, *There was a door in the caverns, M'landan; you kept it closed.*

Where is the danger here, my beloved? Who in this great house would raise a harvest knife to hurt us?

No one she could name, although the fear was there, illogically, perhaps, that some harm would come to him. *You've never closed your heart to anyone, have you?* she had asked, turning from the door.

No, he had answered in his perfect honesty. *I could never do that.*

And through that open door had come a steady stream of crew members, all asking for L'Hlaadin, who spoke with each one according to the measure of comfort and assurance they wanted from him. Darenga sat in a chair by the fire, listening to the soft melodic fluctuations of his voice being translated into every language represented by the 231 crew, a double, triple echo of his song that soothed every ear it entered.

But his hands were magic, too, she thought, and then lay her head back on the thick, cushioned chair and closed her mind against the thought.

Andor.

Another thought that needed to be shut away. Nothing ever completely dies.

They were all sitting on the rug by the fire—M'landan and Darenga and Klayon and Tlaima, who, having helped their priest feed and make their people comfortable, were now taking their own nourishment, drawing up through their proboscises their ration from the deep, narrow bowls.

"What will they find for us that will be like plovaan, Chaeya?" Klayon asked. "Or lumeena, or aldaam?"

M'landan lowered his bowl carefully, the blunt end of his gauntlets pressing like a vise against the curved sides. He retracted his tongue and leaned back to hear her answer.

"I don't know," she replied. "It may be a synthetic of some kind."

"Not real food?" Tlaima set her bowl down on the hearthstones.

"Well, if it were a synthetic that only means that it would be manufactured in a lab instead of a plant. You'd get the same nutrients from it."

Tlaima looked at M'landan.

"What does it matter, my sister? If it is what our bodies need, then we will eat it."

Tlaima looked down and away from his eyes.

"So much is different," Klayon said. "Who would know that you could walk out under the sky and nearly drown?"

M'landan reached over and pulled Klayon against his shoulder with the crook of his arm. "We have been here only the length of two sunfalls, and you think that's all there is?"

"No, I don't think that. I want to see all there is; I'm curious, too. I just commented that it all was different; only one sun, and it is yellow; everything glares when it is in the sky, and now that it has fallen away, it is as dark as the caverns."

He made a movement to turn to the open windows, and M'landan released him. "Look at that," he said. "Stars everywhere, and so bright!"

Tlaima tilted her head toward Darenga. "I have not seen any silver anywhere. Does this planet not have any?"

"It doesn't grow up out of the ground here as it did on M'dia, but there is silver. Although it is expensive. It's available to artists, and I'm sure the university at Amper would supply you with what you need when they see your work."

"I brought only my tools with me, none of my work."

Darenga looked back into the fire. "Maybe the high ambassador would sponsor you."

"How is that arranged?" M'landan asked her.

"Someone requests a meeting with him to explain what is wanted."

"Then that is what we'll do," M'landan told Tlaima.

"It would be better to wait a few days; I think Andor has all he can handle right now."

They censured him, Areia, Bendi Felix had told her.

56

Why would they do that? God knows he worked all his life against us to get the dubious freedom they have now. Why did they do it?

He has enemies in the Council, you know that. They had an opportunity to discredit him, finally.

What had he done?

He was publicly drunk. And he nearly provoked Ambassador Klote into attacking him.

Klote! Was he trying to commit suicide?

The quiet reply: *Perhaps he was.*

She had turned away from Bendi Felix then, and walked to the window to stare unseeing into the afternoon.

Now M'landan leaned toward Tlaima to touch his gauntlet to her cheek. "Then we will have to wait," he said gently.

Bendi Felix entered the room, and M'landan looked up to give him a lilting fragment of greeting.

"Hello," the scientist replied, stopping before him. He crossed his arms over his chest and bowed his head.

It had been the salute of respect of the Maintainers to the Circle members who had been their/leaders for a thousand years. Darenga, watching him, found it ominous that not only Bendi Felix but the crew as well used this gesture to M'landan. She had expected that once the crew was on the ground they would not seek him out anymore—once they were safe and with their feet on familiar terrain. But they had all come. They had all been drawn back to him. And she found herself hoping that it was temporary, that they would stop looking to him for—for what? She wasn't sure what it was they gained from him.

He had changed them all. And she had yet to understand why or how. But she was afraid. Fear charging the atmosphere: the barometer falling, the current at mid-ocean beginning to surge, all the shore in sunlight, but out there stirring—cataclysm. And it was because of these undefinable fears that she instinctively drew nearer to him. And when his gauntlet touched her hand, where it curled into the thick pile of the rug, she realized that this sudden and inexplicable comfort that flowed out from him was the thing that bound the crew to him.

Yet it was strange to see Bendi Felix in obeisance to M'landan, who had never asked it from anyone.

"Please join us. I think there is some plovaan left—"

"No, thank you, L'Hlaadin. I've had dinner. I'm on my way to my room. Did you see the rain?"

"Yes, so delightful! I am looking forward to walking out in it."

The scientist glanced down at Darenga, who was gazing at him quietly. "The Council shouldn't hold us here more than a day or two, do you think?"

"I don't know. I quit trying to guess what the Alliance will do years ago."

"Andor Seldoldon was always very gracious to us," Tlaima said. "He shouldn't have the trouble guiding his members that he does."

Darenga gave her a sharp look. "Why do you say that?"

Tlaima turned to her. The firelight shimmered over the irridescent skin of her face and glanced and flashed in the liquid of her eyes. "He is a good person. His radiation patterns have always indicated it. And he is persuasive, not violent. He is what a leader should be."

Darenga's eyes met Bendi Felix's above Tlaima's head. "It may not be what the Alliance wants anymore."

"Then that speaks to their lack of judgment."

"Sometimes I'm sure they have no judgment at all."

She was dreaming that she was playing a game from her childhood, and, in attempting to win, had fallen off a high narrow ladder onto her back. The wind had been knocked out of her, and, as the other young Lambda clones gathered around, used to this sort of game-time calamity, one knelt beside her and said, "Well, Areia, are we going to have to carry you over the ladder?"

"Don't be silly," she tried to say, but her lungs wouldn't fill. Then she awoke, and there was no end to the dream. She sat up in sudden awful panic.

Instantly, M'landan was up beside her. "What is it, Chaeya? What's the matter?" And when he saw she couldn't answer, saw her sucking desperately at the air, he called out ultrasonically for Klayon.

"She must have a doctor of her own species," she heard Klayon say. "I don't understand why she cannot breathe; there is nothing obstructing the passageway to her lungs."

She was trying to clutch M'landan's shoulder to hold on to him, but her hands had become too deformed, and she could only scratch helplessly at his robe. He lifted suddenly away, moved swiftly to the door, and then was gone, and she was trying to rise off the bed and fell instead to the floor, hanging there on her hands and knees as the spasms convulsed her chest, while Klayon and Tlaima knelt beside her, their voices low with melodies of urgent comfort, unable even with their combined strength to raise her back to the bed.

Then slowly the air began to seep back into her lungs. Still she was afraid to move, afraid that she would disturb the shallow increase of oxygen. But finally, exhausted, she sank sprawling into a sitting position with her arms bracing her body, her head down.

She heard the door swing open, and a startled guzzle from the breathing tubes of Arguns.

"My dear Andor! We disagree with you; we are not monsters! Take her at once. I speak for all of us. You have my permission to take her to Tricreden. You have my blessing. Poor Captain! Dear Captain! You'll be taken care of—you'll be most assuredly taken care of."

Seldoldon was down on one knee in front of her, his hand on her arm, his other hand slipping under her body. "Areia, I'm going to lift you. I'll be careful."

She managed to gasp to him, "Keep . . . my shoulders up . . . I can't breathe if my chest . . . isn't elevated."

"I will. Just try to relax." He stood up with her in his arms.

Her retracted and crippled hands fell like claws across her body.

"I should have come before now," he said.

She said, "I don't want to . . . complicate things for you."

"Oh, dear God," he replied, and tilted her head against his face.

Chapter 8

M'landan had been waiting for several hours in this room. Outside the small window, the mountains folded up from the narrow valley into the bitter green sky, a part of one range among thousands that covered the face of Tricreden, mountain ranges that stretched upward for scores of kilometers, until the sky was only a thin sliver of glass in a cold and brittle universe.

He waited with characteristic patience, for most of the time simply standing near the window, his gauntlets resting deep inside his sleeves as his eyes absorbed all beyond the windows, every shift of light in all its frequencies from ultraviolet to infrared.

He had already adjusted to the torrent of sound that had rushed against his ear membranes, the body sounds of the attendants, the thousand small noises of an unfamiliar structure, the clamor of machinery, insulated to human ears, near-deafening to his. Now he waited to hear what the silence that had met his prayers would reveal. But there were yet many hours to wait.

An attendant had told him there was a bed. He had no idea where it was. The only chair in the room was not suited for him, the contours too small. So he stood and waited and watched from the window the shift of light over a landscape created through the goodness of another distant god he had always sensed existed, but whose voice he had only begun to understand.

Some time later, he recognized the footsteps of the Caretaker, and he turned away from the window as the man came through the door.

"Areia was concerned that you wouldn't have water," he said, and paused with the carafe he held in his hand. He glanced toward M'landan's sleeves. "Do you want me to hold it for you?"

"If you would, please; the shape would be hard for me to balance." He dipped his head toward the container as the Caretaker raised it. His tongue uncoiled from his mouth and sank into the water. After a long moment, the tongue drew back up. "Thank you, I was very thirsty."

"She said you would be," the Caretaker answered, with a thoughtful look at him.

M'landan made no reply, but silently waited.

The Caretaker glanced around the room, walked to one wall, touched a bracket, and a bed suddenly appeared from a long decorative panel.

"Ah!" M'landan exclaimed.

At the Caretaker's gesture, he sat gratefully down on the edge. The man pulled up the chair, sat down, crossed his legs.

"I look at you and I'm amazed," he said.

"That can mean many things," M'landan replied.

The man nodded. "It can. What it means in this case is that Areia is a clone—a *Lambda* clone, and the most respected of that House of the Maintainers. What have you done to her?"

"What do you imagine I have done to her?"

"Oh, it's not what I imagine, L'Hlaadin; it's what I know to be fact. I can't help her, you know."

There was no response from the figure seated on the bed.

Finally, the Caretaker said, "The fluid from your hands altered the structure of her cells. Her body can't accept treatment anymore."

"She will die?" M'landan asked softly.

"Within a few months, I would say."

"Where is she now?"

"In one of the treatment rooms. Sleeping. Once I knew she couldn't be treated, then I could give her some medication for the pain."

"You have an alternative to the treatment—what is it, please?"

The Caretaker gave him a crooked smile. "She said you

were perceptive. I can see it was a typical understatement. Was she correct? You still carry the semen for the next generation of your people?"

"Yes."

"Let me see your arms. Without the gauntlets, if I may. . . ."

He withdrew the bronze coverings from M'landan's arms. The priest silently watched as the Caretaker examined his stumps, pressed his fingers over the drawn skin. He raised and lowered M'landan's arms several times, testing, considering.

"How much do you weigh?" he asked abruptly.

"In your measurements? I don't know."

"Are all your bones hollow? I haven't had access to the M'dian reports."

"Yes."

"I guess you have to be careful."

"A fall can be dangerous."

"Interesting." He let M'landan's arms go, and replaced the gauntlets. "It may be possible for me to make a device that will release the semen, but I'll have to run some tests on you first—get some pictures of your reproductive tract. If what I suggest is possible, I want your permission to record every phase, and that will include your contact with Captain Darenga."

"You have my permission." M'landan had stood up quickly. "How long will it take? How soon will I be ready for her?"

To be able to sleep, to rest, to be without pain, was all that she wanted. But the Caretaker was prying at her hands, and it brought back the suggestion of the pain looming beyond the fringes of the opiates that numbed her.

"What . . . are you . . . doing?" she demanded, barely able to articulate the words.

He ignored her. Said something in M'dian. To whom? "Why must you . . . always be so . . . obtuse?" she muttered, slowly turning her head. And, white-hot through all the drugs, the pain seared her arms, striking her heart and pinning her howling to the bed. And woven into it all, a soft melodic murmur and the heavy scent of honey.

"Did he protect you? Did he keep you from hurting yourself? Did you tell him the effect our communion has on you?"

"Chaeya!" His laughter shivered down her body. "Am I harmed? Do I look bruised and battered? Please, I am all right. Your Caretaker very scrupulously strapped me to a table, and I was quite safe."

His tongue danced across her eyelids, and she put her arms around his neck and kissed his great wide mouth. "Was it good for you, too?" she asked against the sweet, whipping tongue. "Was it good for you?"

"Oh, yes!" he replied fervently, and she remained silent after that because the tone of her voice and the melodies she was forming were too arousing for him, and she dared not risk drawing him into communion again so soon. But he understood both her silence and her need and satisfied her in the only physical way he could.

"Chaeya," M'landan said quietly.

"Mmm?"

She lay against his side with her fingers spread across his cheek in a gentle fan, unwilling to relinquish even that small contact with him.

"There is something I must say to you."

It was spoken softly, but her eyes opened immediately, and she rose up on one elbow to look at him. "I'm listening," she said.

"There is an obligation that I have to my people—to all my generations."

She knew then what he was going to say. "Yes, I know."

"The Caretaker has arranged with Ambassador Seldoldon and his Alliance to have Tlaima transported here."

She sat all the way up, cross-legged on the bed, and shoved the cover around her. "When?"

"The length of . . . three sunfalls. I'm sorry, I have not yet mastered your time system."

"About six hours."

"Yes."

"Why now, M'landan? It's years before the time of conception. Why are you doing this with Tlaima now?"

"We are no longer guided by the cycle of L'M'dia. There are many uncertainties . . . I will not live forever—"

"M'landan, please—"

"Can we avoid the truth? I am not immortal, and there are dangers I am unprepared for. Everything is not clear to me."

She looked down at him where he lay with his head against the pillow. The stark white material made the huge circumference of his eyes seem greater still. Eyes that were dull gray now, almost blind.

"There must be another priest, Chaeya, while I can still teach him the new ways he must know."

She silently studied the folds of the blanket, rearranged it meticulously. "And Tlaima will carry him. You . . . have a deep love for her." She thought she may have expressed it as a question, but the melody was all wrong, the notes without harmonics.

"My love for her is not like the love I have for my other sisters, that is true, but you know that. You know, too, that it is not enough, for *ana-il'ma* must be present. That does not make up the feeling Tlaima and I share."

"She loves you far beyond the love she has for Klayon, even now."

"But it must come from me as well. I bear that love only for you."

So simply said. She had hardly needed reassurance. Had she? Yet the words brought her forward, brought her hands to his face to rest lightly on his cheeks and ear membranes.

"If there is to be a priest," he told her, "he must be conceived in that love, and it must be your hands that admit my seed."

"But that's not possible."

"I know. Yet your Caretaker has suggested a way it might be."

He sat up slowly then, and rested his gauntlets on the copper hair that lay over her shoulders like a shawl.

"What has he suggested?"

"If I were drugged. . ."

". . . I told him if he were drugged he might, for the few necessary moments, be deceived into thinking it was your hands that were receiving the laanva. He agreed with me. So with a few improvements in the prostheses I devised, and a framework to keep him in an upright position, he's ready now for this rather interesting reproductive experiment."

The Caretaker and Darenga had been walking down a long corridor, but now she stopped abruptly and stared down at him. "Experiment?" she echoed. "What the hell do you mean calling this an experiment?"

He gazed up at her with a narrowed expression. "That's exactly what it is, Areia—an experiment. What else would you call it? Whatever romantic or heroic emotion you've tagged to this relationship you have with this being hardly changes it. It is an experiment. And it may work, or it may not. He wants it to. Shall we continue?"

At the end of the corridor was a room with a viewing window. Set in front of this window was an instrument on a tripod, and two attendants were adjusting it.

Darenga, stung into silence by the Caretaker's tone, now glanced at him sharply. "You're recording this!" She pushed by the attendants to look in through the window.

"He gave his permission, Areia—"

The room inside glared with light. A cluster of spectrum bulbs reflected down from a hanging fixture, making a precise balance of light and shadow for the holocopies. At another window, across from her, there was a second camera, trained, as the one beside her was trained, on the center of the room, where M'landan stood encased in a steel framework that ran all the way from the floor to the ceiling.

His forearms were held rigidly in place in front of him by a metal brace. Tubes ran from his body into receptacles outside the stanchion. As he moved slightly, slowly shifting his weight, his head drooping forward, she saw his bare flesh press against the metal bars.

Darenga whirled from the window toward the Caretaker, catching his arm as he jumped away, and wrenching him back around. Everything was suddenly gone. All the years that had laid a peace over her, the gentle instruction that had slowly diminished the anger and resentment and had worn away the violence with the patient pressure of a glacier. All that wiped away. Yet, even as her hands gripped the man, she knew it was wrong.

"You've made your own morality, haven't you? And you think you can satisfy your perversions and do this—sacrilege on him with no one to stop you—"

"Sacrilege, Areia?"

The severity of his tone, as he spoke in Standard Maintainer, halted her.

"Sacrilege? Oh, no! I'm repairing what you nearly destroyed. I come behind you, Captain Darenga, pulling together the pieces."

Her hands dropped away from him.

"My dear Captain, you abandoned the crew, who had been trained all their lives to obey you, and ran down to that planet with all your complaints and excuses, and you ripped that society apart. Even when you saw what was happening all around you, you wouldn't withdraw. And, Captain, what you've sown, you will reap. You be indignant. You be angry. You allow your abnormality to surface in all its ugliness. But know this: through your own cowardice and folly, that being in there depends wholly on you. The only way he can keep this pitiful scrap of his society intact is through your cooperation. *And you will do what he wants!*"

She had taken a faltering step backwards, and now stood uncertainly. "It . . . wasn't like that."

"It was exactly like that, and you know it. And, clone, you have an obligation to that being in there. And, whether it suits your taste and conscience or not, you will perform it."

"You're doing this for yourself."

"Go ahead, keep this up. How long do you think he can stay in that apparatus before he collapses? The drugs I gave him will be maximum for maybe twenty more minutes. I can't give him any more after that; his system won't tolerate it. Look beyond yourself, Areia. You know him better than anyone else. Would he be in there if he didn't believe fully that what he was doing was best for his people?"

"I can't play games," she said.

"And you think this is a game for him? Perhaps you don't understand him at all."

"I understand him. I . . . can't speak the melodies he would have to hear, in that—glass bowl."

"Of course not. Your own sensitivities are more important than the survival of his race."

"Quit twisting what I say, damn you! If I never walked in that room at all; if Tlaima were never to have communion with him—" she brought her voice down, took a breath, drew herself together "—if Tlaima were never to have communion with him, there would still be children."

"Goddamn you! There has to be a priest; have you forgotten that? The priest is the guide and instructor of their society, and their only father. If there is no priest, there is no society. There are only beings who once called M'dia their homeworld, galactic curiosities with enormous eyes, whose ears can hear in frequencies totally escaping the human ear, whose speech is incredibly beautiful music, curiosities who attempt to attach themselves to this group and that because they have no society—"

"Shut up! You're trying to manipulate me. I won't stand for it anymore. You have no control over me. I'm not defined by you or the Circle or the Maintainers anymore. I'm not your tool. You're not going to tell me what I must do or not do."

"Then tell yourself, you stupid woman. You have ten minutes left." And he turned on his heel and walked away from her.

She stared after him, then took a step backward, turned, found the attendants frozen together behind the camera, their eyes on her. She saw the old fear. She ignored them, looked blindly in at the window. Then she opened the door, entering slowly. At once, the figures beyond the windows, the Caretaker, who had made a swift retrace of his

steps and was now entering behind her, all faded to the
edges of her consciousness. Her focus was on the figure in
the apparatus, whose head swayed as he lifted it, his eyes
bright and streaked with the color of clay.

"Why haven't you let him keep his robe? Why do you
have him like this?"

"It would interfere with the tubing." The Caretaker went
over to play with a small instrument on a stand. He lifted
the wires leading to the braces on M'landan's arms, and
shook out the kinks.

"Chaeya—"

"I'm here," she said, moving up to the stanchion to
touch his face. "M'landan," she told him gently, "shield
your eyes; this light is too bright."

He ran his tongue over her hands, and obediently drew
down the nictating membrane over his eye fluid.

The Caretaker was still leaning over the machine, and
Darenga demanded in a low voice, "What is that? What
are you doing?"

"Making adjustments," he answered quietly. "This instrument controls the flow of laanva." He glanced up at
her. "He has some ability to constrict the ducts. The screen
registers the constriction. I complete the closure here;
otherwise too much fluid might be . . . ejaculated."

There was a light tap on a door at the back of the room,
and the Caretaker hurried to admit Tlaima, who came forward with him, her hood pulled around her face, her eyes
cast down. He brought her to the side of the stanchion and
went back to his machine.

Tlaima called softly, "Chaeya?"

She was reluctant to leave M'landan, but he seemed to
be resting quietly, and Tlaima's eyes were on her, huge,
compelling. Darenga went around to her.

"There is no one else to administer the sacred oil,
Chaeya," she sang in a gentle tone. "There is no one else
who should. It would be an impure act for me to accept
eretec without the oil on my body. Will you do this for
me?"

Darenga looked at the small and delicate jar Tlaima had
withdrawn from her sleeve and now held balanced in her

palm. The feeling was fear, and she repressed it quickly, took the jar in her hand, and removed the lid. "What shall I do?" she whispered.

"My eyes, my throat," she replied. "You remember. . . ."

Yes, I remember, Darenga thought. She dipped her fingers into the oil, drew a glistening line down Tlaima's throat, touched it to either ear membrane, rubbed it lightly over her eyelids, this application of the honey-scented oil and the laanva from his hands.

Darenga replaced the lid and set the jar back into Tlaima's outstretched palm. Tlaima bowed her head and did not look up again.

When Darenga returned to the front of the stanchion, she touched M'landan's face. "Are you all right, my dear friend?"

"The sacred oil," he said, and she realized he had smelled it on her hand. He spoke then from a thought it had triggered.

"My poor Areia, there will be no ceremonies for you . . . no ceremonies for my beloved."

"Should there be a ceremony?"

"Oh, yes. A great, long, and beautiful ceremony. A ceremony that would purify and prepare our bodies for *eretec*." He closed his eyes, then slowly reopened them. "Is it enough to say that you are loved by one whose sins have brought him to this?" The head swayed down again. *"Tlay mg salan drae."* Let the truth be spoken.

She leaned forward over the braces and the gleaming prostheses that covered the stumps of his arms, the surgical steel with the soft circular insets, reached forward to spread her fingers over his ear membranes.

"My friend, don't think about these things—"

"In part my desire," M'landan murmured. "In part my desire. I must admit it." He lifted his head again, and the membrane slid back to the corners of his eyes, leaving the surface brilliant, every detail of the room in bright reflection. "I must admit it."

"To me? What do you have to admit?" Darenga saw herself standing before him, her face impassive, cool. *I'm a lie,* she thought. *But he can see beyond it. Can he see now?*

"I wanted what was forbidden to me. I wanted it so much I forgot the purpose of my life. And now my sin is become one with me, and I still love it more than I love my people."

The song descended in the room, a shadow, filling all the bright spaces, pressing down on her as she held his head. They were all forgotten now, the listeners and the watchers.

"You told me once that I thought you innocent in all things, and myself guilty. You convinced me I was wrong, that it was a guilt which, at least, we shared. And, having taught me that, are you deceiving your own instruction and taking all the blame to yourself? Have you always? M'landan, have you always?"

"*Mlo saindla*, Chaeya. My beloved Chaeya. *Mlo saindla*, forgive me. But at *eretec* there must be truth. And the truth is that I drew you, innocent, into communion with me. And I allowed myself fulfillment, and kept you in ignorance. And the punishment you will suffer for my error will be worse than any given me."

The apprehension she had been feeling began now to overtake her. "What punishment are you talking about? What are you saying?"

"The end link of the chain that binds us together is anchored in your flesh," he said. "And if there were a way I could set it deeper, I would do it in an instant. I confess this—" He moved then, in the hard confines of the cage, loose-limbed, slow-reflexed, and staggered against the bars.

"Please—you'll hurt yourself . . . and don't say these things. . . ." She ran her hands anxiously over his face and pressed her lips against his cheek and his mouth. When he felt her contact he opened his mouth, and his tongue uncoiled to flick over her skin, the sweet tongue that gently forced its way into her mouth, bringing a soft tone from her throat that he echoed. He drew his head back. "Chaeya, give me your hands."

She saw the clear picture of herself in his eyes, reaching toward the braces and the metal shields. Then his head

71

slowly lowered, and his eyes closed, closed before he could see the change in her radiation, the bright pulse begin.

"O Loving Gods—" It was begun in the vocative, and as the strong melody filled the room the Caretaker was suddenly pulling her away, pulling her back as Tlaima stepped around and pressed her hands against the shields.

"O Loving Grace, enter—" and in the instant before the air became heavy and sweet with the odor of his laanva, the Caretaker abruptly released Darenga, and she sprang forward and her arms went around Tlaima's waist. Tlaima shrieked, her hands still gripping the shields. M'landan flung his head back and then slumped down into the stanchion, held halfway up on his legs by the narrowness of the enclosure and the brace on his arms.

Darenga, dazed and unaware of what had passed from her body into theirs, set Tlaima on the floor. Then she saw the widening pool of liquid that was slowly dropping from the center ring of the metal shields. She swung around, yelling, "Caretaker!"

He stood staring at her.

"Shut it off! Shut it off!"

Abruptly he snapped around, fumbled at the machine. The slow trickle from the shields stopped.

Darenga looked back to see Tlaima kneel forward and mop at the liquid with her robe in quick distracted movements, then grope through the bars to clutch at M'landan's legs. "L'Hlaadin!" she cried. "Please get him out. His arms will break! *Please!*"

Darenga hurled herself over Tlaima, landing on the lower rung of the stanchion. She grasped M'landan's arms and pulled him part way up. "Open this!" she yelled. "Get these things off his arms!"

"Here, move to one side," the Caretaker told her, and slapped up the pins that held the brace in one piece. The metal sprang apart and M'landan's arms slipped back.

"O, my brother!" Tlaima was calling out in a low frantic song as she tugged at the side bars.

"Release those rear bolts," the Caretaker was telling the attendants who had run into the room at his call. "Get a cart," he said, and, as the section of the bars came away, one of the attendants ran for the door.

"You can let him go," the other attendant told Darenga. "I have him."

"Be careful," she said, and lowered M'landan back into the attendant's arms.

The Caretaker and Darenga came around the stanchion as the cart arrived. The attendants lifted M'landan up onto the pad.

"Keep him hooked up until I find out what's going on," the Caretaker told them.

The receptacles and tubing were tucked in around the blanket they had pulled over him, and all was strapped down.

"Tlaima," M'landan said, very clearly, although his eyes were still closed.

She bent quickly down and lay her hand against his ear membrane. "I am here, my brother."

Darenga could see the movement along his throat as he spoke to Tlaima, but what he said was ultrasonic, and no one but Tlaima could hear it.

"May I take him now?" the Caretaker said to Tlaima with a strange gentleness.

She turned her brilliant eyes on his face. "Yes, but he wants me to come, too. May I do that?"

"Absolutely. We'll go out this way." And he directed her and the attendants to the rear door.

Darenga started after them, but saw Tlaima bend down over M'landan, and saw his tongue flick out against her hand as the group moved out into the corridor. She stopped abruptly. The Caretaker reappeared in the doorway.

"Are you coming?"

"No," she answered. "No."

"Then wait in my office." It was a command.

She turned obediently, as perhaps she always would, and went slowly across the room and out the other door.

Once he had convinced her that M'landan was well, that he was sleeping, that there had been no injury to him, then she took the chair he had earlier offered her and sat quietly looking at him.

"When you grabbed Tlaima," he said, "it had a violent effect on L'Hlaadin, too. Do you know why?"

"No."

"Why did you grab Tlaima?"

"I don't know . . . I don't know."

"Jealousy?"

"You are . . . unclean," she said.

He made a sound in his throat. "Challenge that, then. Challenge what I accuse you of."

"I'm not going to challenge anything. It's a waste of energy to be jealous in a society where one male is the father of an entire generation, with all the specialized relationships that implies. Particularly when the females are all his sisters. Jealousy would be foolish."

He looked at her thoughtfully. "I see," he said. "I don't know what mechanisms operate in the M'dian race per se," he continued, "but I thought you should know that with L'Hlaadin, once his reproductive fluid is exhausted, he will die within a few years."

"How . . . many years?"

"Three, possibly four."

She rubbed her hand along the side of her face, and then, as if she realized the gesture to be too revealing, she placed her hand in her lap. "How much fluid has he left now?"

"My dear," he answered, reading her gesture perfectly, "he doesn't possess a jar with graduated measurements. I can't be accurate. But if it is as he says, that under normal conditions he would have had the capacity to service some five hundred females and still have a small reserve, then when he has impregnated the—what? 150—?"

"156."

"156 females, minus one, then he should be able to take care of you for some years to come."

"I'm not concerned about myself." She looked away. "The earlier reports of the research teams indicated M'dians might be able to live three hundred years or more."

"Conjecture, probably. I haven't read the reports. Team

research isn't always critically accurate. If Andor can get permission from his chain of albatrosses, I could get a good scientific answer for you. But as far as L'Hlaadin is concerned, you have my expert opinion."

When Darenga had finally located the room where M'landan had been taken, she found him asleep and Tlaima seated on the floor beside his bed, with her long fingers wrapped around one of his bandaged arms. Her head rested in the crook of her arm, and Darenga thought her asleep until she looked up.

"Are you all right?" Darenga asked in a stiff whisper. "You weren't hurt, were you? I didn't want to hurt you."

"We were not hurt," she answered, and turned back to M'landan.

That seemed to say it for any question she might have asked, so Darenga stood silently, watching them. There was a low murmur from Tlaima which Darenga could tell, from the melody, was sung partly beyond her range of hearing. M'landan made a drowsy movement and gave an inaudible answer. Darenga felt, as she often had before, an intruder, but she walked to the other side of the bed and sat down in a chair placed back from the sleeping figure.

Tlaima looked at her across the slow rise and fall of M'landan's chest. She had not risen when Darenga had entered, nor had she yielded her position at his side. Darenga understood quite clearly that a different relationship had now evolved, and it was outside the love between priest and Chaeya.

Darenga looked down at her hands as she slowly entertwined the fingers. Her whisper was harsh and dry. "Did it work?" She looked up to meet Tlaima's serene black gaze. "Are you—"

"Yes. I carry the next priest of our generations."

After a moment, Darenga got up from the chair and left the room.

She had formally asked, through all the proper channels, for an audience with the High Ambassador, and he had responded accordingly, meeting her in his reception room with formal courtesy and escorting her into his inner office, where he offered her a comfortable chair, inquired if she wanted anything to drink, and gauged from that brief exchange, and through the tumult of his own feelings, how she wished the interview to be conducted.

He saw that she had adopted the M'dian form of dress and wore the exquisitely woven off-white robe all the M'dians wore, except that her hood was bound with a wide bronze band. She had laid the hood back, and her hair, even in the subdued lighting of his office, burned around her face like a firefall.

He found it extremely difficult to meet her gaze with the posture of polite interest he had assumed. He could tell nothing from the calm expression, the total composure that held her in an attitude of quiet assurance, and he felt that his own dissolution was obvious.

For Darenga, the meeting had been a responsibility that had fallen to her, and she had accepted it, going through official procedures to arrange it, because she was not so imprudent as to think she could presume on their former relationship to make the request that she had come to make. Certainly, he had given her no outward sign that anything but a genuine and friendly concern governed his feelings toward her now, and had not allowed herself, had no desire to allow herself to expect anything else, for the divergence of their lives had been determined by universal uncertainties they both understood.

Looking at him now, she was confused, uncertain of her own feelings, as he leaned casually against his desk, his arms folded across his chest, the dark eyes friendly, the pleasant angular features shadowed slightly by the ends of the long chestnut hair curving along his cheekbones and swaying against the collar of his brown tunic as he bent his head with a polite gesture that indicated he was waiting for her to speak. But she said, calmly enough, "I've requested this interview on behalf of L'Hlaadin and his people."

Seldoldon nodded, and then, because he was unable to stop himself from saying it, "I understand you've become his Chaeya." Friendly, interested.

She replied, "L'Hlaadin has given me that honor, yes."

He finally looked away then, toward the window briefly, his face in profile to her as he raised his head. She remembered the mannerism, what she knew it to mean. But then his eyes were on her again, warm and receptive, and she thought herself mistaken in what she had read into his gesture.

"I wish you the best," he said. "M'landan—L'Hlaadin, I guess I should call him—was always a unique individual. I always considered him a friend—"

"—as he does you."

"Well, thank you, it pleases me to know that." He changed his position, rested his palms against the edge of the desk and leaned his body against the brace he had made of his arms. "In the few weeks you've been here, he's made a strong impression on the Council. They'd like to see him become the M'dian representative."

Her eyes widened slightly. "I . . . don't think he would consent to that. He would tell you, I'm sure, that he serves only those who came with him. He wouldn't try to speak for the M'dian cities."

"An envoy could be sent to consult with the leaders there—"

"Andor—" she hadn't meant to speak his name, but it had come so readily "—you must know the circumstances that surrounded our small exodus."

"Yes."

"Then you can see why he would not consider becoming a M'dian representative."

His gaze came up to hers from where it had fallen to the pattern of windflowers at his feet. "They will send an envoy anway, Areia. If he declines, they'll bring back someone who will serve on the Council. M'dia has become too important."

"Don't let them exploit the planet."

"I have no intention of letting that happen."

"No, of course you don't. Forgive me."

"I understand your concern. A ship will be leaving in two weeks."

"And the Spinandre Fold?"

"The Fold? It's as stable as if it were constructed of granite."

She heard the bitterness then. But he said quickly, "There'll be continuing contact with M'dia now, and the problem of their food supply is not as acute as when you first landed, although they will eventually have to develop a substitute. You have the supplemental list, don't you?"

"Yes, your aides gave copies to M'landan."

"I see you still call him by his original name."

"I'm the only one who does."

He nodded silently.

"The reason I'm here," she said, pulling herself back on the track, "is in part related to the supplemental list. Since we know now there are common plants on Ronadjoun that can be used for food, we would like to know if there is some unused area of the Gemainshaf where we might go to start our own community. It could be anywhere. We need nothing more than the permission to use the land. We have our own tools, and, once our community is set up, we could contribute to the Gemainshaf. You know the M'dian skill in weaving and silvercraft and the other arts that I needn't mention because you are as familiar with them as I am. This is very important to the M'dians, Andor. They need to rebuild themselves, to revive the sense of usefulness and order that has been draining away these past terrible months."

She had come to her feet and was standing now, facing him, her hands plunged into her sleeves as she spoke in a rapid glide of Ronadjounian phrases. "You knew them even before I did. You know how gentle and modest they are in their manner and way of life. I don't have to tell you they would never abuse the privilege if you would grant it."

"I realize that. Your request is reasonable. However, I will have to call together the district heads and explain to them what you want. Since our lands are held in common, there would have to be a general agreement, and the agreement of the community center of the area you would be assigned. But I'm sure they'll consent. Is there any district you might feel more suited to your needs than another?"

"We have no preference, although a region where there is ample water? Springs, or a creek? And perhaps a soft stone they could use for building material?"

"Water is no problem on Ronadjoun," he smiled. "And I'll find out where the largest deposits of sandstone are, although right off hand I'd say Canigou. How does Canigou sound?"

"Any place you think would be suitable for L'Hlaadin's people, and agreeable to your own, will be acceptable."

"Yes. Well, I'll call everyone together, and by the end of the week I'll have an answer for you." He looked down at the rug again. "There's something you should be aware of, Areia. Outside the Gemainshaf there are some rather strong objections to intimate relationships between aliens and humans. I don't know that there would be any serious trouble—there's no legal stand any objector could take on this—but it's possible that hard feelings could develop if the relationship were flaunted, for instance."

"You're telling me not to let anyone know that I am M'landan's Chaeya?"

"It might not be prudent to announce it. Not until people have time to adjust."

"There won't be any reason to tell anyone, unless they come into our community."

"I just wanted you to understand the situation."

"Yes." She took her hand from her sleeve and offered her wrist to him in the old Maintainer gesture. He clasped it. "You've been very gracious, Andor. I thank you for L'Hlaadin and his people, and for myself."

"I'm only too glad to be able to do anything for you, Areia. I just thank God you live."

She stared at him, hearing clearly what he had been holding back.

She slowly withdrew her arm and slipped her hand back into her sleeve. "Goodbye, Andor," she said, and, turning, walked out through the door he quickly opened for her, and on through the crowded reception room to the corridor.

"Call the district heads of the Gemainshaf," Seldoldon told the man at the desk as he watched her go out the door. "Arrange for a meeting on Wednesday at the latest, earlier if we can get them all together." He turned back toward his office. "And give me five minutes now, will you, please."

Seldoldon shut the door and stood there with his back against it. He put his hands out in front of him. They were shaking. "Dear God," he said in a hoarse whisper.

And down the long corridor from his office, Darenga walked away, her hood pulled around her face, her head bowed.

Chapter 9

They were moving to what would be their new home, and it was raining.

They were gathering on the portico of the Hall, their numbers spilling down the steps and onto the crushed shell driveway. Darenga had never seen them quite so animated, so joyous. Their random, interlaced melodies rang down the air as they called to one another, asked lilting questions they didn't wait to hear answered, cried dismay over lost articles, cried delight when they were found. No one stood still, and Darenga, seeking M'landan from a little space near a porch column and the stone face of the building, finally saw him beyond the steps, standing in the driveway in the rain.

M'dian cloth, designed for wear in an arid climate, was highly absorbent, and M'landan's robe was rapidly becoming saturated. But he moved, unnoticing, through the figures that shifted back and forth from portico to driveway as they waited for the signal to begin their walk to the landing field, where shuttle craft would take them all to Canigou.

Darenga watched him, knowing he enjoyed the rain and was finding reasons to stay out in it. Still, even with the wet robe hanging to him, and his hood dark and dripping around his face, he moved with dignity and an air of calm about him that his brothers and sisters swarmed to and, receiving a measure of it, drew back, only to return to it again and again.

You are so dear to us all, she thought, and, at just that moment, he saw her.

"There you are!" he cried out in an admonitory tone that startled her, and came at her so swiftly that she fell back in surprise. "You disobedient Chaeya!" he told her, crowding her against the corner formed by the column and wall.

"L'Hlaadin—" she began.

"L'Hlaadin, you call me! Am I your Holy Guide?"

And then she heard his laughter and the barely controlled excitement that rode in it.

"You are my guide in everything," she replied, not resisting him, feeling the stones cold along her back, his steamy warmth from thigh to breast. She protested, "What are you doing!" laughing now herself.

He had his forearms pressed inward on her arms, holding her firmly and against the wall. He was not strong, and she could easily have broken away from him, but she was so amazed at his behavior that she stayed where he held her, squeezed between column, wall, and his body, staring up at him as his tongue whipped back and forth across her face.

"M'landan!"

" 'M'landan . . . M'landan!' " he echoed, the name distorted as his tongue ran along her cheek.

"What do you think you're doing!"

"Be still! Everyone is looking at you."

"At me!"

His tongue slipped quickly between her lips and then hastily withdrew as she brought her teeth down on it. "Ah, you wound me!" he cried.

"M'landan, what is all this about?"

"Why do you neglect me?" he said then. "All my brothers and sisters look around, and they say, 'Where is the Chaeya that is supposed to be by L'Hlaadin's side?' I must hide my face because I have no answer. They all think it very sad."

"Are you serious?"

"Of course! You were instructed at our joining, were you not? You were told that a Chaeya must remain at her priest's side always, unless he tells her otherwise, isn't that so? And didn't you agree to those conditions?"

"Yes! But—"

"Have I told you to stay away?"

"Yes, you have—"

"*What!*"

"Not in words," she said quickly, and then, because she realized all at once that he was pressing more than her body, she told him sternly, "What else can I think, when you haven't been in our room for weeks, when you've scarcely spoken to me in all that time for either instruction or reprimand?"

"But there were other things that needed my attention," he said softly, and before her brain could disengage her tongue she had answered with all the disharmony that had wracked her since Tricreden, all the suppressed feelings she had sealed in iron below the level of her consciousness, all now suddenly melted loose and floating free, "Yes, Tlaima." She frowned. "You said you wouldn't manipulate me," she said heavily, when he didn't speak.

"I said I would not use the frequencies of my voice to trigger responses in you. All I have done is to ask you questions in such a way that you reveal to yourself what you hide from yourself."

His pressure on her arms released as he brought his gauntlets up to the sides of her head. Still his body leaned against her, and she didn't want him to move away.

"*Mlo saindla* for what I've taken for granted you knew. We have seemed to have become so much as one that I am afraid I assumed too much. And I will tell you now what I should have told you before. The few weeks following conception are crucial for the one who carries the future priest in her womb. She must be surrounded by love, submerged in it; no disturbing thing must happen to the loving cradle that rocks this child. This is the time when the *Augmeena* develops, and if he is to have that gift, his mother must provide the tranquil sea through which it must travel to him. I had only one chance to produce a priest for my people, my beloved, and having done that, I had to ensure his powers."

She caressed his face. "You left me unprepared," she told him. "I thought—"

"You thought I had taken another Chaeya." He sighed.

"You are right to rebuke me. I am neglectful many times when I shouldn't be. My assumptions and my oversights are too gross to name. Say you forgive me for these things."

"Yes," she smiled, "you are forgiven."

His mouth touched hers, and she parted her lips so his tongue could enter. He retracted it slowly and looked at her. "Now I will tell you what it is I will forgive you for."

She drew her head back. "You'll forgive *me* for?"

"You are not blameless in this. I have told you, time and again, that I love you, that there is no one for me but you. Haven't I said that? And don't you know there is but one Chaeya for all the priest's life?"

"Yes," she answered slowly.

"But you ignored these things that were true, and believed a fabrication."

She stared at him expressionlessly.

"Isn't that true?"

"Yes."

"Ask me to forgive you."

She searched his face for the answer to the strange quality she heard in his voice, at the same time aware sharply of the crowd that milled over the portico, their voices rising and falling with the intensity of their conversations, realizing that, here in this cool and stony corner, they were being discreetly ignored. She was aware, too, of the rain falling just beyond the roof of the portico, with a sound as musical as the voices around them. But most of all she was aware of him and what he was generating in her, here, on this porch in front of anyone who might look to see.

"Who would answer?" she replied softly.

His eyes gleamed out at her from the hood. "Whom do you want to answer?"

"The one who loves me most."

He was silent. And then he repeated, "Ask me to forgive you."

"*Mlo saindla* . . . M'landan," she answered, taking the choice away.

"M'landan does forgive you," he said. His head bowed down against her hair, and she could feel his heart pounding as he sang on a low tense note, "If I had hands, I would lock my palms against yours. . . ."

"Yes. . . ."

"I want what it is wrong for me to want."

She closed her eyes, and he touched his tongue to the lids in a gentle stroking motion.

"I want it too."

"The device your Caretaker gave me—"

"—is for your sisters."

"It is for you, also."

"Only when I . . . need it."

"And do you need it now?" And when she didn't answer, he demanded softly, "Do you? Do you need my laanva now?"

She remained silent, not daring to answer.

He stepped away from her then, and turned his head toward the rain, toward the fine misty rain that drifted over the wet lawns and brought with it the smell of salt air, while Darenga stood with her back against the wide rough stone blocks, her shoulder pressing the column. And even with those solid props she felt suddenly off-balance, unsupported. She spread her fingers back over the stone.

"M'landan?"

He turned abruptly. "When we reach our destination," he said, miserably, "when we have some shelter of our own. . . ."

"There's no way to neutralize—"

"I would welcome the pain."

She heard then, in his intricate song, what he might have been able to disguise if he hadn't been so distraught: one pain drives out another, the deeper pain of guilt.

What do I continue to do to you? Darenga thought in despair. *Why must we be linked together this way?*

But she said nothing more, and after a few moments he went to call his people together.

Darenga had never heard a silence like it. They had been quiet when they had gathered after the landing. Even after M'landan's long and emotional blessing of their land, they were silent. In this early twilight, now that the shuttle craft were gone, now that the crews assigned to knock up the temporary living quarters and storage areas were gone, they were left in this lengthening evening, and Darenga thought she understood the reason for their silence.

There had been, she imagined, a kind of unreality to their lives. They had been shuffled from here to there— never very long in any one place, and the temporariness of their lives had almost become a stability. They were adaptable and obedient. But it was with the finality of this last swift journey, the realization that this was to be their home, that the children which would soon be conceived and born and all their descendants would never know M'dia, would never see the two suns of their world or the green sands of their planet, would never tend the beautiful and noble plant that their civilization had centered around for all their generations, it was this that they now faced.

And then someone said, "What moves out there?"

The breeze blew softly through the grass, and everyone looked toward the darker shadows moving at the far end of the ancient lakebed. To Darenga they were only shadows, but she knew the M'dians perceived the heat patterns rising from the forms and could also, even from this distance—a mile or so—hear the movements.

"Soenderbiests," she replied.

There was a little restless shudder in the people around her.

"They won't bother us," Darenga told them, "if we don't bother them."

There were a few dubious little arpeggios that danced for a moment on the darkening evening, and then, at a signal from M'landan, everyone's attention was turned from the animals at the end of the meadow as Klayon and Tlaima began settling the community down for the night.

Living arrangements would be restrictive for a time in this makeshift camp, yet the M'dians, in spite of it, or perhaps because of it, were in sudden good humor.

Darenga could hear them from the tent she and M'landan would share with Tlaima and Klayon. They were so childlike in their excitement, calling goodnight to one another with little indication that any of them would sleep.

Darenga lay back on the mat and closed her eyes, listening to the bright, erratic melodies.

She had dozed off, and now she awoke thinking she had heard M'landan's voice. She stared into the dim light but saw nothing at first. And then, within the tent, she heard Tlaima's voice, low and vibrant, "Is it not a beautiful thing, my brother, to feel the child move inside me?"

By the way her voice caressed the words, Darenga knew she was speaking to M'landan.

"Yes, it is," she heard him answer in a soft wondering tone.

She could make them out now, one large shadow two yards away.

"You have endured great shame, Tlaima," he said then, "but there will be great honor for you and Klayon."

And Tlaima's low, intense reply, "This is our child, my brother—yours and mine."

There was a pause. And, although Darenga heard nothing, she knew M'landan had answered. She did not know what he had answered, and, unwilling to continue an eavesdropper to any more of this private conversation, she turned inward, down, away, wishing they had chosen another place to talk. And with that flight she was engulfed in a sense of emptiness, of impotence. There was no sanctuary in her own strength anymore; she had no strength. There was no sanctuary anywhere.

But the depressing beginning to that night produced a comedy that was almost a disaster. Darenga came awake in a rising leap that pulled M'landan up with her. She tripped over Klayon, fell across Tlaima, who curled up like an armadillo, and scrambled up, hearing again, as she came to her feet, the sound that had catapulted her out of bed.

It was a soft, snuffling lowing which had her instinctively reaching for a weapon she hadn't worn in years. The sound was all around the tent, the questing breathing and wary footfalls of the soenderbiest.

From the doorway she whispered back, "Don't move!"

Outside, she could hear sleepy melodic questions from the nearby tents, and, as Darenga stepped cautiously outside, a soenderbiest lifted its head and breathed sharply through its nostrils. The long, spiral horns swung down. To the side, she saw the shadows move. The animals were all through the camp, and she knew the tents would be no protection if they became excited.

"M'landan," Darenga called quietly, watching the soenderbiest shift restlessly, head down, horns poised toward her breastbone. "Tell everyone to stay where they are. Tell them not to move."

She heard his voice slide up out of her range, and then the sudden stillness all about her. The soenderbiest had raised its head, danced lightly backward, and then lifted its forelegs in a little half-jump. There had been a similar movement in the other animals. Now the soenderbiest shook its head, drew its horns down abruptly, and charged.

Darenga hurled herself out of its path, and hit the ground away from the tent. From that point there was nowhere to go but down the incline toward the meadow, where there would be no cover for her. Then she was waist-high in a nightmare of thick grass that wrapped around her legs, reducing her speed to short awkward leaps. She stopped, swung around to face the animals, because she thought she might have some chance that way.

A sound pierced her ears for an instant and was gone. The soenderbiests veered away, their heads violently swinging from side to side as they stampeded into the darkness. She stared off in the direction they had taken.

"Areia!" It was M'landan, flying down the hill toward where she still stood in a half crouch, her hands spread over the top of the grass as if she were treading deep water. She straightened as he sank into the meadow and waded up to her, his arms opening out to draw her against him.

"You scared them with the frequency of your voice," she said.

"I would have driven them away sooner, but I thought you had some purpose in mind in going out among them," he said, and then added in a breathless little phrase, "You were sacrificing yourself for us."

She swore heavily in Arcustan, because there were no equivalents in any other language to what she felt about herself and the whole situation.

"Why are you displeased with yourself?" His question was tinged with reproach.

"Oh, hell," she said, and, pulling away from him, started back toward the camp.

After a moment, he silently followed.

A plan for excavation of the sandstone cliffs was made; a communication, really, of what almost seemed a genetic blueprint that every M'dian engaged in that project possessed. There was a vocalization, a general agreement, and then the workers gathered their tools, pulled on the heavy gloves they had made while they were still at the Hall, and began.

At least half the community was occupied in the work on the cliffs that rose from the shore of the ancient lake-bed. There were some who set to work constructing carts to carry off the debris, while others were busily erecting scaffolding. Meanwhile, the diggers started into the soft stone, and the first room was already outlined in intaglio.

Darenga took a group out with her into the meadow to search out the plants that would be their food. She had a scribe unit with text and illustrations of the usable plants, and she explained to the M'dians what they were to look for as they walked along. They discovered several varieties in the meadow itself, and others along the bench which joined the woods that sloped down from the surrounding mountains.

Natural agrarians, the M'dians wanted to know the cycles of the plants, and, after a noisy consultation and an intense concentration on Darenga's reading of the pertinent section from the scribe unit, they tied little threads to the most vigorous and well-developed plants they found, began to measure off the first section of the meadow for islands. (*Of course!* thought Darenga, *they would visualize plantings in groups, not rows.*) But they all agreed there was nothing in their repertoire of implements or in their experience that could handle the job of clearing and grubbing which would need to be done on the meadow if they were to cultivate the plants.

"We might be able to barter with the people in Canigou

for a plow and draft animal," said Darenga, amused at the thought of going into the town on such an errand.

"Barter?"

"Exchange something of value that we have for something we need."

They were excited at the prospect, this possible contact with people they had only seen at a distance. "When can we go? What should we take?" they asked, crowding around her.

She laughed. "I don't know. Cloth, I would imagine. That's about all the surplus we have right now."

"Can we all go?"

"Can we go now?"

"We can gather the cloth and be ready very soon."

"How much should we take?"

"L'Hlaadin must be told about this first. Why don't we go back and talk to him? We'll decide what to do from there."

They returned to the camp, arriving at the tent just as a shuttle craft swung in a bright blue arc over the cliff and landed at the edge of the meadow. The high ambassador, casually and comfortably dressed in emerald and brown, came out of the hatch and walked lightly up the slope to meet the crowd pouring down to greet him.

"*J'lai mg manani,*" he said to M'landan. *May you always have generations.* He glanced about the camp. "Looks like you're well under way. If there's anything more I can do for you, anything I can get for you—"

"Thank you," M'landan replied. "I think we have all we need."

Seldoldon nodded. "Have the soenderbiests been a problem?"

"They have frequencies that control them," Darenga answered dryly.

Seldoldon looked surprised, and then he laughed. "With their voices!" He gave M'landan a wide grin. "I can see pioneering is going to be no hazard for you at all."

"It was a simple thing," M'landan answered, with a side glance at Darenga.

Seldoldon took a deep breath. "Well," he said, "are you

ready to check some boundaries? I brought a couple of smallcraft along—"

"Sir, we're ready to unload." A crewman had come up behind Seldoldon.

"Oh, good. Bring it on." Seldoldon turned back to M'landan. "I've brought something I thought you might like to have."

They all stood watching as a box was unloaded from the side bay of the shuttle. It was some four yards high and two yards wide, and had a protective outer layer covering it. The whole container was mounted on a mechipad that the crewmen now began to direct slowly up the incline.

"That's fine. Right there," Seldoldon told them. "You can move it, of course," he said to M'landan. "But the case will have to remain closed. We'll leave the mechipad with it." He handed the control unit to Darenga, and turned back to the crew members gathered around the box. "Take off those panels, please," he told them, and then he went over to help pull them down himself.

There was a sharp collective stroke of sound as the covering came away.

"Oh, Andor," Darenga said, so softly no one heard it.

It was a huge terrarium, and inside the glass was L'M'dia, a small island of it resting on its green native soil. There were five stalks reaching out of the thick purple grass, each topped by a great golden globe laced in black. The black side fronds of the stalk were heavy with buds.

M'landan swung around to Seldoldon, lifted his gauntlets from his sleeves, and drew a wide, encompassing circle above his head. "You have already done so much for us. And now you bring L'M'dia to our new home when we had resigned ourselves to having those things that were so important left only in our memories. You are a generous man, and this is a great and wonderful gesture. What we thought would fade with the birth of our generations now will be kept fresh and real. We will always bless your name."

Seldoldon had been taken off guard by this sudden and deeply emotional speech, and the sweet-swelling approval that had lifted from the M'dians. He gave M'landan and the crowd a gracious bow of his head, and Darenga heard him murmur, "Thank you; you overwhelm me."

As the M'dians began to move around the terrarium to look inside, to press their hands against the glass and sing in a high, wondering melody, Seldoldon explained to M'landan, "The university has been testing L'M'dia. It doesn't adapt well to this climate, although they've had limited success in the arid zones of the planet. I understand that the amount of light, which is only half what it is on M'dia, is the factor."

M'landan was listening closely, Darenga knew, but his eyes were fixed on the slowly oscillating plants within the box.

"They installed special lamps inside the terrarium, which maintain the normal growth rate. The packs that are in there now should last thirty years, anyway. However, there are more at the University if these should prove defective in the meantime. You have the control for the mechipad; as I said, you can put the terrarium anywhere."

"I will remember these things," M'landan said, glancing briefly at Seldoldon and then back to the glass box.

Seldoldon looked over to Darenga, said in a low voice, "I've brought some silver for Tlaima. Where shall I have it put?"

"Silver? That was very thoughtful of you. Where is it?"

Seldoldon retreated a few paces, signaled to two crewmen who stood on either side of a small crate. They lifted it and brought it forward.

"This way," Darenga said, and led them to the tent. She held back the flap so the men could set it down inside.

"You can tell her about it later," Seldoldon said as the crew members withdrew.

"How can I thank you for all your kindness, Andor?"

He looked away from her toward the crowd. "I'm happy to be able to do something for them." He shook his head. "They're so fragile . . . so innocent."

"They're stronger than you might imagine."

He turned back to her. "The strength that illuminates the soul?"

92

"If there is such a thing. And if it could be illuminated."

"That, at least, hasn't changed in you," he said, giving her a thoughtful look.

"What hasn't?"

"Three hundred years of conditioning against religion."

"Not against religion—against non-rational thinking.

"Mmmm," he acknowledged, and let the subject slide. "Are you going with us to run the boundaries?"

Now she could see that two smallcraft had been unloaded from the shuttle craft. "Yes, I'd planned on it."

"I have some commitments for later this afternoon, but we should be able to make a leisurely survey if we left now. . . ."

"Of course. I'll speak to M'landan."

She left Seldoldon and made her way through the crowd to where M'landan stood with Klayon and Tlaima, next to the terrarium.

"M'landan," she called softly.

He turned, his eyes bright and unshielded.

"Andor would like to show you the boundaries before he has to leave."

His gaze shifted from her to the figure waiting further down the slope. "May I remain here? Can you do what is necessary?"

"Yes, if you want me to. It's just a matter of flying over the lines."

"Then we will learn their position from you when you return."

She lowered her eyes. "It shouldn't be too long," she replied.

"No."

She finally turned, and, as she started to walk away, his low song came to her. "My love goes with you," he said.

Although she hesitated, she didn't look back, and M'landan watched her until she and Seldoldon had climbed into one of the smallcraft and it had lifted slowly into the bright air.

"The boundary runs west to the ocean," he said, once they were above the meadow and the cliffs.

93

The sea lay some three miles from the gradual down-slope of the sandstone bluff. In the noonward height of the sun, it spread in beaten silver to the pale horizon.

"Your southern boundary is the Mekinac River."

Seldoldon curved the smallcraft away from the lake bed and settled it down over a gleaming waterway that wound along a gentle ridge which formed the lake basin.

"Looks like the lake must have drained down through the fault line," Darenga said.

"That's the conclusion of the geologists. These mountains you see are within the boundaries."

Beneath their wing, the deeply forested flank of a ridge was slipping away. She looked down as he told her, "This arête is the eastern boundary—the line runs right along the top. It's easy to distinguish and well-defined even on the ground."

They were skimming the trees now, as he pointed out the ridge line. "I did have a lake included that would normally lie outside the boundary. I'll show it to you."

His hands played over the controls; the craft rose, and Darenga could see the broad expanse of water ahead, a wild and quiet lake of inlets and coves, where trees grew down to the shoreline. Seldoldon banked the craft toward a wide beach and set it down. He opened the canopy and raised himself out of his couch. "Let me show you around."

"All right."

He got out, and stood watching her gather the thick folds of her robe.

"Can I help you? That looks like it would be a treacherous garment."

"I've gotten used to it." She stepped easily to the ground and, with her hands on her hips, made a slow evaluative turn. "I see a cabin—well-camouflaged."

He laughed. "Anyone else would have said it was nestled in the trees. But camouflaged or nestled, it's yours. Come on, let me show it to you. By the way, there's some awfully good fish in that lake."

"You sound like you've been here before."

"My family used to come up here, now and then. But, as

94

far as I know, no one's been here for years. It's dusty as hell," he added, as they walked inside.

There was one large central room, an open sleeping loft, an alcove with bunk beds, an enormous stone fireplace, a small kitchen area.

"We used to cook our fish in this," he said and struck a tone on a long-handled pan that hung from the mantel of the fireplace. "If we had time," he said, "we'd have fish for dinner. I'm sure there's some tackle here someplace."

He opened a cupboard door, poked through a closet. "Ever do any fishing?" he asked Darenga.

"Only when I had to," she answered, watching him dig through an old chest that sat in one corner of the room.

"Strictly survival value?"

"That's about it."

He turned his search to a pantry off the kitchen, then came back into the main room. "In the loft," he said abruptly, and was up the ladder and prowling into the upper sleeping space while Darenga looked on in amusement from below.

"Are you really planning to go fishing?"

He appeared at the rail with a long pole in his hand. "No," laughed the high ambassador, seating himself on the flooring at the head of the ladder, "but it's a nice dream."

He sat, examining the pole. "Look at this; I left the hook on it."

"Then all you have to do is drop it in the water."

He looked down at her. "It's a temptation," he sighed. "And if there wasn't a final vote due this afternoon on the SOL 14, I'd yield to it; you'd have a fish dinner."

"SOL 14?"

He set the pole aside and came down the ladder. "It's the Alliance freighter. We need something SOL that's a little more flexible than the Galaxy-class ship."

"You're voting on whether to manufacture it or not?"

"No. *Where*. The vote is on site location. It's come down to either Arcus or Juang."

"I see. And your vote is essential?"

His quick laugh held a note of self-deprecation. "Not

hardly. There's not much question but that it will be Arcus. Even though I live in hope."

"SOL craft assembly on Arcus. Interesting. How long do you give yourself before you're in another war?"

"I know what the danger is."

"What happened to the Galaxies of the Solar Force?"

"They're under Arcustan and Arkdikh control. Although we can't prove it."

"So now you have a free Alliance, and all the fear and anxiety that goes with it."

He looked directly at her. "Your way was not the right way, Areia. We have an Alliance that's imperfect because its members are imperfect. But now the survival of all our worlds depends on our mutual cooperation, not on the threat of instant annihilation if we don't follow behavior prescribed by an oligarchy of genetic machinery. We'll make our mistakes, Areia, but we'll make them in a free society."

"Well," she said, turning away from him, "in eight years our arguments haven't altered."

"Can you change a principle and keep your self-respect? I can't, and neither can you. And that's the way it is. There's no reason why we can't remain friends in spite of it."

"No, there's no reason." She went out onto the porch and waited while he closed the door.

He came up beside her and took a deep breath. "I don't know whether it's a particular species of tree or flower or grass, but the air smells better here than anywhere else on this planet."

"The compelling power of memories," she said.

He was looking out toward the glittering water. She saw his head rise. "Yes, they are compelling," he replied.

A bird called from the high branches of a nearby tree, and they both looked up, a half-automatic response that faded as the song faded.

"Well," Seldoldon said finally, "what do you say we walk down here a little way before we go?"

He led her along the shoreline, pointing out his boyhood

fishing holes, giving her a short geological history of the lake, informing her of the plants which could be used with safety by both her and the M'dians. And all the while his voice flowed on, pleasant, friendly, so familiar, so warm.

They came to a little stream that emptied into the lake. "Thirsty?" he asked.

Darenga shook her head.

"It's perfectly pure."

"No, thanks. Go ahead if you like."

"Lectures always make me thirsty," he grinned, and went down on his belly beside the stream. He pulled his long hair to one side of his neck and dropped his head forward to drink. One of his hands spread into the shallow rushing creek, and the billow of his sleeve turned deeper green as it dipped into the water.

As she watched, his hair slid down from where he had twisted it back, and she knelt down to gather it up away from his face. When he felt her hands touch him he lifted his head.

The little starts and laps of the stream filled the silence. He rose slowly, sitting back on his heels, his hands spread over his thighs, as he looked at her.

"I still love you," he said. "And I can't change that."

M'landan had said, *My love goes with you*; he had known that there was this moment she was to face. And suddenly his presence, never very far from her, shone on them both.

"There are feelings I still have for you that I can't change, either," she answered. "But so much has happened to me—and to M'landan—that I can't even begin to explain to you—"

"You don't have to. I love you, and I want to see you happy. I thought it would be with me. But if it isn't, I wouldn't get any pleasure denying you what happiness you can find with M'landan. I wish only the best for you, Areia."

She looked away from him. "I didn't know something like this could be so difficult . . . I want you to know that

97

I'm concerned about you. About the way things have gone for you. May I say this? I'm sorry that the Alliance, in their regressive way, found it fit to censure you. I don't think you deserved that."

He drew her up from the ground, put his arm around her, and started them walking back in the direction from which they had come. "I deserved some of it," he told her. "I was unbelievably stupid."

"I can't agree that you would do anything stupid."

"Thank you, but in this case, I was." He took his arm away and strolled beside her, his head turned down thoughtfully. "I'm afraid that stupidity has cost me what it took all the years to build up. I don't think I'm ever going to be as effective as I was before. Sometimes I think I've been fooling myself all along."

"I wish I could be encouraging, but you know my thoughts on the Alliance."

They had reached the smallcraft, and she turned now to face him. "Andor, you are a good man—in all that over-worked phrase means—and if there is justice anywhere in this universe, it will recognize your goodness and assure you the true freedom you've always wanted."

He took her hand and kissed it before she could draw back. "Areia, I will do anything that it's in my power to do for you and all of M'landan's people."

She slipped her hands deep into her sleeves and answered, "My people as well, Andor."

"Yes, I realize that now—your people."

"I'm very grateful for what you've already done for them. They are so at the mercy of anyone who might take advantage of their weakness." She stopped speaking because the thought was one that could make her cry, and she saw no purpose in that. But he knew the depth of her feeling, and said, "No one will take advantage of them. I'll see to that. Go ahead and build your community. Live in peace."

There seemed nothing more to say after that, and so they got into the smallcraft and rode down a long and silent arc back to the cliffs.

Chapter 10

Darenga's little group of farmers had selected and tagged all the plants that would be used for seed, had measured and marked off the positions of the islands they would plant, and now, with the large-eyed silence all M'dians used when they wished another to mark their patience, they turned to Darenga.

Standing in the hip-high grass under the zenith of the Ronadjounian sun, and harassed by little moisture-loving insects that had never evolved on M'dia, Darenga didn't get it at first, and so she just stared back, automatically fanning a reassembly of gnats with her hand while her mind sought a reason for the silence. And then it came to her—the plow.

She laughed. "Well, all right. I guess we're ready for it now."

They gave her a quick, approving chirrup, gathering around her in excitement and little trills of laughter. The male Atin and his shoma-mate Reen came up on either side of her.

"May we go now, Chaeya?" Atin asked.

"We have everything ready." That was Reen.

Another male, Laak, said, "We've had it ready for—" he hesitated, counting "—four *tda* sunfalls."

It had become their way of measuring time—*tda*. On M'dia their white sun, Baandla, had touched and swung up from their horizon four times—four sunfalls—the equivalent of a 24-hour day. Now the addition *tda* meant *here, in this place, on this planet*. Four days.

"Go get the material, and I'll tell L'Hlaadin we're going."

They rushed off, eight figures flying ahead of her up the slope toward the tents, as she walked along behind with a smile twisting down the corners of her mouth.

She found M'landan watching the builders. Two outer rooms had been roughly carved, and small groups of M'dians were doing the finishing work while another crew was hollowing out a third, inner, room that was slightly larger than the other two, the dimensions being prepared under M'landan's direction. It was to be the room where L'M'dia would be kept.

"It's almost finished," she said.

He looked down at her, startled, he had been so intently watching the activity. "I did not expect to see you," he said quickly, his voice revealing his pleasure.

"I'm sorry, I didn't mean to sneak up on you." Her Songspeech translation of "sneak" broadened his mouth in a smile. "No, I'm sure you didn't. Is everything going well in the meadow?"

"I just came up here to tell you we're going to Canigou for the plow."

"Ah. And you are all ready? You have everything you wanted to take?"

"They're getting it now."

He turned and walked back with her to where her group was coming together, with their arms full of cloth.

"This won't work," she said, watching them stagger, trying to balance the heavy rolls. "You'll never make it beyond the tents."

"Perhaps a cart could be spared . . . ?" Atin directed his hopeful question to M'landan.

"Explain what it is you want to them, my brother," M'landan answered, and Atin and Reen hurried off toward the construction area.

"You must keep in mind the Chaeya's instructions when you are in the town," M'landan told the others. "Do only what she tells you to do. Respond politely if someone addresses you, even though you don't understand the language. The Chaeya will translate for you if it's necessary. Keep your hands in your sleeves unless something is handed to you. They must not think you are without manners."

There was a solemn little tune of agreement among the listeners.

Darenga looked down at the ground and hoped M'landan would not say anything to her which would require her to speak, because she would have had to explain why she sounded so amused. But Atin and Reen arrived then with a cart that was still slightly damp from the quick scrubbing they had given it, and immediately everyone was engaged in packing the rolls of cloth into it.

When it was accomplished, and after an excited farewell to M'landan, they started off.

It was five miles to Canigou, all downhill, and Darenga had to restrain them every inch of the way. Eventually she took charge of the cart and made them all stay with it at her pace, while their lilting voices carried on their bright and endless speculations.

"What can a city of humans be like?"

"Like the great Hall?"

"Or the little metal dwellings they gave us?"

"Or the dwellings of cloth!" This in a high glissade of laughter from Reen that was echoed through the group. For the sensitive eyes of the M'dians, who could detect heat sources and, even more precisely, the tiny fluctuations that were a visual language of their own, the tents were only a shelter from the elements, nothing more.

"Some of the houses are stone, others are made of wood," Darenga said.

"They have to have big houses," Laak offered *ex cathedra*, "because they have young all the time. *Eretec* over and over, and every male is a priest."

"Where did you get an idea like that!" Darenga glanced back over her shoulder at him, fascinated by this rumor.

"Why, in the books, Chaeya," he replied, as if he were citing an unchallengeable authority.

"Books? Oh, the anatomy lessons." A term for the simple and graphic polyfilmpacs that were used in information exchange with newly contacted planets. She continued to pull the cart along. "Every normal male is capable of carrying out that function," she said, "but they're not all priests. In fact," and she knew this addendum would cause trouble, "males who have chosen to be priests have vowed not to produce children."

There were little sucks and releases of sound around her.

"The word 'priest' doesn't have quite the same meaning here," she said, and explained, as clearly as she could, the difference.

"Will we see one of these strange priests?" Reen asked her. "What do they look like?"

"Like everybody else. Sometimes they wear a brown garment when they're acting unofficially. During ceremonies they have more elaborate clothing."

"And does everyone have a different costume for what they do?"

"How do we tell them all apart!"

"You recognize me, don't you?" Darenga laughed.

"But your hair is like fire!"

That made her consider something she hadn't thought of before. And as the M'dians continued their deliberations on what they could expect to find in Canigou, she was planning how best to give herself a low profile.

Since she would have to do the talking, it wouldn't be easy. She decided to let someone else pull the cart into town, and walk beside it with the others, instead. She pushed her hair way back and pulled her hood forward, so a casual observer would not readily see the color. Her eyebrows and eyelashes she could do nothing about; she only hoped that the sight of a group of M'dian giants descending on the town would keep attention from falling on her.

And they did cause a modest sensation. Canigou was far enough from the Gemainshaf Hall that the sight of an alien was not a frequent occurrence. And so they came bearing their goods to market with a growing, but politely distant, citizenry trailing along the sidewalks of either side of the main street.

She had to keep giving the command, "Shield your eyes!" to them, because in their excitement they wanted to see more clearly than they could with the membrane down.

"What *are* they saying!" Atin exclaimed.

"They wonder what *you're* saying," she replied. "Someone thinks your voices are pretty."

Atin called out in an elegant melody, "May *your* generations have beautiful voices!"

"Oh, Atin!" Reen admonished him. "No one spoke to you!"

"That's not so; they're all speaking to us."

"Stop here, Holta," Darenga told the one who was now pulling the cart. "I'll go in here and find out where we can get a plow."

She had halted the whole procession in front of a low stone building that had a slowly rotating cylindrical screen mounted on the roof.

"What is this place?" Holta wanted to know.

"Community communications," Darenga answered her. "If there's an old plow anywhere in Canigou, they'll know it here."

"Look, everyplace has steps—steps up, steps down. How does one get a cart in and out of the dwellings?" Atin had started toward the sidewalk with Reen right behind him, and the others were making motions to follow.

"Just a minute." Darenga realized that this wasn't going to work at all, that she couldn't leave them alone. "Come on in with me," she told them, and they all trooped along behind her as she went up the steps, their little parade watched by the people who were trying not to appear as if they were watching.

Darenga went in through the door, hearing Atin sing, "You are beautiful, too," in response to someone who had said, "Look at that sucker! He must be ten feet high!"

She marched across a big, comfortable room where the three or four people who had been inside were trying to look as if the sight they were seeing happened every day.

The woman behind the wicket smiled with bright courtesy when Darenga walked up. "Can I help you?"

Darenga, remembering Seldoldon's earlier warning, had abandoned the idea of presenting herself as L'Hlaadin's Chaeya, even though that was a custom that was expected to be honored. Instead, she identified herself as translator for the M'dians, who were seeking information about any plow that might be for sale or trade. She kept herself faced so she could carry on a conversation with the woman and watch the room at the same time.

People from outside were beginning to saunter in on one pretext or another to carry on half-articulated, half-heard dialogs while they stared at the M'dians, whose brilliant and unveiled eyes stared back.

"The co-op has new plows," the woman offered.

"We don't have any money, only trade items. What we would like to have is a used plow in good condition."

"I may have a listing here—" she ran her fingers over a lighted board. "Are you from Amper?" she asked Darenga pleasantly.

"No." Darenga's accent was close to native Ronadjounian, but not close enough. "Earth, originally."

"Earth? Where?" She leaned back, her fingers hovering over the board, and seemed prepared to continue the conversation for some time.

"Northern Hemisphere."

"Chaeya?" Atin asked then, "may I talk to them?"

"Oh, their voices are *so* lovely!" the woman behind the wicket said. Her face came forward almost to the screen. "I voted for them to be allowed to live up there, you know. We are the planet that is headquarters for the Alliance, and yet Canigou isn't really exposed to the different beings who live on our world. I know it will be a good thing. Especially for the children. They have to learn how to get along with aliens. It's the only time in my life I've voted against the abbot, but, well, you have to vote for what you think's right, don't you?"

"Yes," Darenga replied, and turned away to answer Atin. "Not right now. We're going to leave as soon as we find out if there's a plow around here."

"How nice to be able to understand that language, and be able to speak it too—or sing it, I guess I should say. Was it difficult to learn?"

Darenga looked back through the screen. "I lived with them for several years."

"I have the feeling I've seen you before," the woman replied with a thoughtful frown.

"I don't think so. The plow? Were you able to find one?"

"Oh! Yes, Jean Thivierge has two, and he's willing to trade." She looked up inquiringly.

"We have cloth."

"Cloth? I don't imagine—no, I shouldn't say that. It would be up to him to decide. What kind of cloth is it?"

"M'dian. It's woven from fibers of one of the native plants. It's a very fine cloth, doesn't soil easily, very sturdy, too. This robe I'm wearing, I've had for eight years."

The woman came around from behind the cage, and Darenga, thinking it would be wise not to bring too much scrutiny to bear on herself, moved ahead of her, guiding her to the group of M'dians, who stood in the middle of the floor.

"All of these robes have had considerable wear," she said, bringing her up to Atin, who was overjoyed. "She wants to look at the material of your robe," she told him, and stepped aside as Atin delicately lifted a fold for the woman to examine.

"Do you like it?" he sang in a soft pleasant tone. "Our weavers are very skilled." He glanced about to include everyone in the room in his comment.

"It's . . . very nice," the woman said, responding to what she understood of the sound. She stared up into the enormous, bright, black eyes as she automatically felt the cloth he had held out for her.

"She likes it! I know she likes it, Chaeya!"

"I think so. The rest want to look at it, too."

The woman relinquished her position to some of the other townspeople who had come forward, and Darenga asked, "Where can we find the person who has the plows?"

The woman was hardly interested in her anymore. Her eyes were on the M'dians. Atin and the others were revolving slowly to the inquiring and careful hands that touched their robes, and listening to the people trying to communicate in primary phrases which they responded to with little lilting runs of encouragement.

"At the end of the street, turn right. It's the third farmhouse on the road."

"Do you know if he's there now?"

"His light on the board was lit. He's home."

"Thank you," Darenga said, and, calling her group together with a quick little phrase, led them back out the door.

By the time they had reached the third farmhouse Darenga knew that Farmer Thivierge had been notified they were coming. But even if he hadn't, he would have known anyway, by the company that was strung out like a comet's tail behind the cart.

The whole crowd sifted in through the wide gate. A tall old man came down from his porch, unsmiling but not unfriendly, chary in his movements and expression. He held himself with a grizzled confidence. *A man with standing in his community,* Darenga thought. He said, "What can I do for you?"

Darenga answered, "We understand you have two plows for sale or trade."

"I have."

"We'd like to see them."

"They're in the shed," he replied. He hadn't looked toward the cart, although Darenga knew he was fully aware of what they carried in it. He turned away, and she indicated to her group that the cart was to be left and they were to follow.

The door to the shed was laid back, and they all crowded into the dim room. The M'dians lifted their eye membranes and stared around, as Darenga was doing, at the walls and the neat rows of implements hanging from pegs and racks, at the heavy benches and the long-handled tools, all cleaned and polished and well-used.

The room itself was a testimony to the possible condition of the plows, which were parked to one side, near the work benches. Both had power packs, but one appeared to be manual, with fittings for a draft animal, and the other fully pack-run, with an operator's seat and small platform behind.

After a close inspection of both plows, and a test of their packs, Darenga said, "The fullpack plow would be best for our needs. We have M'dian cloth to exchange for it. It's in the cart." She started for the door.

"I don't have any need for cloth," he replied brusquely.

Darenga came back around. "That's all we have to bargain with. We want a secondhand plow, but we can sell our material and buy a new one, if we have to. We offer you four rolls. I think if you'll come out to the cart, you'll find the trade is a fair one."

"I'll take a look," he replied.

They all walked back out to the cart. Thivierge was hardly unaware of his neighbors' interest in the rolls that were being examined by them. When he came up there were greetings, but the crowd grew quiet as he did a slow walk around the cart and then, taking an endpiece of one upright roll, ran a section of it through his fingers, turned it over, tested its strength, looked closely at the weave.

"Is this the only color you have?" he asked Darenga.

The M'dians had picked up the concentration of the townspeople on what the old man was doing, and were standing to one side, watching, their focus shifting from him to Darenga as they waited.

"This particular community of M'dians use only the natural color of the material for their robes, but they have dyed it for other uses. However, that was on M'dia. I don't know what they would use for dye on this planet. They haven't been here long enough to look into it. You might contact the university at Amper. I'm sure they can give you some information. Let me add that material made from this plant is limited. All they have is what they brought with them, and there wasn't very much to begin with. They'll weave other cloth, of course, when they get their looms constructed, but it will be from other fiber. When the supply of this cloth is gone, it's gone forever."

Atin began a sweet, compelling phrase then, directed at Thivierge, but Darenga told him, "Let him make up his own mind."

The melody ended on a little note of regret that drew an empathetic murmur from the crowd. Thivierge appeared not to have heard any of it. But he said, "You've seen the condition of the plow you want—it's like new, none of the parts are worn. I take good care of my equipment. It's an HD 400; you won't have trouble with the power packs, like the older 300. And every part on it is replaceable. I couldn't take less than five rolls for a piece of equipment like this."

He stood back with an air of finality, and slipped his fingers into his slanted pockets. His thumbs tapped rhythmically against the double seams.

"What you say about the plow is true," she said, noting his mannerism, "and I've already told you we'd like to have it. But four is all we can offer you. As I said, our supply is limited, and there'll be no more." She gave him a thoughtful look as he slowly shook his head, his eyes on the ground, his thumbs working the seams. "If you really feel that four rolls is not a fair price, then I can promise you a choice of one roll from among the material that will be woven when our weavers begin to use their looms again. It won't be this fiber, of course, but the quality of the weaving will be the same."

"And how long would that be?"

"I can't tell you, because they're still looking for plants they can use. But once they've found some and begin weaving, it won't take long."

"Pardonnez-moi." A man in a brightly patterned blouse and green trousers, characteristic of dress in Canigou, stepped forward. "But could they not use wool from the alpar?"

"I don't know," Darenga said, and directed the question to Laak, who was standing beside her. "Do you know if the weavers could use animal fur?"

"Are the animals killed?" Holta asked, aghast.

"No, they shear off the wool. The animals aren't harmed."

"They have never used animal fur," Reen answered. "We would have to ask them, Chaeya."

Darenga addressed the man who had asked the question. "The weavers have never used animal hair before. We don't know if they would or not."

"I have an alpar compound. Maybe we could work a trade—I'll give them the fur, and we share on the cloth."

"I'll relay your offer. What is your name?"

"René Gendron. And," he added, "I voted for your admission. My compound is east, toward the mountains."

"I'll remember."

"And what is your name?" Thivierge asked Darenga.

She looked into the old man's impassive face. "Areia," she replied.

"No surname?"

"Areia will do."

"You live up there with them?"

"Yes."

He grunted, "You can tell them they have a plow. And I'll take the first roll of cloth that comes off their looms. From alpar wool, if they'll weave it. But if they won't, a good roll of something else."

She nodded. "I'll get word to you as soon as the looms start producing."

"You want to take the plow now?"

"Yes."

She started after the farmer, but Atin called her back around. "Chaeya! What is happening?"

"He's going to take the cloth; we'll take the plow."

"Oh, can this be more wonderful! Do we take it now?"

"Stay here with the cart, and I'll bring it out."

Atin turned back toward his brothers and sisters with an excited flick of his tongue and a swift flourish of melody that rang like a bell, while the farmer led Darenga back into the shed. He turned around. "Here's my hand on a good trade for both of us," he said, and twisted his hand away at the last instant and, automatically, she gripped his wrist.

She stared at the hard blue eyes that leveled on her from below the thick gray eyebrows.

"I thought I knew who you were," he said.

"And now that you're sure . . . ?"

"You did for us once, and I respect Lord Andor as I did his father and his grandfather." He abruptly let go of her

109

wrist. "There are some that don't," he said cryptically. "A word of warning to you: the closer you stay to your reservation, the less trouble you're going to make for yourselves."

"What kind of trouble are you talking about? Do you mean opposition from the abbot?"

He looked at her. "I've said all I'm going to say." He turned away. "If you're planning to use this plow on the bottomlands, set it shallow and let the sillion rest a couple of days and then go back over it. It takes longer, but the plow won't have to be unstuck every ten meters, and the power pack won't wear out on you. There'll be better aeration, too. What are you going to plant?"

"Bishop's bread, marsh staff, and jimasette, primarily."

"Weeds!"

"It's the only substitute the university found for the M'dian's native food source."

"Well, everyone to their own."

"Yes," she slowly replied. "Tell me, Jean Thivierge, were you one of the ones who voted in favor of the M'dian settlement?"

"I was."

She bowed her head slightly. "I'll remember your advice —both about staying home and about using the plow. Now, if you'll open both those doors, please, I'll drive this out."

And back through town, with Thivierge's message still fresh in her mind, she noticed what she hadn't noticed before in the crowd of townspeople; she saw the few here and there who had drawn back, who watched and listened with sober expressions and unyielding stares. Her apprehension began to grow.

The five miles back to the cliffs took twice as long as the trip into Canigou. The whole group wanted to learn how to operate the plow, and, once she had shown them, they all had to have a try. Before long she found herself hauling the cart alone while the M'dians took turns at the plow, one in the driver's seat, two on the platform, and the rest following closely, all flying ahead of her at ten miles per hour, their robes flapping, their voices all in joyous counterpoint. They would rush on with the plow, stop to switch places while she caught up, and then take off again ahead of her. Every now and then one would politely offer to pull the cart, but she would decline with a wave of her hand, and the one would rush back to the rest for another turn.

They pulled into the grounds as twilight was deepening into evening, and as they came through the tents and buildings they could see the brightly lit terrarium, the globes glowing like lamps in the surrounding darkness of the cliffs.

M'landan was standing near the box, his bronze hood shooting back darts of golden light. He looked up as Atin, at the wheel again, brought the plow into the camp and stopped it a careful distance from the terrarium.

"And is this what you will use to tend our fields, Atin?" he asked.

"L'Hlaadin," Atin replied, "they call it 'tilling.' " He looked about as his brothers and sisters came gathering around. "It is our own machine," he told them. "Our very own."

"What was Canigou like?" someone asked him, and the group that had gone to town joined in a chaotic answer as Darenga came up to M'landan and set the handles of the cart on the ground.

"And were you allowed to pull this all the way from town?" he asked her.

"They offered to help."

M'landan made a little noise of disapproval in his throat as they walked away toward the cliffs unnoticed.

"Did you give many rolls of cloth for the plow?" he asked as she stopped to wash her hands and face at the temporary lavabo.

"Four rolls and the promise of a fifth as soon as the weavers find something to weave. Someone suggested using alpar fur; would they do that?"

"Are the animals killed?"

She laughed because it had been the same question, with the same note of horror, that Holta had asked. "No, the wool is shaved off. It grows back quickly."

111

"Perhaps the weavers might. You will have to ask them."

"I thought I would later."

They walked slowly on toward the new rooms, glancing back, now and then, at the scene illuminated by the terrarium.

"Atin is very excited," M'landan said.

"He wants to start plowing right away. With him at the wheel, of course."

"He seems to have forgotten how to restrain himself." He looked down at her. "The inner room is finished," he said.

"That was quick."

"You were gone all day." Faintly, ever so faintly, so she was not entirely sure she had heard it at all, complaint.

She sat back in the window opening of the first room and looked up into his dark hood. "I got some advice with the plow: a friendly warning that we stay on our land. Apparently some of Canigou was opposed to our settling here, and the leading opposition, as far as I can make out, comes from—"

"—the religious leaders."

"Yes, that's right. Was that a guess?"

"It is not hard to reason out."

"There was only a suggestion of it at Canigou."

"Perhaps we should give some thought to remaining here and not going into the town anymore."

"We could get by if we never saw another human being again."

"You are very adaptable."

"I'm realistic."

"Ah, yes, I know."

She started to say something, then let it go. "When does L'M'dia move to its new home?"

"At first light," he answered. "Everything is prepared. If you will guide it in. . . ."

"It'll take at least an hour to bring it up the slope. I'll have to move it very slowly. If the stalks start swaying and the globes strike the sides of the terrarium, they'll probably burst. I don't know how Andor got them down here in one piece."

"With the great care he takes in everything."

She searched the dark hood, caught only the liquid gleam of his eye fluid, could discern nothing there. "I'll be glad when we get it safely into the room."

"As will I." He paused. "When it is finished, we will begin *eretec*."

She looked down at her feet then, and crossed her ankles. "What do you want me to do during all this?"

"Stay with me," he answered, as if he were surprised that she would ask. "That is the place for the Chaeya at *eretec*—beside her priest."

She was silent, and he drew closer to her.

"Chaeya, there are certain rituals we have at *eretec* which are very important, but I cannot perform in many of them. There are some things which would be allowable for you to do for me, and I would have you do them, if you would."

"You know I will; you don't have to ask me."

He bent forward and touched his forehead briefly to hers. "You are the one dearest to me in all the world," he told her softly, "and I would have your hands do for me what mine cannot—administer the sacred oil to my brothers, to the ones who will be called father in my name."

He sat down beside her and laid his gauntlet on her hand where it rested on the sill. "*Eretec* is a time of great joy for us, and we will keep it a time of joy, although nothing is as it was, although this new generation which will proceed from this time must live in a way yet to be decided. We already love these children, and now there is no limitation to the time we will have to spend with them. They will not have the sorrow and loneliness their parents suffered at *Maleelonos*. Is one ever prepared to see those loved so dearly die? But it will not be that way with them."

His gauntlet raised to her head and pressed lightly against her ear. "Ah, Chaeya, it will not be that way with them."

The words expressed gratitude, but the melody was a lament so sad it constricted her throat. She was unable to reply, and he went on, his voice shifting from the minor key.

"My brothers have a sacred role in our society, for although I am the father of the flesh, they provide that constant, loving presence and guidance that I can never give, not to so many, not even to that one who will be my son through the special love I bear for you. It was not meant for me—through all my possible paths, it was never meant for me."

"M'landan. . . ." She turned her head away from the grief in his voice, and stared up through the window at the dark and glittering sky. "What can I do for you? If there is anything in this universe I can do to ease your burden, please let me do it!"

"I distress you; *mlo saindla*, that is not what I intended."

He put his arm around her, and she sank into its comfort, powerless against the physical limitations that left her unable to hear all the frequencies and rich intonations which would have made clear what he had been revealing to her. Her response had been too simple, too centered on herself, and he had reacted in love and concern, and the purity of that instinct drove her down into herself, and in that sudden isolation she couldn't tell him she did understand. She said, "M'landan—"

"Yes?"

"The child that Tlaima bears—"

"I love you."

"Please—"

"You have contributed more than you may ever be able to realize."

"M'landan," she cried out softly, "I am so alone," and, having said it, got up and walked away, and in that moment nothing on the Ronadjounian planet would have drawn her back.

Chapter 11

Darenga rose with Tlaima and Klayon, before sunrise. She had not slept; M'landan had spent the night in the cliff room. And now, as she saw him standing near the terrarium, where the rest of the camp was gathering, she felt wretched and ashamed, although she was not sure why.

He said nothing to her, but it was more a silence of preoccupation, and she kept her own silence, drawing her concentration down on the task of moving the terrarium up the slope. It was a more onerous task than she had anticipated. She had been right about the dangerous swaying inside the box: the most minute unevenness in the ground would send a shudder up the stalks. The M'dians saw this danger and began a sweep ahead of her to clear the way as the mechipad moved the terrarium along by inches.

Her fingers never left the control cartridge, as her eyes moved back and forth from it to the terrarium. And she swore roundly every time the stalks were set into motion, although she tried to curb it into Arcustan out of respect for M'landan, who walked beside her. The machine finally reached the cliffs, and she moved it into the inner room, where the floor had been trampled and smoothed until it shone. Then it was rolled into position, and it was done.

Darenga sighed, let her hands drop to her sides. They all stared at the terrarium, the soft, reddish glow reflecting over their faces. After a moment, she stepped forward and replaced the control cartridge in its slot in the undercarriage of the mechipad, thinking, as she did, that it would probably never be used again. A thousand years from now the terrarium would still be in this same place, but worshiped by whom?

She went back to stand beside M'landan while he offered a prayer of gratitude for the safe arrival of L'M'dia to its permanent place. When this was done, and they had come back out into the sunlight, M'landan stopped, looked out over the people. Darenga stopped beside him, and he glanced toward her for an instant, his eyes unshielded. Then the membrane came down as he turned his face so it was obscured from her view. He lifted his head, and there was an abrupt rippling movement in the crowd. M'landan became as suddenly still. The people were kneeling and beginning a soft chant, an insistent question that rose toward him in increasing volume until it broke around him with tidal force. "Father . . . ? Father . . . ? *Father?*"

He stood transfixed by the strange plaintive quality of the sound, a sound which, from its first tone, drove Darenga into a vague, but demanding, restlessness that was impossible to act on. She felt a compelling need to respond, but there was nothing in her experience to guide her.

And still the irresistible question, "Father . . . ? *Father?*"

M'landan lifted his head once again, and, seeing his throat moving silently, Darenga understood then that it had been an instruction from him which had triggered their reaction in the first place and set in motion what had held him amazed. Something instinctive? something learned? an expectancy conditioned into them in their childhood? But her childhood had not been spent with the M'dians, nor had her genetic coding been determined by their elders. Still, every nerve in her body was responsive and electrified.

And now a soft and haunting chant from the female voices, "Father of our generations whose precious seed is life, bless us now."

On a low, constant note came the corresponding prayer from the male voices, "Brother to all brothers whose love joins us all, Holy Guide, pray for us."

As the final note faded, the sweet lyric chant of the female voices repeated their orison, followed by the deep and haunting prayer of the males: "Father of our generations, whose precious seed is life, bless us now. . . . Brother to all brothers, whose love joins us all, Holy Guide, pray

116

for us. . . . Father of our generations, whose precious seed is life, bless us now. . . . Brother to all brothers, whose love joins us all, L'Hlaadin, pray for us now. . . ."

And, clear and achingly beautiful to Darenga, who was drowning in the frequencies she could hear and stimulated to distraction by those she could not, came the deep baritone voice of M'landan, "O Loving Gods, thou hast found our conduct pleasing. Thy will hast guided us to this place and hast set for us the time of *eretec*. We thank thee for the continuance of our generations. Thy love is truly deep and abundant that thou wouldst grant us this joy."

It was as though his voice had drawn together all the fibers in her nervous system and laid them smooth again. She felt her entire body relax, and she saw that it had affected the crowd below them in the same way.

M'landan concluded his prayer, the whole company came to its feet and cried out in a quick rising phrase, "L'Hlaadin! Permission . . . permission!"

With raised arms, he inscribed a double circle on the air. The crowd rolled back, shifted, dispersed with low, excited melodies, melting back into the camp in groups and pairs, a number breaking away from the main group and going to the building where the stores were kept. With a gentle call, M'landan drew Darenga away from this scene, and, as she followed him up the slope to the cliff rooms and the cool shadows, she saw the M'dians emerging from the building with jars of lumeena carefully balanced in their arms. She turned to M'landan with a question, but his arms came swiftly around her and his tongue darted all about her face.

"Why do you . . . hide this excitement from . . . your people?" she asked him between lunges his tongue made at her lips. He coiled it back into his mouth with a soft little noise.

"There are things I would reveal to no one but you, my Chaeya. Do you feel my joy? What a gracious gift we are being given! Our generations will continue, and they will have their priest to guide them. Are we not blessed above all others in this great and beautiful universe?"

117

"I think you deserve more than any other being the happiness you feel."

"And you, dear Chaeya, my beloved and faithful Chaeya, what do you feel when you see your priest in ecstasy over something so strange to you? Tell me what you feel."

"I try to understand."

"Yes," he agreed, much calmer now. He touched his mouth to her hair and sang quietly, "That is true. And it must be the greatest measure of *why my eyes hold only your image, why my ears hear only your song—*"

"My brother. . . ." It was Tlaima, softly interrupting. She stood in the doorway, her hands in her sleeves, and even in her voluminous robes the heaviness of the child inside her was visible. She came slowly into the room as M'landan turned. "There is much to do before sunfall, my brother."

"*Mlo saindla,*" he said ruefully, "I didn't mean for you to search me out. I will come at once." He turned back to Darenga, who had stepped away and now stood near the window quietly watching them.

"There are rituals I must follow," he told her. "Preparations I must make for *eretec.* I will return for you this evening, and then we will go together to my sisters."

"Do you want me to wait here for you?"

"I ask it of you, yes."

She bowed her head in silent assent, and then watched as they left the room together.

Alternately through the long day she heard the rise and fall of their voices from the shrine room and, later, Klayon's voice. The melodies were solemn, supplicating, filled with gratitude. They were a curious counterpoint to the festive score that rode the outer air. If *eretec* required serious preparation from the priest, it demanded nothing more than merriment from the other participants. And, at a point between the two, Darenga sat watching and listening, her head resting against the edge of the window opening as the bright Ronadjounian sun rose to the top of the sky and slowly disappeared behind the cliffs. And for the first time in years, she went down into alpha: she lay on the ledge with the brilliant oblong of glassy blue sky and black cliff to her right and went plunging down into alpha until the blackness inside her mind reversed and it was the room, with its smooth, rounded walls dappled with reflected light and hung with the glaring oblong of blue, which rested behind her eyelids, and the blackness which filled the space around her body, both enclosing her and leaving her free, buoyant on space, anchored in darkness, herself fluid and contained, washing up the sides of this weightless space she had formed of her own body. It kept out the light confined inside her skull, that small circumference that delicately bound so much. And, having set the boundaries, made the darkness, confined the light, she wept.

She had been standing for a half hour or so, her shoulder leaning against the wall while she watched the shadows beyond the window deepen, and heard the voices fom the camp grow gradually quiet until the hush became anticipatory, heavy. She saw a figure go by the window, and Klayon appeared at the door. He held a narrow rounded case in his hands. Darenga straightened away from the wall.

"I will leave these with you, Chaeya," Klayon told her. "He wishes you to—" he hesitated "—mount these." He gave her the box.

She stood in the middle of the room, staring at the case in her hands. He left unnoticed.

Only the shift in silence, that sudden alteration in the reflection of her own soft breathing, that and the brush of his robe against the stone as he came through the doorway, announced M'landan's presence. She looked up and sensed immediately his constraint, and, understanding it, she walked over to the ledge, set the case down, and opened it.

The Caretaker had improved on his original design. The prostheses he had developed for M'landan had been refined now, so that no additional control unit was necessary; it was all self-contained and governed by the autonomic responses of M'landan's body, these metal gauntlets.

119

He had come up beside her, and when she turned, he held out his arms so she could remove the cloth. She ran a small sterilizing rod over her own hands and over his wrist stumps. She unclipped the thin tubes that had been implanted into the duct openings in his wrists, and carefully inserted the sensors into the tubes. It was painful enough that he winced and drew in a quick breath, but she went about this work matter-of-factly, carefully fitting the shields, securing the prostheses at his elbows, and testing the firmness of the shields by pressing her palms against the circular inserts. She realized then what she was doing, and took her hands away. He stood motionless, and when she said, "M'landan. . . ." her voice trailing off because she didn't know what else to say, he told her sharply, "Call me by my name." And she understood the unfamiliar tone for what it was, an attempt to compose himself.

But because it seemed suddenly very important, she replied, "Your people put a name to the comfort and hope they were given when they were confused and afraid, and it was L'Hlaadin. But your name is M'landan, and it's in that name that I find my comfort. I'll call you nothing else."

He looked surprised. And then he said, "You have a bitter wisdom, Chaeya. Yes, you are right—my name is M'landan. That is the truth. That is what I must remember."

She was following after him before the swift agreement he had made, as if he had in fact been reminded of something, struck her. The sweet melodic glide of his name had become so familiar to her that its literal meaning had long ago lost its significance. But it came now to her as clearly as if it had been spoken aloud. M'landan: One-Who-Is-Sacrificed. And a feeling of dread so strong welled up in her that she reached out and lay her hand on his back.

Without turning, he said softly, "Do not be afraid for me, Chaeya."

"But I am afraid."

He stopped then, on the slope a few meters from where Klayon and Tlaima stood waiting, and looked over at her as she came up beside him. "When this time is over, Chaeya, you and I will go to our own room and we will talk about everything that has been troubling you . . . and me."

He drew one arm out of his sleeve, and the shield gleamed in the light from the brilliant bridge of stars overhead as he reached forward to press his wrist against her ear. "They are waiting; we must go."

When they started down the slope again, Klayon came forward and placed a large, open jar of oil in Darenga's hand. It was wide and heavily ornamented with silver, beautiful and alien. It felt warm against her fingers.

Klayon and Tlaima drew aside, and Darenga and M'landan walked silently to the first tent. Two M'dians held the flaps aside while others looked on. Darenga entered first; it was the order they were to follow throughout the night.

It took a moment for Darenga's eyes to adjust to the dim light inside the walls of the tent, and even when they had, the figures were indistinct ghosts floating against the dark background. She stood to M'landan's right as he knelt before the figures. Bowing his head, M'landan said, "Quanti, my sister, treasured daughter of Quualaa and her shoma-mate Bavair and our father Lodan, will you consent to this union with me?"

The gentle answer, "My brother, Father of Generations, I consent."

"Samar, my brother, grant me this union with your mate, our sister. These children she will bear will be yours to love and to guide in the sacred traditions of our people. I beg you, in the name of our generations, to grant this union."

"I grant it, knowing these will be my children, and I make this promise, to hold them in love, because through our blood they are made my flesh."

M'landan bowed his head deeply to Samar, and then rose in a soft flow of robes to stand directly in front of Quanti. There came a soft and purring tone from his throat, a sound Darenga had never heard before; it drew a restless movement from Samar and a sudden intense silence from Quanti. And then there was a breathless, long, and upward-sliding run of melody that quickly vanished out of Darenga's range of hearing, but not before she had recognized her own voice in Quanti's song.

The metal shields glimmered in the darkness, Quanti moved forward, and the thick and sudden odor of honey filled the close air of the tent. Darenga's reaction was swift and confused, and so instantly and savagely stifled that it immobilized her. M'landan's voice drew across the violence of her response.

"Bless and divide this seed, O Gods. Increase us as thy wisdom choses."

The pale sleeves of his robe returned to his sides. The dark oval of his hood turned toward Darenga, and she jolted herself into motion, touching the cool surface of the oil and reaching out as Samar bent his head toward her. She pressed her fingers against his forehead as M'landan intoned, "I pass the fatherhood to you."

"My brother," Samar responded with a deep tremolo. He put his arm around Quanti, and their pale figures melted toward the entrance, faded and were replaced by two other figures.

And it was the same again and again, the solemn and reverent requests, the respectful answers, the autonomic mating response, the heavy scent of honey that sent her plunging down inside herself, and then her fingers in the smooth and clinging oil.

They walked in the fresh and moist Ronadjounian night toward another tent, and she drew a deep and vital breath as she looked up at the stars burning in the sharp clear air.

"Endure this," he said to her gently, "for my sake. There is no passion involved in it with me. It is my obligation."

"I know." She turned her head toward him. "Does everyone see my reaction?" she asked, with a trace of bitterness impossible for her to filter out.

"No. You hide it well from everyone but me."

They had come to the second tent, and were given admittance, and it was all repeated again. And again. Until the tents seemed to crowd forward and surround them, and the M'dians move before them as if it were they who stood in one place and the procession was drifting past on a sea of honey fragrance and oil.

She dropped the jar and watched it slowly fall, the silver figures revolving in the air, the droplets shivering out from the mouth, riding singly on the heavy air and falling, falling, drop by glistening drop, irretrievably into the fabric of the tent floor. But she was too slow in reaching for it, and the noise, the terrible engulfing sound she had been hearing, had been feeling, had been remembering, prevented her muscles from obeying the commands she was trying to give.

She thought, *The oil is sacred. It's blessed. My God, my God! what have I done!*

And then she was nauseated and cold. She turned away from the hoods that were like openings into infinity, and stumbled forward, suddenly on fire. From somewhere Klayon appeared, and she drew back from him as M'landan cried out, "Do not put your hand on her! Let her go! Stand away!"

She didn't hear him. What concentration she was able to marshal under the total sensation of sound was directed toward reaching a point of isolation. Her body rang. She careened into a building, fell to her knees, and then managed somehow to pull herself up and go forward again. It was too familiar, this disruption in the nerve impulses, this flood of sound that governed even her sense of touch so that she slid over a rolling sheet of sound so terrible it made her cry out in pain.

Klayon had backed away from her when M'landan had called out to him. Now he stood by with his arms out from his sides, his body leaning anxiously forward as he watched her stumbling on an erratic track toward the cliff rooms. He swung his head around to M'landan. "What is wrong? What has happened to her?"

Darenga was feeling her way along the wall now, her hands stretched out in front of her. "Tell them to wait," M'landan replied. "I'm going to her; keep everyone away."

Klayon stood, indecisive, then backed away, his face still turned toward the cliffs. "Yes, L'Hlaadin," he answered. Behind him, the M'dians were gathering silently among the tents and buildings.

M'landan walked quickly up the slope to where Darenga moved blindly in the direction of the rooms. He stayed a few paces back, and, as she fell, he stood waiting. She tried to rise, but was pitched forward by the thick material of her robes. He made a movement as if to help her, but drew back with his arms held stiffly away from his body. The steel shields glimmered at his wrists with the rapid motion of his heartbeat.

He knew his people were watching, so he held back, perceiving what they could not—the figure struggling to its feet in a violent blue radiance that lit the cliffs with its brilliance, the glorious light that was the vision and illumination of his life and purpose.

He dared not touch her, as much as he wanted to, even to end the fear and misery that sent her staggering toward some unseen safety ahead. Then she had found the door opening to the second cliff room and disappeared into its darkness.

He moved swiftly through the doorway and found her standing at the far curve of the wall, her hands pressing desperately against the smooth stone. She was crying softly, whimpering, like an injured child, and the sound of it dulled his eyes and brought him forward. Now, out of sight of his people, he approached her as her head fell against the wall; his arms folded around her and the radiance that flowed out from her entered his body and was contained.

He screamed. Darenga sank back abruptly and slipped through his fragile arms to the floor. He collapsed over her, still screaming, and then he was silent.

The room was dark, but when she opened her eyes Darenga could see the rectangular form of lighter darkness that marked the window opening. She anchored her gaze on that visual sensation, held to it, as she felt the smooth floor against her cheek and its reviving coolness, caught the earthy smell that mingled with his faint sweet odor.

She was weak and dizzy; the rectangle of light moved in arcs above her head, but she didn't want to close her eyes, didn't want to relinquish the sensation of sight. But the motion was unpleasant. She was becoming aware, too, of the restrictive pressure against her ribs.

"M'landan." It was more an exhalation than a name.

His voice answered, clear and grave. "Yes, Chaeya."

"I'm so sick."

He moved slowly, drawing back so that he was sitting beside her. "Is there something I can do for you? Shall I call Klayon?"

"No. Let me lie here . . . where it's cool." She exhaled slowly, drew a breath. "I was burning to death." Her voice sounded faint, drained. "You knew this would happen."

"I knew."

She began to cry, too exhausted and sick to cover her face. She lay where she had fallen on her side, one arm stretched above her head, the other palm up beside her back. "Why did you do it this way? You know I wouldn't refuse anything you ask. Haven't I proven that?" She cried uncontrollably for a minute, and then said, "When we were joined, your instructions were that I was to accept the oil on my skin, even though we both knew it was poison to me. And I did what you asked."

She rolled onto her back and put her hands over her face. "Why don't you let me know how I'm being used?"

He bowed his head, his shoulders bending forward. "You may not question . . . my reasons. . . ." He was crying now, too; she heard it in his voice, and with her head reeling from the motion she pushed herself up from the ground to reach into his hood and cover his ear membranes with her hands. She lay her forehead against his and felt his tongue uncoil along her cheek.

"Oh, my dear and loving friend, if this is what provides your visions, then I'll gladly do it. Dear God, I'll drink the oil, if that's what it takes. But let me know; let me participate; let me understand!"

"Have I not told you before that you cannot share what you do not believe in?"

125

She drew her hands from his hood and put her arms around him. "What shall I believe in? Which god? Yamth? Baandla? or this new and unnamed one? Why isn't it enough that I believe in you?"

"I haven't discarded the gods of my world, Chaeya. They've become part of a greater knowledge and a deeper faith. And if it is me that you believe in, then you believe in the instrument, not the source, and any explanation I would try to give you would be meaningless and a cause for argument only." He lowered his head. "I would have you believe in what I believe, but since you do not, I must accept it, knowing there is a wisdom allowing it for a purpose not known to me. It has never been clear to me why you are the source of this sacred power when you resist—" he stopped. There was a long pause. He lifted his head so he could look into her face. "—when you resist every suggestion that the gods exist, even when you realize I am one whose voice speaks their will."

"I don't resist, M'landan," she told him, understanding his abrupt silence. "Because I know there's nothing for me to resist. In all the time we've been together, there is nothing that's happened that can't be explained by very solid, non-miraculous physical laws. And none of it has anything to do at all with whether gods exist or not. If you see visions when you touch me at a certain time, it's because of something else, some need in you that is so powerful it creates what you want to see. I don't mean to shake your faith—"

"Dear Chaeya, you don't."

She sighed deeply and, getting unsteadily to her feet, walked over to the ledge and sat down. He remained on the floor, his robes a pale circle around him.

"I don't mean to challenge your beliefs," she said. She leaned her head wearily back against the stone wall, and looked up at the ceiling. "We've skirted this issue for so many years—"

"I have always been willing to talk about it."

"Not entirely. Oh, you will up to a point, and then you slide away on the excuse of my disbelief."

"It is not an excuse, Chaeya. You simply would not believe most of what I would say, and some of it would cause you pain."

"You aren't so delicate with your brothers and sisters."

"But they believe! They have been given instruction from their childhoods, and have grown up in their faith; they were nurtured by it. They acknowledge the gods' existence; they see what you do not allow yourself to see."

"You said it: they were conditioned to believe what you tell them."

"And you were conditioned to disbelieve."

"I was trained to be objective and not look for mystical explanations in physical events. But I have been dishonest with you and that training, because there have been times when I allowed you to assume certain things about this relationship we have without saying anything."

"And what assumptions have I made?"

"That I am some sort of instrument of your gods."

"We are all instruments, Areia. We are manifestations of a goodness beyond our comprehension, and we act within that characteristic."

"But don't you see? You're judging all beings from your own perspective, from your own behavior. Did goodness guide the actions of Claufe, who destroyed man, woman, and child in order to free himself from the Maintainers?" Old wounds torn open; it was evident in her tortured song. M'landan turned his head slightly away. "M'landan, did Trolon reflect that goodness when he cut off your hands and drove you from your own planet?"

"M'dians have a choice, as all sentient beings have a choice—to either act according to that goodness that is our inherent nature, or not to. And as you have observed in Trolon—since you use him as an example—rejecting that goodness carries a heavy penalty. He is unable to rest or to find any peace. Nor will he, until he is repentant and can receive absolution through his priest."

"That isn't an answer to my question."

"What answer do you want? Is it a physical revelation of the gods in their persons? What more manifestation of their existence do you want than yourself?"

She stared at him across the dim room where he sat on the floor with his arms resting in the folds of his robes, so calm, so patient and serene, and she thought, *The one thing you want, I'm unable to give.* But she said, "I'm a manifestation of careful genetic engineering."

"That is no argument. Do you think the gods are less concerned with what science has manipulated than with what is randomly created? Whether lumeena is placed in a vial or a bowl can it be anything more or less than lumeena?"

Darenga clasped her hands between her knees and turned the fingers over, as though she were studying them. "I suppose," she said quietly, "we could talk about this till the end of time, and it wouldn't change how either of us think. I did demand an answer from you, and you've tried to give it." She looked up from her hands. "I can't accept it; you're right about that. And I'm sorry if it . . . distresses you. It seems almost a cruel joke."

"There are many ways that lead to the gods. Some are . . . painful, none are easy."

"You're speaking about yourself."

"Yes."

"And for you, I was part of the pain."

"I allowed myself to love you, to act against the commandments placed on me by my gods through the nature of my body and by tradition. That brought pain and dishonor, but it also brought me to a greater understanding of my purpose and into the *ana-il'ma* that has opened my ears and my eyes to what no other priest has been able to perceive. There was guidance in that for me, Chaeya, even when I had erred. But the end purpose for you, it has not been given me to know."

"And the end purpose for you?" She had asked it with a little intake of breath and quick vibration of her heart—adrenaline released at some interchange of signals from body to brain that she was not consciously aware of—a reaction *ex animo* . . . and unsuppressible.

He didn't answer right away. The pale hood turned

toward the window, and even in the darkness the bronze threads ran with captured light.

"What was your vision, M'landan?"

"You have no belief in such things."

"I would still like to know what you experienced."

"A matter of scientific curiosity?"

"Are you mocking me?"

"I'm preparing you with your own armor."

"It isn't necessary. What did you see that causes all this reluctance?"

"My death, Chaeya."

"Oh?" The note jangled on the air. She tried to diminish it. "What value can that sort of foresight have? Aren't visions supposed to be spiritual revelations?"

"Yes, of course. I only mentioned that part of it which affected me strongly."

"You seem good-humored about it." She drew one knee up and wrapped her arms around the thick folds of material that covered it. "And when is this event supposed to take place? and how?"

"I am always amazed," he sang in a gentle tone, "why you pretend one thing, when you know your radiation reveals to me quite another."

"All right. This disturbs me, but the thought that you might be harmed in any way disturbs me—it doesn't mean I believe in your visions."

"Ah, Chaeya," he sighed, "it's just as well that you don't."

"Well, you've told me this much, you may as well tell me the rest."

"I will tell you this much—I will die old."

"Well, that's a marvelous bit of fortune-telling!" But, in spite of herself, she felt relieved. Distressing events, even imaginary ones, being pushed far ahead, out of mind.

"Then you are comforted?"

She exhaled, dropped her chin on her hands, where they cupped one over the other on her knee. "I prefer natural events in their own time," she answered, and was quite willing to bury the thin apprehension which quivered at the edges of her perception, and to forestall the things she had wanted to talk to him about.

And so she retired to their pallet, still not feeling well, and M'landan went back with Klayon and Tlaima to conclude what he had begun.

Chapter 12

Atin had no sooner touched the plow blade to the soil when the bridge crew of the 231 came walking over the lip of the hill and into the camp, led by Bendi Felix. They all still wore the bright blue uniforms of the Galaxy personnel, and they were carrying their duffle bags.

Now what the hell! thought Darenga, riding on the platform behind Atin. She gripped his shoulder, leaned forward. "Stop the plow," she said into his ear membrane.

He looked around at her in surprise, but obeyed.

"This will have to wait a few minutes," she told him, jumping down from the plow, "until I find out what's going on."

Atin saw then the blue figures, who had stopped and were setting down their bags and looking around at the M'dians, who were hurrying toward them from all parts of the camp. "It is the crew!" he cried delightedly, and came instantly down from his seat to the ground in a flurry of robes. "They have brought their things, Chaeya! Are they going to stay?"

"Oh, God, I hope not," she replied, striding along ahead of him.

He flew up beside her. "But they are welcome, aren't they?"

"Yes, of course. I didn't mean that quite the way it sounded."

M'landan had already reached the crew members, and his bright greeting to Bendi Felix carried down the slope to where Darenga and Atin and the rest of her group of farmers were coming swiftly along.

"We have something for you from Ambassador Seldoldon," Bendi Felix was saying when he saw Darenga. "Areia!" he called out in Songspeech. "We stayed away

131

much longer than we thought we could." He gripped her wrist, then embraced her warmly. "It's good to be here with you all again."

"I'm glad you feel that way, although I'm not sure what your being here means." That was truthful enough.

"Let me discharge my pleasant obligation here, and then—" and he turned to M'landan with a gracious bow of his head—"we lay ourselves on your mercy."

He signaled, and Ohl, the navigator, and Lapides, the communications officer, came forward with a huge box suspended on a pole between them.

"How did you get here?" Darenga asked. "You didn't walk from the Hall, did you?"

"Only from the coast road; it wasn't far. One of the Gemainshaf trucks was continuing south and brought us that far."

The box had been set at M'landan's feet. Bendi Felix lifted back the lid.

"Hanj!" It was a collective breath.

M'landan leaned forward to look into the box as Darenga came up beside him. Rows and rows of hanj pods hung suspended in specially constructed racks.

"He said he was arranging for the rest to be sent down to you."

M'landan looked up at Bendi Felix. "Again the generosity of the ambassador has given us a measure of the life we have left behind us."

Generosity, yes, and perhaps something more. Darenga looked down into the box at the dark pods that had held Seldoldon addicted for so long.

"Where would you like these put, L'Hlaadin?"

"If you would be so kind—in the first metal building beyond the tents. It is a temporary storage area."

"Your permanent buildings will be in the cliffs, then?"

"Yes. There are three rooms completed now. Would you like to see them? And L'M'dia?"

"L'M'dia?"

"Andor brought an island down in the shuttle," Darenga explained.

"That would be like ~~him~~," Bendi Felix said, as they exchanged a glance.

Some of the other crew members, having particular friends among the M'dians, were beginning to cluster together, and now edged along with Bendi Felix and M'landan toward the cliff rooms, so that the whole community was moving upward in a bright melodic wave which spread out in front of the sandstone cliff and the rooms carved from the rock.

Once M'landan, Darenga, Bendi Felix, Klayon, and Tlaima had sat down in the room M'landan and Darenga had taken for themselves, Bendi Felix said politely to Tlaima, "You have blossomed since I saw you last. When is the child expected?"

She hesitated. "In thirty-three *tda* sunfalls."

He nodded and touched her arm. "What a delightful event for you and your people: the first M'dian child born on Ronadjoun."

There was little he could have said that would have pleased anyone in the room more. And Darenga, hearing M'landan's little tone of pleasure deep in his throat, wondered why she had never thought about the birth of the child in just that way.

Bendi Felix's blue eyes touched her face briefly, and then rested on M'landan. "L'Hlaadin, we have asked to be released from our obligations to the Alliance. There was never much question of my release, but since those members of the bridge crew who elected to come along were still in service, it was necessary for them to go before a number of hearings to convince members of the Alliance that they were sincere about their change of views, that the interests of the Systems' Alliance were no longer important to them. And so, finally, today, they were discharged, and we came straight here."

"What change of views, Bendi Felix?" She asked the question even though she already knew the answer.

"I think we've known better than most," he replied quietly, "just how senseless everything has become. We died, in effect, and now that we are counted again among the

133

living, rather than to go on as before, we decided we would determine the direction our lives would take from now on."

The crew had been filtering into the room, and now all sixteen original members of the last flight into the Spinandre Quincunx stood quietly around the walls as Bendi Felix continued.

"We would like to stay near you and your people, L'Hlaadin. Let us make our home here. Let us follow you."

There was a tense silence. Then M'landan said, "You are always welcome, my friends. If you want to live here, it is your home. But how are you to follow me? You have no belief in my gods."

"Then teach us, L'Hlaadin," Bendi Felix said softly. "We want to become part of this community—this *loving* community that is guided by you. Teach us, L'Hlaadin. You'll never find more attentive students anywhere."

"This is . . . unexpected," he answered. He looked all around, his eyes shining. "And you all feel this way." It was a statement, not a question. It was plain to him in their radiation.

Darenga's sense of disaster renewed itself, although there was hardly a reason for it; hadn't the Alliance discharged the crew? And she wondered how much the final decision had been influenced by Andor Seldoldon. And the thought came as well—how much the decision was induced by the Arcustan and Arkdikh faction who must have rejoiced to see a Galaxy bridge crew disposed of so neatly and so finally. They must have been astounded at their good fortune.

"There is one empty tent," M'landan told them. "If you are very careful not to roll over on one another, it may hold six. Perhaps during the daily rain, the remaining number could seek shelter in the other tents."

"We brought some survival gear with us," Ohl said. "It's part of our regular pack."

Lapides added, "With the one tent you have, sir, there'll be plenty of space. Just tell us where you want us."

"Wherever you like. It will be temporary. And you will have your own rooms in the cliffs."

M'landan stood, and everyone seated along the ledge came immediately to their feet. "We welcome you into our midst." He raised his arms. To a person, the bright ring of blue folded their hands and bowed their heads.

"Look up," M'landan gently instructed. "Look toward the source of all wisdom and light." And he drew the circle slowly in the air.

No one spoke. It was as if they had, at that instant, while the light glinting from the metal shields still burned on their retinas, given themselves wholly over to his care.

They had been as quick to adopt M'dian dress as Darenga had been. As soon as the tailors, who had been pulled from their temporary jobs at the cliffs, could seam together their robes, the crew discarded the blue uniforms and became full-fledged members of the community. Most of them opted to help at the cliffs, because that's where their strength could be utilized for the common good. But at least two decided to help prepare the food, which was perfectly safe for all crew members except Darenga, for whom it was deadly in any form.

The new crop they would be harvesting in another sixty days, having finally completed the plowing and mounding and seeding, was flourishing in its new island habitat. Nothing Darenga had been able to say could talk her farmers into planting in rows, and she finally decided they probably knew more about such matters than she, even on a planet where everything was unfamiliar, and resigned the argument, letting them do what they wanted. It had turned out beautifully.

Jean Thivierge had appeared at the edge of the fields one day, to Darenga's surprise and Atin's absolute delight. He was impressed, and said so in his brusque way. He was still skeptical about the crop—weeds, he continued to call it—but he noted the large seed heads of the marsh staff, the long closed flowers of the jimasette, whose fragrance unfurled with the blossoms at the rising of the brilliant nebula

L'Epervier, the net, and the large broad-leaved bishop's bread, which was already forming bigger than normal fruits at the ends of the twig streamers, all the result of careful seed selection and cultivation.

"You're pretty good for weed farmers," he said.

Darenga translated. Immediately Atin and the rest wanted to take him over the area of the entire lake basin; they settled on a tour of a representative sample. Thivierge was curious about their method of planting, and Darenga translated as faithfully as she could, and was rather surprised herself to learn how much was dictated by their religion.

Thivierge also wanted to know if he could see L'M'dia, and Darenga, anticipating his interest, gathered up one of the weavers as they walked to the cliff room shrine. They spent some time there while Thivierge walked around and around the case, staring up at the plant, at the five golden balls that seemed to glow from within, at the long stalks and the black fronds bent away from the stalks by the weight of the tiny bulbs, at the lush purple grass that covered the dark ring at the base of each stalk.

The weaver answered all Thivierge's questions about the processing of portions of the plant into cloth, and then left to return to her job at the construction site. When she had gone, Thivierge said, his eyes still on the case, "And with this plant we could live forever, just like you."

"Where did you hear that?" she demanded.

He looked at her and laughed in a short, gruff explosion. "Who hasn't heard it? You know it's true. There was a fight over it for years."

Darenga remained silent.

"Isn't it true?"

"Ask that question of the proper authority; I can't answer it for you."

"You mean you won't answer."

"I have no information to give you."

He grunted, looked back toward the case and stared into it. "It killed off the adults," he said, shaking his head. "How does something like that get started?"

"If you're talking about evolution, I doubt if anyone will ever know with any certainty. As long as there was another generation to take the adults' place, nature was satisfied. The survival mechanism was kept intact. This will be the first generation to live out its normal lifespan."

They walked back out into the sunlight to find M'landan at his morning instruction of the bridge crew. They sat on the ground before M'landan, who acknowledged the on-lookers with a melodic greeting and then resumed his lesson.

They stood for a while listening, and then Darenga led Thivierge away, where their conversation wouldn't disturb the class.

"So that's L'Hlaadin," he said, looking back. "What's he saying to those people?"

"They wanted to know more about his religion," she replied. "He's explaining it to them." She hoped he wouldn't pursue his curiosity any further than that.

"I've heard a lot about him." He stopped and turned to look at the group on the hillside.

"Oh?"

"When we were making up our minds on whether to let you stay here or not. There wasn't anything said about you." He glanced over at her. "I have a nephew who works at the Hall," he told her. "I know more that goes on there than you think." He made a motion with his hand. "That bunch up there—they're the ones who came in a couple of months ago. Used to be a Maintainer crew. Your crew, in fact."

"They were discharged. I'm sure your nephew must have told you that, too."

He lowered his head and looked up at her from under his thick gray brows. "I'm not the only one in Canigou who has relatives at the Hall. And you might want to know that the Hall priest is from the abbey here."

"And the priest carries rumors back to the abbot?"

"I'm just saying there's more than one line of communications in and out of Canigou."

"We've stayed on our own ground. There shouldn't be any concern about us."

"There's concern among the ones who were against giving you permission to settle. And now, with the Maintainer crew. . . ." He shrugged.

"Won't we ever be allowed to live in peace?" she said.

"What's the answer, Captain? I don't know." He turned again to the figure on the hill, and stood listening attentively. "His voice . . . I can feel it." He raised his large hand and spread the fingers across his chest. ". . . strange."

He took a few steps forward, and then stopped.

Atin came in from the side. "Chaeya? Were you coming back to the fields with us?"

"Go ahead, I'll be along in a few minutes."

In a warm and delicate song, Atin said to Thivierge, "We were so pleased you came. We would be happy if you would return."

Darenga relayed his message to Thivierge who nodded quickly and said, "I will," and watched as Atin moved lightly away toward the lake bed.

"They take you off-guard, don't they?"

She smiled. "They are disarming."

He looked around at her. "What's the name he called you—*Chaeya?* I've heard the others use it."

"It simply means 'The Loved One.' "

"Oh." He stared at her. "I don't mean this in an unfriendly way, but how did you get that name?"

"Do you mean 'how could a clone be loved'?"

"Well," he replied drily, "you weren't exactly loved before, not on this planet. Although you did some good things for us at the last, I'll admit that."

"The M'dians are a loving people. They look beyond the surface."

M'landan, having finished the morning's instruction, had started toward them, still carrying on a conversation with a few members of the crew, who followed and then veered off as he reached Darenga and Thivierge.

"I am L'Hlaadin," he said to Thivierge. And when the man reached his hand out automatically, M'landan drew out one arm from his sleeve and touched Thivierge's wrist lightly; his adaption of the Ronadjounian handshake.

138

Thivierge stared down at the shield, lifting his eyes to M'landan's face only after he had replaced his arm into his sleeve. "Sir," he said, his lips barely moving.

"This is the man who traded the plow to us," Darenga explained.

"Why has he come?"

"I'm not sure. He came to the fields first. It may be that he's curious. He has been friendly to us."

"Have you offered him food and water?"

"Mlo saindla," she said, "I haven't." She turned to the man beside her. "L'Hlaadin wants to know if you would like something to eat or drink."

"No, I had breakfast before I left."

He stood without moving, staring up into the bronze hood. "Is it true?" he asked in a hoarse whisper. "Does he know what you're thinking?"

Oh, God, Darenga thought, recognizing the superstitious awe in his voice. "It's nothing supernatural," she told him quickly, "he just has more sophisticated sensory equipment than humans do. His eyes can detect light rays all across the spectrum, and thereby any heat sources. He can hear changes in a voice that indicate the tension and general mental state of the person speaking to him—when they're speaking his language, of course, since he doesn't understand any other." She added, "It's nothing mysterious; the M'dians are born with this ability." She wasn't sure if he was listening to her or not, he was staring so intently at M'landan.

"But I've heard about his powers."

Darenga put her hand down heavily on his shoulder. "What powers?" she asked him, Standard Maintainer.

His head came around, startled.

M'landan said, "Chaeya—what is it?"

"What powers?" she repeated.

"I heard he prophesies. That god speaks through him."

"That's nonsense. He worships *gods*—in the plural— M'dian gods represented by the two suns of his world. Now he worships this one." She glanced angrily up at the Ronadjounian sun, and let it burn an instant into her eyes.

139

"If you believe it's a god, then your abbot does have something to worry about."

Thivierge's glance went back to M'landan. "That's not what I heard."

"What exactly did you hear?"

"That he knows events before they happen, and that God speaks through him—like the old prophets—that he knows what you're thinking—"

"I've just explained that," Darenga told him, restraining an impulse to shake him, to nullify her growing fear.

M'landan had picked up her emotion. "Tell me what he said." It was not a request.

"He seems to think—" She stopped. "He has heard that the gods speak through you—his god, he means—and that you can foretell events."

"Why does that make you afraid?" It was a gentle question that required no answer. He turned to Thivierge. "I am L'Hlaadin," he said. "I am the Globe and the Stalk. My voice speaks the will of the gods. What I am allowed to see of the future is through their grace and the Chaeya's fire."

It was his voice of invocation, deep and ringing, and it immediately drew the attention of the M'dians, who had been going about their tasks, and the crew members, who responded with an animal-like intensity—heads up and turned in his direction, bodies coming slowly around.

"Repeat to him what I said," M'landan told Darenga.

"He's not going to understand. He's not going to know what you mean by these things. It will confuse him."

"Is it not the truth?"

"It's your truth."

"Ah, for one trained in logic, you are quick to create your own contradictions. If it is truth, how can it not be truth?"

"I won't tell him, M'landan. He's already deaf with his own superstitious hopes, and I won't amplify them."

"Then you are disobedient."

"Well," she said in surprise, "then I will just have to be disobedient."

"I understand that love guides your decision, but it is still disobedience. You will go to the cliff room, my beloved, and you will wait for me there."

Trained to obedience, Darenga stood irresolute. "You didn't listen to me once before, M'landan," she said. "Are you going to make the same mistake again?"

"My path was unclear, then," he replied. "I had no guidance. Now the way is very clear."

There were M'dians all around now, and Thivierge glanced at them uneasily. The bridge crew was also there. And Bendi Felix.

"The danger is real, my dear friend. Listen to me this time, please!"

"I hear everything that you say. Now will you hear what I say? Truth is not silenced merely by refusing to speak it. Go now, beloved Chaeya, do as your priest has asked you."

Without replying, Darenga turned and made her way up the slope. Behind her she heard the voice of Bendi Felix quietly repeating M'landan's words. She went past the first room and into the second, where the sandstone walls insulated her from the sound. She sat down on the ledge and put her head in her hands.

When M'landan came in three hours later, Darenga was asleep on the pallet. He stepped lightly and soundlessly around the pallet to the window opening, and gazed out over the metal storage sheds to the rising line of mountains.

He had been standing there for several minutes when Darenga said, "Well, my most dear and loving friend, what have your gods accomplished this day?"

He listened carefully, but there was not the sound of mockery that he had expected, only a sad resignation. He went over to the pallet and sat down in front of her.

Placing one bronze gauntlet on her hands he asked, "Do you suspect a plot?"

She laughed at the grave way he had spoken, catching only in the final vibration the tremolo of amusement. "We're laughing," she said, lifting back his hood so she could see his face clearly, "but . . . ah, M'landan, I have such a feeling of dread about all of this." She lay her arms along his and tucked her fingers into the material of his sleeves, her eyes on the shiny black liquid of his eye sockets, seeing herself leaning toward him.

"You have told me this several times, and I have wondered where you acquired this information about future events." The tremolo again.

"I've lived for over three hundred years, and I've observed events and beings of all kinds who create those events for their own—usually selfish—reasons. You cannot share your beliefs with people who won't be able to handle them wisely. There is going to be trouble; I can already feel it."

"Chaeya, I will not go into Canigou, nor will I allow any of us to go where there is one in the town who is opposed to it. But neither will I turn away anyone who comes here seeking to understand."

"Did he ask you any questions about what you had said to him?"

"He was not able to formulate many questions, I think."

"But there were some?"

"Yes."

"Tell me what they were, please."

"Perhaps we should start with the one which disturbs you most. He asked what 'Chaeya' meant."

"And, of course, you told him in detail."

"Why is that distressing? You are the Loved One. You are my mate. Were we not joined with the blessing of the gods?"

"He can't understand what you mean by that."

"What is there so difficult to understand?"

"M'Landan, Jean Thivierge is unimportant in this; I worry about the abbot's reaction. He's already opposed to our being here. Do you think it will help us for him or the others who think as he does to discover our relationship."

M'landan was thoughtful. "How very strange that it would make a difference to anybody that we are joined."

"No, it isn't strange. Humans mate for the purpose of

142

continuing the species. If species intermate, there are no offspring. This doesn't glorify god, it only satisfies lust. At least, that's the way the religions view it. You know Andor warned us about this."

"Still, it is curious to me."

"My dear friend, they thought they were giving land to a quiet group of M'dians who would be confined to this basin and seen only now and then. Now, they'll find out that in the bargain they got the one Maintainer they hated and feared most, and all her crew. The abbot will find that in addition to these aberrations—that's what we were called by the religious community—there is also a union between species. He'll never tolerate it."

"Yes . . . perhaps you are correct in your reservations."

She sat back abruptly, surprised that he would agree so quickly. "I wish you had realized it before you spoke to that man."

His eyes brightened from the murky color they had assumed. "They will learn it anyway," he said. "Others will come, and they will learn it all."

She sat looking at him with her hands clutching her knees. "Do you want this?"

"I have no choice. It is the will of the gods."

"Yes, you have a choice! You don't have to tell them anything. Would your gods object to that? M'landan, let it be known the humans here are going back to the Gemainshaf. We can post a guard on the road. Whenever anyone comes up here, the crew members and I can stay out of sight until they leave. They'll think we went back to the Hall."

He sat very still, his eyes going slowly gray. "I will give you a choice. You may go back to the Gemainshaf and take those members of the crew who wish to leave, or you may stay here as my Chaeya. It is up to you to decide, but it can be only the one or the other."

With her mouth stiff, she replied, "Would it be better for you if I left?"

"It would always be better if you are with me. It may not be better for you, so I must give you the choice."

"Oh, my dear friend, that is no choice at all. Do you think I want to live away from you? But god knows I don't want to bring you any more harm."

"Which god?"

"What?"

"Which god do you call as witness to what you say?"

"It's . . . an expletive. It doesn't mean anything."

"You use it often, and I have always been curious to know the god you have in mind when you cry out in that way."

"I'm not thinking about a god when I use it. I'm emphasizing my sincerity."

"Ah," he said, lying back on the pallet, "I am disappointed."

"Disappointed?" She turned so she was facing him. She crossed her legs beneath her robe, carefully adjusting the folds over her knees.

He had taken the place where she had been, settling himself on the pillows, and now looked up at her with his whimsical expression. "I thought you might have discovered a new god."

"Are you serious?"

"No, I'm not serious, Chaeya. But I find it remarkable that you call on a god who has no meaning for you."

"How long am I to stay here?" she asked him, dropping the subject.

"You are free to go now," he answered, yawning with a slow uncoiling of his tongue. He closed his eyes.

She started to get up.

His eyes flew open. "Wait!" he told her.

Disguising a smile, she resumed her seat. "I'm here and waiting."

"Come and kiss me," he sang. "Come and put your hands on me."

"I have fields to tend," she replied, leaning down to stroke his face.

"Listen," he told her.

She listened. Everything was quiet. Only the distant and random melodies of conversation. The songs of birds.

144

"No one is working. The time is ours."

"So you had more than one reason to send me up here."

"Were you angry when I sent you away?"

"You should know the answer to that."

"Not always. Sometimes you hide it very well, even from me."

"No, I wasn't angry. It was perfectly within your authority to order me away. I was disobeying you. And—I must be honest with you—I probably will disobey you again."

He said nothing, and she began to stroke his face and throat until she felt a vibration along her fingertips. "Are you speaking?" she asked softly, bending over him. Her hair came around both their faces.

"Not words," he answered, and sang the melody within her hearing range, a tender, low, and swaying phrase that he repeated over and over.

"I love you, my dear friend," she replied to it. She unfastened both their robes and lay down beside him, and he turned toward her so their bodies touched, the pale slender body that was so light, so vulnerable against her strong and solid flesh.

"Most precious and most loved," he sang as her hands caressed him. "Most precious and most loved."

"Your skin is so cool—"

"And yours is warm . . . and bright now; I see what you are beginning to feel. . . ."

And it was as he saw it. She had known the change was occurring, that her normal sexual energy was no longer being directed toward human intercourse, but rather toward the acceptance of his laanva, and that he shared this drive, was the focus of it, made it even more immediate. She had, when he had revealed his distress on the portico of the Hall the day they had left, made up her mind that she would avoid any situation that might increase his sense of guilt. But he was next to her now, his tongue gliding down the line of her throat, and his melodies were so soft and urgent.

"Take the gauntlets away . . . take them away."

She said, "No," but he came up on his knees and held his arms out to her. She pulled off the gauntlets. The metal shields were hard and cold and then instantly fire.

He had made no sound at all, but lay quietly back on the pallet with his head on the cushions and his brilliant eyes fixed on her face. She swam down toward him through layers of fragrance, trying to reach him before the convulsions began.

But he was quite calm, his arms folded across his chest, his tongue flicking out to her lips as she leaned over him. Then he shuddered, closed his eyes, and moaned softly. But the usual severe reaction didn't come. His arms went around her neck.

"Chaeya . . . there is no pain!"

She looked down into his face, still fearing the convulsions, thinking there had been a delay in his reaction. But as the minutes went by she realized that there would be no reaction, that somehow his body had adjusted, had adapted, and at the same time she knew it was impossible.

She glanced at her hands. Turned them over. Perhaps her body was producing . . . something. But that was impossible, too.

And then his arms came away from around her, and his hands slipped under her hair, and she felt his fingers cupping over her ears.

"There are always miracles," he sang, and in the strange acoustical chamber that his hands had formed the sound transformed into notes so pure and clear they rang down the very structure of her atoms.

"You are the miracle," she said, and took his hands, seeing each slender finger and the thumbs, hands so graceful in form and motion, hands supple and expressive, turning now to reveal the whorl of tiny holes in the palms. She laid her cheek into his hands and held them tightly against her face.

"Your love encloses me," he said tenderly.

She kissed his hands, pressed her mouth against first one palm and then the other, feeling their texture and sweet taste on her lips, the abrupt sweet and rushing liquid in her mouth and throat, searing her tongue and stopping her

146

nostrils. She couldn't breathe for an instant, and then she reeled back, her fingers at her throat.

Her lungs ballooned, saturated with honey fragrance. She began to cry. "M'landan—" she reached out, and he took her hands, pulling her up with him. His fingers touched her hair and her eyelids, then lifted her hands away from his chest.

"I don't want to stop you," she sobbed. "It's going to kill you, and I don't want you to stop. What kind of terrible love is this?"

"Take my hands," he told her. "Take my hands."

She shook her head, crying hard now, but she lay her hands on his and watched his fingers lock around her wrists. *"Mlo saindla,"* she cried out, "I never meant to do this to you!"

And the pain again, hard and violent, without letup, continuing, continuing as she tried to pull away, while his face, serene and beautiful within the hood, turned down to hers, watching from an incredible distance as she sank down through an endless green fall of sand.

Chapter 13

There had been so many hallucinations in such a constant stream that she was completely unaware of the difference between dream and reality. She was having a conversation with Bendi Felix. She was sitting by the window, animated, rocked forward with her hands gripping the edge of the ledge. She was making a point. Bendi Felix was beside her, his legs crossed, and he was leaning back against the corner of the window opening. By the half smile and gentle expression on his face, the relaxed way one hand rested over the other, she knew he was getting the better of the argument. She never found out what the argument was, for between one utterance and the next she was out of the dream and into the clarity of mind that marked her return to reality.

She came to her feet. "Where is M'landan?" she asked. "Is he all right?"

Bendi Felix stood up slowly, his eyes evaluating her face, her posture. "Yes, he's all right. He's in the fields. Are *you* all right?"

"Yes, I think so. But I'm hungry—terribly hungry." She looked down at herself. "Good God! am I thinner? How long have I been hallucinating?"

"This is the twenty-ninth day."

She was holding her robe against her body, her hand flat against her stomach. She looked up at him. "Twenty-nine days!"

"We couldn't get you to eat regularly. I'm going to tell L'Hlaadin you are aware now. He's tried to stay here with you as much as he could. He'll be very relieved to know you're back with us."

"Wait," she said, as he started for the door. "I'll go with you."

She was faced now with the evidence of the hiatus in her life. As they came out into the sunlight, she glanced back and saw the number of dwellings that had been finished. Now the rooms hung like clusters of grapes down the center of the cliff face. And the same delicate bridge architecture of the M'dian caverns connected the clusters here. Yet there had been something added that hadn't been part of the exterior design of those cavern dwellings, for the outside of each room was carved with slender representations of L'M'dia and what she recognized as the plants that were growing now in these fields, on this planet, and all the carvings were touched with the lovely soft pastels of the homeworld of the M'dian people.

"It's beautiful," Darenga said.

"Yes," Bendi Felix replied. "The homesickness that creates art."

"What else have I missed?" she asked, looking around and seeing that most of the tents were gone, with only a few remaining, and those concentrated in one small area along the slope. Now she looked into the fields and saw that the plants were nearing their maturity. There were people wandering around the shaggy green and color-shot islands—M'dians, of course, she noticed Atin and Holta right off, but there were also humans, from Canigou. And then she saw M'landan coming swiftly through the islands, alerted, she knew, by a silent call from the workers at the cliffs. It was a joyous little melody that came up to her, and the refrain went on, even after he had his arms around her.

Once they had established to each other's satisfaction that they were both well and undamaged, they went back up the slope, Darenga's arm about M'landan's waist, his arm resting across her shoulders and the bright red hair, while behind them the humans from Canigou stared silently after them.

"I'm not really sure what was hallucination and what was actual," Darenga said.

They sat on a ledge in the new gathering room, a high

and airy loft near the top of the complex. The fields stretched below them toward the rising mountains, where the first clouds were drifting in from the ocean. Within the hour there would be rain.

M'landan's eyes had gone dull, streaked with gray. "When there was no pain for me . . . *mlo saindla,* but I thought only of myself . . . it is unforgivable, this desire. I am ashamed . . . the things I did . . . I am ashamed." His gaze fell away from her face, for, even as he spoke of his shame, the desire still rode in a low harmonic in his voice.

Her whole body responded to it. "There was nothing you did that I didn't want myself," she replied, her eyes fixed on the smooth-rubbed floor.

She heard his quick-drawn breath, and she looked away out the window into the cloud-darkening day, looked down toward the fields that stretched in a long and gradual slope toward the soenderbiest meadows and the mountains beyond, down where she could see the humans moving now from the fields and toward the cliffs.

"What are the people from Canigou doing here?" she asked, having found a subject.

He seemed as eager as she to find a distraction. "They came as visitors, bringing small gifts of food that we had to refuse, but which our human members gratefully accepted. They have been coming every morning since then."

"Every morning? For your instruction?"

"Yes. Please don't concern yourself about this. There have been no unpleasant incidents. They have been extremely polite, and the questions they have asked, when they have asked them, have been framed in a respectful way. It has given me great pleasure to have them here. And it is as it should be."

"As it should be?"

He sat calmly, watching her, but said nothing.

"Has Thivierge been back?" she asked then.

"Often. And he has put many questions to me in private. He seems reluctant to speak in front of the others."

"Do you know why?"

"He is uncertain about his beliefs—as they all are."

151

She sighed. "I feel like I've been in hibernation."

"I have missed you," he said.

"We must decide how we are to extract the nectar, Chaeya," Atin said.

They were standing in the warm darkness of the fields where the islands hung thick and heavy with fruit and unopened blossoms. In the sky above the cliffs, a halo burned out in a bright aureole: the slow rising of the L'Epervier nebula.

All the farmers had been sifting through the islands, testing, examining, their attention focused on the furled blossoms of jimasette which would this night first open to the light of the nebula. There would be ten nights, then, of ripening and peak harvest time, and they were making the final decisions on how.

"Does it have to be taken out through the throat of the flower?" Darenga asked.

"We don't know, Chaeya; we will have to wait until the flower opens and the nectar is released."

They had explained to her how they had tried breaking open the receptacle at the stem end of the long, trumpet-shaped flower, but there had been very little liquid, and it had been bitter-tasting. So now they were waiting for L'Epervier to rise and for whatever metamorphosis must occur.

Its light had already touched the mountains and slowly widened down their flanks toward the basin and the far end of the meadow where the soenderbiest grazed. Darenga sat down to wait on the ground of the slope. Behind and around her, a few M'dians were gathering to watch as the sky began to brighten. A robe brushed her arm, and she looked up to find M'landan standing beside her. All around his head, L'Epervier glowed with a silver, gauzy light.

"The flowers have begun to open," he said.

She stood up, drawing a faint, dusty sweetness into her nostrils. One by one the blossoms were turning their petals outward, their small globes expanding and rising through the dark island foliage.

Darenga followed M'landan into the fields, where they

joined Atin and Reen, who were lifting and examining the blossoms, closely watching the degree of their movement, and inhaling their fragrance with judicious nostrils.

"What have you learned?" M'landan asked.

"The flavor is much improved, L'Hlaadin," Reen answered. "It is slightly sweet, not unpleasant at all, and smooth, very smooth. Will you taste?"

She lifted the stem of the blossom wheel she was holding, and he bent forward toward the open petals glowing against the dark leaves, his robe taking on the same luminescence as the flower, and the motion of his head tracked by the needle-thin flashes of copper in his hood.

His tongue extended down into the tubular flower, probing into the nectar grooves of each petal, a quiet, patient task which took several minutes. And all the while Darenga stood stunned and scarcely breathing as she watched him siphon the nectar from the flower, his face tranquil and beautiful in the starglow.

"Come here, Chaeya," he sang gently.

In the curious light, he had straightened and looked toward her without her observing the motion. "Would you taste it, too?" And, like a fledgling, she tilted her face up to him and received a small and luscious measure of the nectar.

"Perhaps we should consider using it as a substitute for hanj," he was saying to Reen and Atin, while Darenga, feeling as if she were in a dream, still rolled and tested the flavor over her tongue.

"Yes," Atin mused, "it might ferment well. But how are we to remove it from the blossom?"

M'landan raised back the flower with his gauntlet. "The grooves were filled," he said. "Perhaps the receptacle fills as the light increases. You may need a tool that would pierce it."

All three bent their hoods over the flower. "Grooved, maybe," Atin conjectured, "so the nectar would flow down—"

"—with a container to hold it, so several plants can be emptied."

"Can we make the tool?" Atin asked M'landan.

"We will see—"

"Look!" Darenga was turned toward the meadows, staring out over the bright black and silver of the fields.

From the distance were coming thin streams of light, rising and falling with the contours of the islands, drifting up, circling, spiraling down into the foliage and marking everything with light.

"What is it?" Atin asked, his eyes blazing.

"Some insect, I think," Darenga answered.

They all looked up as the first shapes fluttered down toward the blossoms.

"Moths," Darenga said.

"Oh . . . oh!" Atin froze as one lighted on his sleeve and spread down its wings.

"It glows!" Reen breathed.

The black-lined silver pattern was severely defined, and the edges of its wings luminous. Its feathery antennae teased back and forth as it held its balance, then it suddenly lifted away toward the blossom near M'landan's shoulder.

"Is this like a butterfly?" he asked, tilting his head to watch the moth uncoil its proboscis down into the nectar groove.

"Yamth! It's a small brother!" Atin exclaimed, and sank immediately under a quick and soaring rebuke from M'landan.

"But see!" Reen cried, "it drinks as we do!"

"Their ancestors were hitchhikers from Earth," Darenga said. "When the rebels were brought from Quebec to this planet, they came along and adapted."

"We will share our harvest with them," M'landan said, "these who have also lost their homeworld. The islands nearest the meadows will be theirs." He looked once again at the moth, then turned his head toward the cliffs, calling silently. Then he and Atin and Reen went back to their discussion of the extraction problem, while Darenga listened.

In a moment Tlaima appeared and, as Darenga watched, made her slow way down the slope in their direction, moving with awkward grace.

Because of the child she carries, Darenga thought. *The child that is so precious to us all.*

"Such a lovely fragrance," Tlaima said, when she reached them. "It must fill the whole world. And what are these!"

"Moths, Tlaima," Atin answered. "Look, look at their tongues!"

And after Tlaima had been introduced to the moths, and was given a taste of the nectar, and after her Klayon, who had anxiously followed her, Tlaima said, "This nectar tastes so—silky. But it is very rich. More than a tongue full would make us sick."

"L'Hlaadin thought we might make a hanj of it," Atin told her.

"Well, that would be a good idea—if it can be done," Klayon replied, taking another sip.

"What did you want, my brother?" Tlaima asked M'landan.

"Can you make a harvest tool for them?" he replied, and described what was needed.

"I will try," she answered. "I'll go now, and see what I can design."

It was some time later when Klayon appeared in the field and spoke briefly to M'landan, who turned immediately and followed him up the slope toward the cliffs. Darenga, sensing what was up, as the others did, came out of the islands and on up to the cliff room, arriving there just as M'landan was coming out of Tlaima and Klayon's room.

"The child is coming," he said, and then reannounced it to the quickly gathering crowd. "It will not be for several hours," he told them. "When the time is close, I will call all of you."

The people dispersed with excited little exclamations to him and gentle touches of their hands to his face and arms. He accepted it all, these gestures of love and support, with quick phrases of gratitude, then he and Darenga entered their own room to wait.

They waited in silence.

After a while, M'landan got up from the ledge where he had been sitting and left the room.

For a long time Darenga paced about, making up her mind whether to follow him or not, whether to assume that he would accept her presence. But the need not to be alone with the undercurrent of unwanted feelings that had overtaken her was more compelling than her respect for his desire to be by himself. She followed him.

He had not gone to Tlaima and Klayon's dwelling—that would have been against custom: the priest did not approach the mother of the first born until she was actually delivering, when he would go in to insure that life would properly begin for the son who would be both the servant and master.

M'landan had gone to the shrine room. She came into the doorway, which streamed a foggy light into the corridor, and stood hesitant, one hand on the door facing.

He was kneeling at the thin silver cord that fenced off the terrarium, motionless, his robe spread out around him, cowl pulled forward, arms deep in his sleeves, a figure isolated and alone.

She knew he was aware of her, but since he made no move to indicate it she remained for another moment at the door. And then, slowly, as if she might still change her mind, Darenga walked over to him. Still, he did not acknowledge her. She felt again an intruder, unsure whether she were breaching a serious code or merely being impolite. There was always that uncertainty, for all the years she had been with him, there was still so much that was clouded, obscure in his religion. And he was so tightly bound to that religion that it was impossible to consider him apart from it. And yet, if she could have put into a container what she knew of it—that thing that was inseparable from him—it would scarcely have filled a very small vial. Her deliberate choice; she hadn't wanted to know. She had, in fact, avoided any knowledge of it, as if it were something inferior, backward, this integral part of the being she loved. All these years he had lived half of himself for her because that was all she would accept. And she understood then, more than she ever had before, his vast and undiminishing love. And her own loneliness.

"M'landan," she said, unwilling to force acknowledgment from him, but needing to hear his voice, "is she in any danger?"

"Danger?" came the echo from inside the hood. "No . . . no, she is in no danger."

"The child?"

"There is no danger for either of them." He answered her questions and resumed his silence.

She waited a moment, and then turned away and went back to their room to sit at the window opening and watch the glittering slow and drifting fall of L'Epervier toward the mountains.

The fragrance of jimasette drenched the room, lingering even as the blazing edge of the net was slipping into the dark juncture of earth and sky, and the blossoms began to curl into slender tubes.

There had been activity in the next room, but subdued, rarely vocal. And it seemed surprising to Darenga, who admittedly had little experience in these matters, that giving birth would be such a quiet process.

Samar and Quanti looked briefly in at the doorway, then disappeared and returned with M'landan.

"It is time, Chaeya," he told her.

They entered the next room. Tlaima lay on a pallet that had been placed on a platform and turned away from the door. She was covered with a cloth of intricate and beautiful design, whose colors shifted in reflected shimmers over the damp and glowing skin of her face.

It was like human birth, this M'dian birth. Klayon, the physician, calmly tended his mate, aided by Sklova, who moved efficiently and cheerfully about at Klayon's sometimes brisk commands.

"He begins, my brother," Klayon said to M'landan.

M'landan immediately went to Tlaima, and she arched her head back so she could see him.

"Our child," she said in the faintest whisper.

Darenga heard. If Klayon heard, he made no sign.

M'landan lay his gauntlet against her cheek, and she

reached up and took hold of it with both hands, lacing her long fingers around it, moving them beyond the metal shields the material covered until they touched his skin.

Darenga looked away to Klayon and watched the smooth and confident rhythm of his movements, concentrating on the thought that, although this marked his first delivery, he behaved as though he had been doing it all his life. *Genetics again?*

Tlaima's fingers, caressing now.

Our child. Our child.

"The head . . . oh, how beautiful!" An utterance not from the physician, but the surrogate father.

Tlaima moaned a little, and Klayon glanced up. Darenga saw the quick, anxious expression on his face.

"A few moments more," he told her.

"Yes," she answered, her fingers wringing at M'landan's arm, "a few moments more."

And then Klayon made a slow, steady, dipping motion, and Tlaima gave a long, audible sigh and lifted her head. Klayon raised his arms.

Darenga saw the baby shape first, small and pale and streaked with green M'dian blood, its arms and legs close to the torso but slowly changing position, alive.

"Is he all right?" Tlaima asked.

Klayon looked up from the child with a dazed and joyful expression. "Yes . . . yes. He is . . . beautiful."

Sklova came behind him and drew the cloth over Tlaima's legs as he moved forward to lay the child in her arms. He stepped back then, as M'landan came around to stand at Tlaima's side.

For a moment he stared down at his son, this new and silent child, displaced and innocent in an alien land that was to be his homeworld. If Darenga had ever understood M'landan's love and wishes for his people, it was at this moment, when she saw him perceiving this image clearly for the first time, and sensed him registering that small pattern of radiation and finding it acceptable to everything under heaven.

Tlaima lay perfectly still, radiant and tired, her eyes on

the figure above her. And in her face was revealed what Darenga had known all along had never been resolved.

M'landan lifted his arm and held the gauntlet suspended over the child. "Thy name is Audane, for you will truly guide a new people."

"Thy name is Audane," Tlaima responded, "and your father will live in you, for his light will shine through all the generations and not be extinguished."

It was not expected, Darenga could tell from M'landan's reaction and the sudden silence and immobility in Klayon and Sklova. But the naming of the child and the formal benediction by both natural parents was immutable. It would stand forever, this declaration of love and ascendancy.

M'landan accepted what she had said, and bent toward the small form.

"Thine eyes are perfect and receptive." His tongue stroked the lids, which closed over the black and luminous eyes the instant it touched the skin. "Thine ears are open to what they are blessed to hear."

The head, large for the body and yet so small, responded to the tongue that circled over its ear membranes, and the motions to Darenga seemed curiously alert.

"Thy mouth will speak the truth," and with a swift, inward thrust, M'landan's tongue plunged deep into the tiny throat and as swiftly retracted. The baby choked, recovered, and began a high and undulant tone of bewilderment that quickly wavered out of Darenga's auditory range. Tlaima blinked and drew in her breath.

"Thy hands . . . thy hands—" he faltered "—thy hands will serve thy people and continue our generations."

Now his voice, which had been softly muted, took on a different, more familiar timbre. What would follow was to be an instruction from the gods.

"Thy hands will provide life for . . . Mia'iana."

Mia'iana—Mother of Visions.

Darenga stood as if she were paralyzed. He had proclaimed that she would hold the same relationship with this priest as she did with the father, that she would be the catalyst for his visions, and he would keep her alive; the laanva from this baby's hands would one day be her only source of life.

The only source. It was a delayed explosion that shattered the remainder of what she had been. Leaving one life that had been designed and organized, even her thoughts and the motions of her body predicted and regulated, she had entered another, and in the flow of love around her she had not recognized the direction in which it carried her.

M'landan ran his tongue along the tiny fingers of the hands Tlaima was holding together for him, and the word came involuntarily from her—*"No!"*

There was a shocked little tone from Sklova, and quick movement from Klayon.

M'landan straightened slowly. "Tlaima is a treasured sister and special recipient of love and favor," he said. "But she has forgotten that possessiveness is a grievous error and the cause of misery in all beings created by the grace of the gods.

"This child will serve all his generations. He will guide a race dedicated to the gods, a brother and sisterhood of many species, and he must learn to serve and instruct them all. And his way will be made easier by the one beside me. Tlaima must content herself with being the One Mother, and not seek to gratify her own needs. Hear me, my sister, beloved in a special way, you will offend your gods and bring dishonor upon yourself if you continue in this manner."

Tlaima's eyes had gone gray as she silently listened, her fingers still wrapped about the hands and soft arms of her son. But she answered him resolutely. "It is a harsh judgment the gods make on me, my brother, for following the natural instinct to protect this child from danger—an instinct they placed in me."

Klayon stepped toward M'landan. "Please, L'Hlaadin, she is tired—"

M'landan raised his arm, and Klayon fell silent.

"Did I speak for myself or for the gods?"

Her gaze didn't waver. "You spoke for the gods, my priest."

"Will you accept their command?"

"I accept."

M'landan stared silently down at her, then leaned forward until his face was close above hers. "Thou art loved, Tlaima; inside this heart, thou art loved."

Her hand came up to his face and lay against the round curve of his cheek. She sang in a low and vibrating tone, "And thou art so dearly loved."

He tilted his head into her palm and then drew away to look again at the child, who had grown quiet and had closed his eyes. "He is so small . . . and perfect. You have accomplished a great and wonderful thing. And you must rest now."

"Yes, my brother," Tlaima answered with her eyes bright and clear. She looked past him to where Klayon stood patiently, his arms at his sides.

M'landan followed her gaze, and there was a silent exchange between him and Klayon. Then he moved back, allowing Klayon to take his place. Klayon leaned eagerly forward to grasp Tlaima's hand in one of his and lay his other gently on the child. M'landan eased back to Sklova and put his arm around her shoulder.

"You have always been kind and thoughtful, my sister, and tonight you have been blessed in measure to the goodness you have always shown us."

"Do not overpraise me, please. I wished to do this for my own satisfaction, too, L'Hlaadin. It is an honor to attend the one who bears the young priest."

"I approve of your modesty and truthfulness, Sklova. It makes what you have done even more praiseworthy. But the gods have seen into your intentions, and they have proclaimed them good."

He brought her around to face him. "You are tired, too, my sister. Go now to your dwelling, and sleep well."

He saw her to the door, and then turned back to Darenga. She walked toward him woodenly, and preceded him out into a paling night that still bore a faint and exotic fragrance on the air.

Chapter 14

"Mia'iana?"

"You will get us both into trouble, Audane," Darenga said.

She had come up to the cliff room to change her robe; Atin, whose enthusiasm for driving the plow hadn't diminished in the four years he had been using it, had managed to dump them both into the muckiest part of the fields. So she had bathed, changed her robe, and lay down for a moment on the pallet before she started back to the fields.

She lived alone in the room now. M'landan had taken another, and had forbidden admittance to anyone. She had honored that injunction.

I have no control over my desire for you; it has begun to guide everything I do. If you are to live, I must remove myself from you, and provide the laanva only when your body requires it. You do understand this, don't you?

She had understood, and had silently accepted, because she had known the anguish that had brought him to that decision, a decision she knew he had come to the night of his first son's birth. And in all that time, her body had not shown the signs of Life'send. So the days and nights had sifted one into the other and the months, and now she counted his absence in years. Each time she saw him, each day their particular duties brought them in contact, their separation was as fresh and painful as the day he had announced it. But she gave no outward sign, and looked for none in him. She simply continued to exist for the rare moments when he would come to her room, and she would place her fingers in the sacred oil and then stand with her head bowed and her eyes closed, waiting for the fire that would bring his vision. And for his arms around her. And then he would leave quickly, and she would be alone again.

163

A terrible and familiar loneliness. She would have preferred to die. But the choice was no longer hers to make.

With her eyes closed and her mind engaged in her thoughts, she hadn't heard the child enter. But now she heard him move near her head, and felt him lift a strand of her hair.

"And are you going to reprimand me, too?"

She opened her eyes. He was kneeling at her head, one small hand holding the long copper hair, the other stroking it. He had inherited his mother's rainbow skin, but his father's expression. He looked down at her now, with his great dark and solemn eyes, and set his mouth into his father's wistful line.

"You behaved foolishly, Audane. You frightened Mia and Taath, and you caused your father great anxiety. And you didn't set a very good example for your brothers and sisters."

"I was not disobedient, Mia'iana. And I was not hurt."

"Because no one has made a point of saying you should not try to ride a soenderbiest in no way absolves you from a charge of disobedience—" she started laughing. "Why do you come to me? You know you were restricted to your quarters. Go away."

His own laughter shimmered all around her. "I know you are trying to say things you are expected to say, and I do realize I made somewhat of an error. But it was a thing I enjoyed, and I wasn't afraid. The animals can only do what my voice directs them to do, and I surely wouldn't direct them to harm me."

"And when you gave these excuses to your father, what did he tell you?"

"Mia'iana," he evaded, "I am tired of staying by myself."

"What did he tell you, Audane?" she persisted, sitting up now and coiling her hair over one shoulder and out of his reach.

The child sank back on his haunches and wrapped his arms around his legs, his bright, convex eyes mirroring her image as she sat waiting for him to answer.

"He told me I have no right to do anything that would endanger myself."

"What else?"

"He said many things, but it can all be reduced to one. I am unique, and when he is gone, I will be the only way for my people to reach the gods."

It was not something she had wanted to hear, not said in that way, and the child was aware of it.

"You did ask me," he said in Ronadjounian, his voice a sweet flow over the most melodic of the human languages.

"Go," she answered harshly in Standard Maintainer, which he understood, but would never speak. "Go do as your father instructed you to do."

He got up and tucked his hands into the sleeves of his robe and walked slowly to the door. "I will say a prayer for you, disagreeable Mother," he sang in a low and solemn tone, "one that will improve your temper." And then he was gone, with his laughter left glittering down the air.

Darenga got up from the pallet and stood, rubbing her fingers in an absent way and doubting if any sort of discipline would ever curb the child's strange un-M'dian predilection for adventure. She went out then, and, going past his chamber, saw him in a small and pious attitude of prayer, the screens carefully drawn aside so she would see. She stopped, reached around the entrance to release the screens.

"I will tell my father your arm entered my chamber," he called out.

"Behave yourself, Audane," she answered, and walked on.

When she got back to the field, she found Atin regroomed and impatient by the plow, waiting according to her stern instruction. It struck her then how alike Atin and Audane were in this one respect, this little streak of recklessness that they shared—this uncle and nephew.

She came up to the plow and stood staring at it with her hands on her hips. One side of it was caked with thick mud where it had fallen during the wild turn Atin had made.

"That's a real mess," she said, putting as much disgust into her voice as she could without overdoing it.

"It will run," he answered.

"No, it won't. The mud has clogged the vents."

"Then we'll clean them out."

"Not 'we,' Atin."

He was silent, considering what she had said. Then he lay his hand on her arm. "I'm very sorry, Chaeya. Must you stay angry?"

She relented. "I'm not angry, Atin. I just don't want you to kill yourself. But since you turned the plow over, it's your responsibility to clean out the vents. And the plow won't run until you do, so you'd better get started."

Atin was cheerful enough about it; the thought that he would soon be aboard the plow again was enough to take the sting out of anything she had said to him. So while Atin scraped and dug at the vents, Darenga walked back along the ground that they had already covered, observing it for the degree of dryness in this particularly moist area that was near the meadow. It was the last remaining strip that needed to be prepared for the island plantings, the plantings that had been going forward for several days, Atin and Darenga plowing ahead of the others, who were seeding the islands. She walked back along the track to where Atin had just completed clearing the plow vents.

"It's too wet to continue, Atin. We'll finish tomorrow—if it's dried out enough."

"Oh, Chaeya!"

"It's too hard on the plow motor, Atin. We don't want to have it break down."

"No, certainly not. You are right. Shall we go help the others—who is that?"

He was looking over her shoulder toward the cliffs, and she turned to see a small group of figures coming over the hill. Atin raised his eye membrane briefly, then closed it again to the afternoon sun.

"You can tell better than I at this distance," Darenga said, shading her own eyes.

"I can tell they are human, Chaeya. And I can hear

them speaking Ronadjounian. They are not familiar to me."

"Well, they're probably from Amper. Let's go on over to Reen and the rest."

They left the plow and walked back across the freshly turned earth and into the drier section that had been formed into islands. The farmers and their children were scattered along the area near the slope that was terraced now, in shallow graduated basins that brimmed with flowers and vines and overflowed onto the paths that were thick-cushioned with carpet moss. Fast-growing silka trees had hung their lace along the paths, and their pale yellow racemes glowed like lanterns in the shade.

It was into this landscape that the group Darenga had been watching as she and Atin came across the fields had come and now stood glancing about. She saw them clearly now, three men in the dark brown clothing of the Abbey.

"You go on," Darenga told Atin, "I'm going up there to see what they want."

She came up the pathway at a moderate pace, assessing them as she approached. All three were in their forties, alert, poised, and with the particular freshness and healthy complexion that sometimes attends the monastic life. They had seen her coming, and stood politely waiting as she came up to them, her hair free and blazing even in the cool shadows of the trees.

"I am the Chaeya," she said. "May I help you?"

"How do you do? I am Brother Timothy," said one, with a pleasant smile. "And this is Brother Andre and Brother Guillaume. We have a message to deliver to the M'dian called L'Hlaadin."

She was wary, and regretted now her haste in identifying herself. But having imagined this contact, and been prepared for it for years, now that it had happened she found, instead of hostility, a pleasant and agreeable attitude in these three representatives of the religion of Ronadjoun, and no reason to refuse them.

"Wait here, please," she told them. "I'll tell L'Hlaadin you're here."

She walked on up the path to the dwellings, and down the corridor past her own room, and deeper into the structure to M'landan's room, and then stood outside the heavily screened door and called his name.

In a moment the screens were drawn aside and he stepped into the corridor.

"There are three monks here from the abbey with a message for you," she told him. "They're waiting on the path."

"Thank you," he said.

She dropped her gaze and started back along the hallway and into the sunlight, and would have turned aside to go back to the fields, but his voice, low and sweet, came from behind her. "Stay with me, Chaeya, please."

She hesitated long enough for him to come up even with her, and they walked together along the soft moss to where the monks stood beneath the trees waiting.

"*H'gala tayntau*," M'landan greeted them, in the old manner.

They looked toward Darenga. "He's giving you the M'dian greeting," she explained. "It means 'share our harvest.' "

"Does it require an answer?" Brother Timothy asked.

"The traditional response is, '*J'lai mg manani*,' may you always have generations," she replied, gauging him. "But it is a matter of form."

"If you would tell him, please, that, in the absence of our abbot, we wish him God's grace and salvation."

They all inclined their heads respectfully as Darenga repeated what they had said to M'landan.

"Your abbot is kind," M'landan responded in a perfectly neutral tone.

Out of the corner of her eye, Darenga saw Audane come slowly out of the shadows of the cliffs.

"Our abbot has sent apologies that he couldn't make this request in person," Brother Timothy said, "but he would like to extend an invitation to you to visit the abbey and discuss matters of mutual interest. He suggests two days from today, when there will be abbots from some of the other houses in attendance, who would be pleased to meet with you. You would be most welcome to spend the night. We can send the abbey car for you."

Darenga translated this, with misgiving evident in her voice.

M'landan said, "Tell them I will accept. No car will be necessary. I will walk. Ask if I may bring one of my assistants."

She did not ask if she could go, she had long ago learned that he would not allow her to presume to protect him. Still, the uneasiness was in her voice, and he recognized it but made no comment.

"They agree," she told him, and then, after their formal goodbyes, watched them move sedately back along the path toward the hill.

"You are quiet, Chaeya," M'landan said. "Have you no warnings for me?"

"No," she answered.

In the silence, Darenga stared at the play of light and shadow across his face as he looked down at her, the play of gold and black, the fluttering light that struck against the liquid of his eyes, brimming now.

She drew in a startled breath and stepped toward him, but he turned away and walked back up the path toward the dwellings, going right past Audane, who stood quickly aside as his father's robe brushed his body.

Darenga stared after M'landan until he had disappeared into the deep shadow of the corridor. Then she retreated a few steps and sank down onto a bench and sat with her back straight, her hands folded together in her lap, her eyes on a point between the moss-covered path and twelve years of her life.

Audane's hand came lightly down on her arm, and she looked into his face. "My father is afraid," he said.

"I'm afraid, too," she answered.

"I know you are. But you are afraid for him; he fears the passage of time. I don't know why."

His hand still rested on her sleeve, and she would have put her arms around that small and comforting form, but at that moment a group of his brothers and sisters appeared on the path, and because it was not the time set

169

aside for him to speak with the other children, he retreated swiftly back toward the cliffs, his body already assuming the same floating grace that was his father's.

Dear God, Darenga cried out silently, *let me die!*

Klayon had gone with M'landan. And they were away for the night, and for the following day, and when evening came and they still hadn't returned, Darenga went to the outer structure of the dwellings, up over the narrow, un-railed bridges toward a room in the central cluster where she stopped in a doorway.

"May I come in?" she asked.

Bendi Felix looked up from a scribe unit he was concentrating over and stood up.

"Of course, Areia. Come sit down."

"What am I interrupting?" she asked, taking a seat on the ledge.

"I was just doing some calculations on the Altide Cluster and the Caldine Nebula. Nothing that can't wait. How is the plowing coming along?"

"We finished the last strip today." She looked out the window and down over the twilight fields.

Bendi Felix sat quietly, observing her profile and the filaments of hair that burned along her cheek where they had come loose from their tie. The features had softened over the past years, not a condition of age, which never touched her, but of what he had imagined to be a relaxation of spirit. Surely no one, human or M'dian, had ever been as close to L'Hlaadin as she was, as close to the center of all comfort. Even now that L'Hlaadin had taken a cell and lived apart from her, his love still flowed out to her, and if she seemed unaware, Bendi Felix assumed it was simply the undemonstrative and stoic nature of the Lambda clone, a nature that had sometimes, indeed, been their only defense.

Now she turned to him. "They're not back yet."

"They will be."

"I'm uneasy about this whole thing. You know the harassment that follows any human who comes up here."

"That's why he went—to arrive at some kind of under-standing; you know that. He won't be harmed."

She looked out the window again. "How is it that you're able to believe in his gods, Bendi Felix?" Her eyes came around to his face. "How can you do it?"

"How can anyone not believe, who's spoken to him and seen the beauty that surrounds him?"

"What kind of impossible leap of faith—or delusion—have you made that lets you believe all this mystical non-sense?" Her tone was so mild it seemed almost indifferent to Bendi Felix, who was taken thoroughly by surprise by her question.

"Nonsense!" He stood up. "Areia, how is it you have lived so close to him all these years and not received what he has to give? You've made yourself a shadow at the source of light."

Now she rose, her mouth tight. "And you've manufac-tured a little ascendancy and placed M'landan near the top, whether he wants that or not. You've reconstructed your world, Bendi Felix, to suit yourself, and you've brought the whole ignorant bridge crew with you. Let me tell you this: as you pointed out, I know him better than anyone else, and he is not some messiah, but only a being whose love for us is greater than what we've ever come to expect in our long and jaded lives. It demands nothing from us but that we know ourselves better and give some of what we have received from him to others. He would create a chain of love and concern that stretches from him into infinity if he could—"

"A chain of ascendancy?" Bendi Felix interrupted qui-etly.

"You damn fool!" she yelled. "You're all going to kill him!" And with that she stalked from the room and down the tier clusters to her own room, where she jerked the screens down into position and then paced to the center of the room. And with no further place to confine herself, she stood there, her chest heaving and her fists clenched, star-ing angrily into space.

M'landan and Klayon returned late that night, so quietly

Darenga didn't hear them at all until their voices, speaking from the next room, drew her into the corridor. The screens on Klayon and Tlaima's room were down, so she didn't enter, but she could plainly hear their voices and the voice of Bendi Felix, and that of M'landan, whose song held a strong note of bewilderment.

"There was only one who came to my defense when all those assembled began to question me and then would not let me speak."

"Who was that, L'Hlaadin?" asked Bendi Felix, and Darenga could hear his anxiety.

She waited for the answer, wondering why she had not been summoned to this gathering, this critique that was being held over an event of major importance, why Bendi Felix was included and she was not.

"One named Geoffrey of Rouyn. He would have allowed me to speak, and I was given a translator for a while, but it was so adjusted that I could understand what they were saying, but they could not understand me. There was only one time when a translator which relayed my words was put in front of me, and that was when I was asked if I knew a human called Areia Darenga, who had been a Maintainer clone of the Lambda House. You can see their direction."

Darenga, about to turn away, swung back.

"What did you tell them?" Bendi Felix again, his voice reflecting what Darenga was suddenly gripped by.

"At the time, I had no idea what such a foolish question meant. But there was only one way it could be answered."

"So you told them you did know her?"

"Of course."

"But you didn't say anything else?"

"I answered their questions."

"My brother," Tlaima's soft voice asked, "what else did they ask about her?"

"There was great anger at me that was being suppressed, especially by Abbot Roenay, who wanted to know if she lived with us. It was clear to me, finally, what information he was trying to extract from me through this devious questioning. So I eased the burden he had placed on himself and told him that she lived, as she had lived in our community for the past several years, as my Chaeya, the Loved One, who in human society would be called wife."

There was a little half-moan from Bendi Felix.

Klayon's voice came in. "There was a terrible outcry at that," he said. "They were all very disturbed. But there were many who acted as if they had accomplished some goal. They mentioned a law. It was very confusing. They did not treat us as guests should be treated. And for a while it seemed they might try to detain us against our will. But the good abbot rebuked the ones severely who were about to lay hands on us, and we left then before they changed their minds. I am glad to be home."

Darenga turned and went back to her room.

There's no reason for me to stay, she thought. *And every reason for me to go.*

She sat down on her pallet and wrapped her arms around her legs.

If they had been that close to daring to hold M'landan, then whatever source they had for silencing him was powerful enough to suggest that they might be successful next time. Apparently she was the weakest point, and their channel to him was through her. That made the necessary action clear enough. Now all there was for her to do was to make the simple decision between leaving unannounced or confronting M'landan to ask for formal permission to be released from her vows to him. The latter would at least be honorable for them both. She waited: she had been through it all before.

It was some time later that she heard him say goodnight to Klayon and Tlaima, and then to Bendi Felix, who stood outside in the corridor talking to him for a few minutes before they said goodnight again. Then she heard Bendi Felix walking away and M'landan's light step passing her door. She came through the screens into the corridor.

"M'landan," she called softly.

He was already down the hallway, but he turned when she called, and came back toward her.

"May I talk with you?"

"Of course."

"Do you mind if we go down to the gardens?"

"If you wish."

He walked beside her, letting her guide him down the pathways, and she knew he was assessing her radiation, and was aware from that why she had chosen the upper pathway that led on through the trees and to the road. But he waited for her to speak.

There was hardly any need for a preamble, so she simply stopped, and he stopped with her.

"I ask you to release me from my vows, M'landan. I want to go back to the Gemainshaf."

"I am your life, Chaeya. Is that what you want to walk away from? Have these last years been so cruel to you?"

She couldn't answer that, because there would have been too much bitterness, so she remained silent.

"Don't you understand that the gods have placed a stricture on me? In releasing me from my physical pain, they have justly given me the greater pain of knowing that to indulge my own desire would be to end your life. In their mercy, they have turned my own fires inward. That I burn now, will save us both a later torment—"

"I don't want you to say any more, M'landan." She looked away.

"I must ask this: if you do not wish to remain here, will you return when your body needs my laanva? Will you come back then?"

"I don't know," she answered. And then, bitterly, "It depends on how afraid I am of dying."

"Chaeya, will you listen to my last plea? The visions—this gift you give me through the grace of my gods, this gift that my son will need to guide all the people who will come together under his guidance—it is needed." He hesitated. "I did not see that you would choose to leave me. This moment had not been revealed to me. Oh, there is uncertainty—vagueness . . . except that Audane will be what I cannot be. And you are so much a part of this plan—" He swung away from her in a sudden gesture of helplessness and frustration. "Why has this been hidden from me? What bearing has this on what is to come? Why do you want to do this?"

He brought his wrists together, and there was a dull and solid tone of metal.

Darenga stared at his back. "Why are you wearing the shields?" And when he didn't answer she demanded again, "Why are you wearing the shields, M'landan?"

He answered her then, without turning. "Because I am forbidden to come in to you."

She didn't say anything for a long time. And then he said quietly, his back still toward her, "I will not hold you to your vows. You are free to go." He paused. "You have my blessing—and my love, wherever you go."

He started back up the path, and she stood motionless watching him. Then she suddenly ran forward, catching up with him at the edge of the garden.

"You let everyone know they were not to enter your room," she said breathlessly.

"That is true," he answered, without looking at her, as he continued up the path.

"And you told me—" she waited as they passed Tlaima and Klayon's room, then she brought her voice down to a whisper "—you told me we had to separate."

"That is also true."

They were silent as they walked by Audane's cell and on down the dark corridor. Abruptly Darenga stopped, and as abruptly turned about and went back up the corridor to her room, pushed the screens aside, and went in. She turned on a small dim lamp that sat in a niche in the wall, and then lay down on the pallet with her arms across her face. She lay that way for several minutes, and then she sat back up, looked around her. She got off the pallet and knelt on the floor and began rolling the material up. She secured it with strips of material that she looped out to fit her shoulders. She was adjusting these when she heard the screens move aside, and she looked up to see M'landan in the doorway, his arm holding back the patterned material against the stone.

"Aren't you forbidden to come in to me?" she said, and continued to retie the straps on her bedroll.

"Yes."

"Then what are you doing here?"

"Will you treat your friend so unkindly?"

"What do you want me to do? I don't understand the rules. I don't know what's allowed or what's prohibited. If you're not supposed to be here, then what the hell are you doing here?"

"I . . . wish to enter."

"But you can't."

"No."

"But you enter when you want your visions."

"That is different. I am not . . . coming in to you then. . . ."

They stared at each other.

Darenga looked away. She gave a final testing upward bounce of the pallet to her shoulders, and then walked over to the wall and turned off the lamp. Then she walked out the doorway, where he still held back the screens, and on into the corridor.

"I will go with you for a way," he said.

They walked silently through the upper garden and over the hill, where the path became a road. The stars shone brightly, illuminating the landscape with a pale white light.

At the bottom of the hill the road branched away to the west, toward the ocean, and she expected him to turn back, but he gave no indication that he was going to return at this point, and so she said nothing and they continued on their silent way.

Finally, after they had gone two miles in this silence, Darenga said, "I don't know what else to do."

"Stay with me."

"Why didn't you ask me to come in and hear about your trip to the abbey?"

He looked down at her, his great eyes reflecting the soft glow of the night. "It would have been . . . upsetting for you." He observed her more closely. "Ah," he said.

"Yes, I heard. It's something that's been threatening for a long time. But it should abate once the word gets out that I am living at the Hall."

Now he stopped in the middle of the road and flung his arms around her. "You do this for us, not for yourself!"

"That's not entirely true," she said, happy to be in his arms, but unwilling to let him think her motives were entirely altruistic. But he knew that, too.

"I know you have felt alone and abandoned, that you wondered what there was of each day that made it worth the effort to go on to the next."

He was comforting her as she had heard him comfort his children, the voice soothing and warm, a loving caress, but the words told her that they had shared the bleakness of the past four years.

"How do I comfort you?" she asked. "How do I understand you the way I want to understand you? I don't know why the others find it so easy when I'm not able—" She put both her hands on his throat and looked up into the brilliant reflection from his eyes. "How does Bendi Felix see what I can't? We had the same training, we have the same respect for logic and analysis. How has he accepted something so far removed from reason? I wish I could. I wish that I could believe—"

"You distress yourself with this. You think to please me, when that is not what I would want at all. For you to believe in the gods is not a thing that should be done for my pleasure—although I would certainly be pleased—but I realize you wish to do this out of love for me, and it must be done for yourself. To believe in the gods is a solitary decision and a solitary act of faith that has nothing to do with an obligation you feel toward someone else. That would be impure and incomplete. You must give yourself entirely to their love and guidance. Depend on them as you have tried so long to depend on yourself. . . ."

She lowered her hands and slipped her arm through his, moving them forward again on the road. "You love so completely and so unselfishly that I wonder how you can see how I feel."

"Are you making a comparison that makes your love seem selfish and incomplete?"

"I think my love is selfish, yes. I want your attention exclusively. I . . . have been jealous." She added quickly, "Although I've realized how really stupid that is. I've tried to reason it out."

"And you think I've had no feelings of jealousy? of exclusivity? Do you think you are the only one who wages this kind of interior battle?"

"My victories have been slight."

He thought about this. "Chaeya, what would you say was my greatest fear?"

She looked over at him, remembering all at once what Audane had said. "The passage of time," she told him.

He halted quite suddenly, and turned to face her. "That is an acute perception," he said. "What do you mean by it?"

"M'landan, let me tell you first that I don't believe you have visionary powers. I'm sorry, but I don't. I think you have a keen, extrapolative mind and an extremely sensitive insight. And together with your training and your beliefs, you create a state of mind that presents visual images of what your mind has reasoned. And you have attached that state of mind to me. You've made it a condition of your association with me. You've made me your . . . thrice-traveled circle, your charm. But I have no powers. My body has an unfortunate resistance to L'M'dia, and my reaction is simply that—an allergic reaction to a toxic substance. Nothing else. And I submit to it; I allow this deception because—" she lowered her head "—I want your arms around me. I want to feel you against me. I need you. . . ."

That had been too impetuous, too ill-thought out. She pushed her hands into her sleeves and turned away.

They had reached the road bordering the ocean, where beyond the shoulder lay the shore and the calm and softly rolling waves that darkened a narrow and receding tidal mark.

"Is that painful for you to say to me? That you need my physical presence?" He put his arm around her. "Come, let's go down by the water. It is lovely, this ocean. We will sit down where we can watch it while we talk."

She let him choose the place, a small copse of talfa, lush with sea grass and small twining flowers that were black in the starlight. They sat down.

"Now let us begin again. You were going to tell me about my greatest fear."

"It was not my perception, it was Audane's. But if I think about it, I can see why that would be your fear. It's a common one for every being who can think and who can understand mortality."

"That is generally true." He studied her for a moment. "You seem to have believed once that I was able to see beyond the present."

"There was a time when events confused me. When I couldn't act on the situations that confronted me. It was disorienting. For a time. It isn't now."

"And you see everything quite clearly."

"I think so."

"Ah, you think so. Then there is room for doubt?"

"No, M'landan."

"We shall see. Let us use the reason you are so fond of citing. When your hand touches the sacred oil of L'M'dia, what happens?"

"I have an allergic reaction."

"And what form does that take?"

"I feel hot—that's not quite accurate—I feel like I'm burning up. It's like the accident on the ship when my legs were pinned under burning debris."

"I remember the first time you had a reaction from L'M'dia. You took a small drink of hanj. I was very young, but I remember that your face and hands were suddenly swollen until your features were unrecognizable. Then you fell to the floor, unconscious."

"Yes, that's the way it happened the first time."

"And when we were joined, the oil that was placed on your skin caused auditory sensations."

"That's right."

"How long did it take for these sensations to go away?"

"The first time I was given an injection by the medic. It took two or three hours for the swelling to go down. There were complications, though, which took me several days to recover from."

"I remember. But the second time, how long did that take?"

"It went away gradually—during several minutes, I would say."

"Yes. And then, while we were still on M'dia, you first experienced this burning sensation that you attributed to the oil and your allergic reaction."

She nodded.

"How long did it take for it—this allergic reaction—to go away that time?"

"It went away immediately."

"Ah, you are so reluctant! Here is reason; we are working at this through reason. Say what you are leaving out. What event happened that the burning ceased immediately?"

"You put your arms around me. But—"

"But we could say that is coincidence. And yet every time since, when my body comes in contact with yours in the fire, the burning ceases. Can we reasonably conclude that all these times have been coincidence?"

"I don't think it's supernatural."

"Of course not! It is perfectly natural! There is nothing more natural than that you are the catalyst that initiates my visions."

"If you are speaking along the lines of chemical possibilities, it very well could be that your contact, perhaps a chemical or electrical haze on your skin, detoxifies me. . . ."

He watched her staring thoughtfully into space. "I seem to have reasoned you away from my intended point," he said wryly.

She gave him a quick look, and then laughed. "You take it well."

"I am patient," he said.

She sobered at that, and raised her hand to his face. "Yes, you are," she said.

"And now we have come all this way to end up as we always do—"

"And that's what you fear."

She hardly knew where the words had come from. They had been spontaneous, but she had known instantly they were correct even before he confirmed it with his arm laid across her hands. She pressed her forehead against his gauntlet and felt the hard metal beneath. Her mouth went suddenly dry. He was very still.

"If it's my salvation you want," she said in a low and frantic tone, "pray for me now."

"I cannot."

She rose up abruptly, flinging his arm aside. He was instantly up beside her. When she started rapidly away from him, out of the trees and onto the smooth hard stretch of beach, he called out, "Run! Run away from me now!"

And the tone of his voice pressed at her, and she began to run, and with the physical exertion, the strength she felt flow into her body, the rhythmic, sure, and steady pumping of her legs and heart and lungs, she experienced a curious and lifting freedom.

It felt good to run, to know again her own power and command, the way her muscles answered to the strain she was putting on them in this sudden, swift demand to flee.

And then his voice from close beside her, "Run, Areia—run away from me!"

It seemed an animal reaction, then, of fear or confusion, some inner-welling, dark, and ancient response that sent her flying forward. And yet it was not enough, this burst of fear and adrenaline, for his voice again, "You cannot out-run my love."

And she understood his lesson then, and the dreadful love he bore her.

She slowed, with the thought finally coming to her mind that, even on this smooth and unobstructed shore, he might fall. She came to a stop, breathing heavily, loose-jointed and exhausted.

He stepped around in front of her, unruffled and not out of breath at all. "Look at me, Areia," he said. "Look at me now," and when she did, he knelt on the sand at her feet, bending forward until his head almost touched the ground.

Immediately she crouched down and lay her hands on his shoulders. "What are you trying to do to me?"

His hood came up slowly, and she saw his eyes go gray. "You would have me pray for you, and I will show you that I do."

His head tilted back as she came to her feet, dismayed,

and then he turned his face up and lifted his arms toward the sky.

"O my Gods!" She had heard him use this melodic supplication only once before, this tone of intimacy, his voice in a low harmony with the surging of the ocean behind her. "Thou hast given me, thy servant, the power to see beyond my time, and thou hast guided me in this knowledge, even when I have erred in thinking myself above thy laws, I, who of all thy creatures has been entrusted to guide my people. Yet thou hast seen fit to join me in love to this one who, still in darkness, has asked for my prayers. Thou knowest that my prayers for her are unceasing. Thou knowest that I plead daily that thou wilt show her mercy in the time ahead. Though thou hadst chosen not to reveal this separation to thy servant, who was ill-prepared and saddened to hear of it, still I will accept it and praise thee, knowing thou wilt draw all life to thy loving kindness and mercy."

The prayer ended, but the sad, submissive cadence was repeated again and again by the waves. He got up slowly from the sand, bracing his gauntlets against his knee as he rose to stand silently looking down at her.

She had been totally moved by this plea on her behalf and what it told her of his concern for her. A little more disclosed, a little more of him allowed to her perception— all so piecemeal, all so arbitrarily given by events.

She put her arms around him and kissed the wide mouth and the softly vibrating throat. "Let me go on, my most dear and loving friend. Let me go now, please."

He complied immediately, stepping back and placing his arms in his sleeves, his eyes leaden and lusterless. "I will keep you no longer," he replied. "Go in my love, and the gods' special grace."

And with nothing more that could be said, Darenga turned and walked away down the beach without looking back. And no song followed her.

Chapter 15

Darenga was hurled headlong into life at the Gemainshaf, almost from the moment of her entrance through the Hall doors.

She had been two days traveling on the road, finally catching a ride with a loquacious supervisor of a surveying team who was returning to Amper from Brouage. He dropped her at the portico and drove on, anxious to return to his family after three weeks in the districts.

The evening rain had begun a few miles south of the Hall and was washing across the lawns and against the inner pillars of the porch as she leaped up the steps and in through the wide portal of the entrance hall. She had advanced a few yards onto the multicolored stone floor when Seldoldon's chief assistant came in from the hallway leading to the communications room.

He stopped. A suprised look crossed his face, and then he came quickly forward. "Captain Darenga?" It was more a question than a greeting.

Darenga swung her bedroll to her other arm. "Hello, Jacques. Will you please inform Lord Andor that I'm here? And may I wait in the Jendi Room? I see there's a fire going in there. . . ."

She waited by the huge fireplace, holding her hands up to the burning talfa logs, feeling the warmth from the flames, seeing in their high and crackling dance the images she could not hear.

"Areia!"

She turned, as Seldoldon came across the echoing room in his long and easy stride, the firelight flashing against the gold chain that swung down his chest.

"I thought Jacques was mad—'The evening wind sometimes brings more than rain.' It's so good to see you again."

183

The pleasant flow of Ronadjounian. A voice at least familiar. He would have taken her hands, but she buried them in her sleeves, and so he hugged her instead, then stepped back to give her a quick survey.

"You look tired," he said. "I hope you didn't walk from Canigou."

"Not all the way." She went over to a nearby bench and sat down. "A surveyor gave me a lift and a rundown of all the gossip in Brouage."

Seldoldon chuckled, but she saw his eyes appraising her. "I think I know the one you mean—a short fellow with a bald spot he tries to cover, rather unsuccessfully."

"That's the one. I didn't need the conversation, but I appreciated the ride. I was two nights sleeping on the ground. I feel like an earthworm."

"Well, let me get someone to take you to your room—" he pressed a small plate in a panel near the fireplace and came back over to her. "Have you eaten?"

"No," she confessed.

"I'll have something sent up. May I join you later? Or would you rather rest?"

"No, please come up."

A servant had entered, and now stood waiting to one side.

"Take Captain Darenga to—" the slightest hesitation "—her old rooms, please."

"Is there something I could change to?" Darenga asked, glancing down at her stained robe.

"Certainly; what would you like? Or shall I have your robe cleaned and returned?"

"No . . . something else." They looked at each other.

"I'll see that you get something right away."

"Thank you," she replied, and followed the servant out of the room.

When she emerged from the shower, she found an array of clothing on the bed. She slipped on a pale green gown, and then went into the other room to sit by the fire and comb her hair dry. Outside the windows the rain was still coming down, striking the panes with a bright, musical sound. She got up and closed the heavy drapes and went back to resume combing her hair. It was almost dry when there was a knock at the door, and Seldoldon entered, pushing a cart. He rolled it to where Darenga sat by the hearth.

"I see you found something suitable," he said cheerily.

"Yes, thank you. What've you got there?"

"I've brought a hodge-podge of food; I wasn't sure what you were eating these days. Or drinking. There's wine here, and milk, and water—if you must—and in this urn is catspaw—"

"Catspaw! Yes, I'll have some of that—it has been years. . . ."

She thought she was hungry, but she had been able to eat very little. Now she sat with the old familiar spicy odor of catspaw drifting up from the cup she held in her hands, and watching Seldoldon sipping from a glass of wine that had the ruby clarity of pomegranate seeds. He looked back at her as he leaned down to set his glass on the hearth.

"I drink," he said in answer to her silent question. "And I'll probably get drunk tonight, but no one will know it except Jacques. And tomorrow . . . well, tomorrow is tomorrow."

"What's happened, Andor?"

"May I ask you that question?"

"I've left."

"Just like that."

"It was a little more painful than that."

"Will you tell me why you left?"

Her green eyes were steady. "You didn't mention when you got the approval for our—" that wasn't acceptable "—for the M'dian settlement that the abbot was opposed, or that he had a good number of supporters."

"Damn! What kind of trouble have they made for you?"

She told him of the events leading up to M'landan's visit to the abbey, and the visit itself. Seldoldon listened intently, and then refilled his wineglass before he spoke again.

"I don't know why he thinks he can summon an inquisition. M'landan is protected by the laws of the Gemainshaf. I'm going to find out what the hell's going on. There's no need for you to leave the settlement. You've more than paid your debt to us."

She stared at him. For some reason it had never occurred to her that anything could be done. She had assumed that it was a situation that could not be reversed, that her life was being moved in a new direction. Perhaps she was becoming too fatalistic. Perhaps she could simply not face being near someone she was no longer allowed to express her love for. Her mind swept back over that final evening, and she realized, with a premonitory chill, that the possibility of a change in the momentum of events in Canigou had not been part of M'landan's argument, either.

"Do what you can," she replied. "But may I stay here, now?"

He came out of his chair, then, and took her hands. "Why do you think you have to ask? Of course you can stay here—as long as you like."

She sat with him holding her hands, hardly hearing his words, confused by the sudden powerful surge that his contact was generating in her. She looked into his face, at the pleasant, angular features, the dark skin and eyes, the long, chestnut hair glowing in the firelight, hair soft as eider.

He had stopped speaking, caught by the expression in her eyes, so unexpected. He reached up and took her face in his hands and tenderly kissed her mouth.

She lowered her head. "Please . . . Andor, will you go now . . . please." She closed her eyes, heard him stand up, heard the soft chime of the chain at his shoulder.

"I'm sorry. I didn't mean to offend you—"

"You didn't offend me. Please believe that. I'm . . . undergoing a change; I'm trying to cope with it." There was nothing else she could say about it.

"I understand. Will you allow me to see you in the morning? Will you let me reassure myself that you forgive my crudeness?"

"Yes, in the morning."

She hadn't looked up, and did not open her eyes until he

had gone out the door. Then she stared down at the hands that lay in her lap with the fingers curved above the palms.

In the moment he had taken her hands, her body had automatically responded; she had expected the swift and fiery pain of laanva. And when his hands had released hers, the sudden passion he had aroused was gone, and she was left weak and stunned by the violent upheaval in her body.

"Oh, God!" she cried out. "How can I live away from him!"

In spite of her mental turmoil and despair, the exhaustion of her body finally overtook her mind, and Darenga slept soundly and awoke refreshed. And hungry. She dressed in a Ronadjounian brocade, and had to readjust her stride to the freedom that trousers afforded her. Strangely enough, she would have liked to have had her robe, but wearing it would hardly convince anyone that she had abandoned the M'dian life.

She looked at herself in the long mirror and held out a thick coil of her hair. It had grown so long that it now reached below her hips. No Lambda clone beyond her tenth year wore her hair long. If she were to be assimilated into the group in the minds of observers, her hair would have to be cut. She ran her fingers down a strand, watching the light from the window run in copper through her hand. But not just yet. She tied her hair back quickly and left the room.

She went to the dining room, found only a servant dusting the wooden floor with a mop gleaming with oil.

"The dining room is used only for formal occasions now," she told Darenga. "Everyone eats in the Alliance cafeteria. Do you know where it is?"

"I can find it, thank you."

Darenga walked back out into the wide corridor and down a branching hallway, bearing eastward through the various turns until she came to the room that announced the wing of the Systems' Alliance, where it was early enough not to have more than a few ambassadors' aides going quietly about their business.

Darenga had no trouble finding the cafeteria, which wasn't crowded, and would have picked up a tray and gone down the line, but she caught a flash of red hair and bronze uniform and instead made her way through the room to the biped area, where two Lambda clones sat relaxed at a table.

They looked up as she approached.

"Well, Areia."

Darenga glanced at their nameplates, answered, "Hello, Gail—Judith. Mind if I sit down?"

The one named Gail reached over and pulled back a chair. "Not at all. How are things in the provinces?"

There was that suddenly remembered and easy oneness that they shared—the brains and bodies identical—almost. And now their silent acknowledgment of the deviation. She was the aberration, the genetic anomaly that had committed murder, had bolted from discipline and celibacy and self-control. She knew the difference was visible, even under the automatic pose that fell over her like a mantle, knew it was clear to them.

"The crops are planted; the sun shines; the rain comes on schedule. How is it among the stars?"

Gail leaned back in her chair with a grin. A minute difference there, too; quick to smile, optimism always apparent. "The machinery still runs, with a little patching here and there."

"I'm surprised to see you on the ground. What's the occasion?"

Gail glanced at Judith, who said, "I have a cargo to ferry at 0930. So I had a little leisure time."

"We just came in from the Spinandre," Gail told her.

"M'dia?"

"Uh-huh. Some life-giving elixir and a new ambassador."

"A new ambassador? What's the ambassador's name?"

"Trolon."

Darenga's eyes held steadily enough.

"Know him?" Gail asked, and Darenga knew she had been expecting a reaction. The Lambda game of bait and disconcert.

"I know him. Why has it taken three years for a choice of ambassador to be made?"

"A little internecine problem."

"What do you mean?"

"Well, from what I could understand of it, there was a struggle, very low key, of course, between what remained of the Ilanu M'dians and the M'dians of Klada. Apparently no other city was seriously considered in the search for an ambassador. The priest at Klada was involved in this through his mate, Laatam, whom he yielded to in the end, although he wanted one of his own city to be ambassador. But his mate is one powerful personality, and Trolon was picked. He wouldn't have been my choice, but then, I just run the ferry boat."

Gail leaned forward, then, and said in a low voice, "Just what the hell are you doing back at the Gemainshaf?"

Darenga met her eyes, saw something she had been missing—a tension that expected an answer far different than the one Darenga could give. "What do you think I'm doing here?"

Gail and Judith exchanged an intelligence without looking at each other, but Darenga sensed it.

"Helping out an old friend."

Darenga smiled. "Which old friend?"

"How many old friends do you have in this madhouse?" She made a little noncommittal gesture as they watched her. "I'm innocent," she said finally. "I really don't know what you're talking about."

Now Gail and Judith looked at each other and then back at her. Gail put her elbows on the table and glanced casually around. "How out of touch have you been?" she asked, bringing her eyes back from a slow circuit of the room.

"When I came in last night, it was the first time I had seen Andor, or had any communication with him, in three years."

"He didn't call for you?"

"No. Why don't you tell me what's going on?"

"You knew about the freighter assembly on Arcus, didn't you?"

"As a matter of fact, the last time I saw Andor was when the vote was coming up on it. He didn't hold much hope of it being defeated."

"It wasn't. Arcus has the whole show, and they've maneuvered things in Council so the controls on their production are a farce. Some old gopher runs up there every six months for an inspection tour that's a joke, a report is filed, and everything is copacetic. They're building more than freighters, of course."

"What proof do you have?"

"Sightings from the 152. We've filed rolls and rolls of reports, but they're ignored."

"Who the hell is ignoring that kind of information?"

"Well—here's the Alliance at work: all worlds' democracy in action—Klote and Leend and all their friends from Dendom—you know the group—have been packing the committees and, as we all know, it takes a majority vote to release any incoming information to the Assembly —formally, that is, officially."

Judith broke in. "And there was the little dance with the reports."

"Somebody sabotaged them?" It wasn't difficult for Darenga to extrapolate the erratic intrigues of the tidal pools of the Alliance; she had dealt with them too long.

" 'One of the maintenance people overturned a chemical solvent over the spools, so sorry.' They never did find the guilty maintenance person. We just sit and wait. We're running on down time anyway."

The bitterness in the clone's voice was clear, and Darenga's first response to it was an old one, well-conditioned: a clone must indicate non-acceptance of another clone's emotion. It was triggered by this confrontation with an old life. But there was a stronger response, now, that overrode it. Darenga lay her hand on the bronze sleeve. "How do we take up a life that has any meaning?" she said, and saw this image of herself withdraw, curl down into the interior woman where there was safety.

Darenga took her hand away. "We were perfectly made, weren't we?"

190

There was a heavy silence.

"So what does all this mean in terms of immediate warfare?" Darenga finally asked, pulling everything back to normal.

"They're going to get rid of Seldoldon," Gail said matter-of-factly. Then she added, "He's backed this organization all his life, and his family before him, and the whole thing's about to dump him. But I won't like to see it."

"He'll get to see his dream of free choice and self-determination lead the whole galaxy right into a holocaust," Judith said.

"It's the reason he can't kick himself free of alcohol or hanj."

Darenga looked at Gail and felt a strange sense of loyalty to the man whose life and hopes they were so casually discussing.

"Oh, it's covert," Gail told her. "But it's still common knowledge; especially since his censure."

"I don't know how he can put that stuff into his body," Judith said with mild distaste.

Darenga turned to her. "You drink catspaw," she said.

"That's not the same thing," she replied. "Catspaw is mood-specific; if we're down, it brings us up; if we're up, it calms us down; it takes care of the genetic rough edges." She laughed, low and husky.

"You said they were going to depose Seldoldon," Darenga said, turning to Gail. "How do you see them accomplishing that? Doesn't he have any support in the Council?"

"DHO and Tren still back him, and there are others. But it's a tenuous balance. And you know something, Areia? I think I've brought back with me the gram that's going to tip the scale against him."

Darenga sat with her hands folded on the table, her thoughts racing ahead of what Gail was suggesting. And she saw a balance being set that the clones sitting with her had no knowledge of.

"You know what a pig's worth our lives are going to be if the Arcustans and Arkdikhs take over. We'll go, and the Caretaker and the treatment facility right along with us."

Gail leaned back in her chair and braced her fingers lightly against the table edge. "And that will be the end of all that."

Judith looked at her chronometer and stood up. "Well, I've got a shuttle to make. It was good to see you again, Areia."

"I've got to be going, too," Gail said, coming to her feet. She stretched, and adjusted the holster belt at her waist.

"I see they've never given you back your side weapons," Darenga told her.

"Hell, no. We'd be dangerous. Well, Areia, you may as well go back to the pastoral life and enjoy it as long as you can. Maybe it is better to die happy and in ignorance." She held out her arm and Darenga clasped her wrist.

"Why die at all?" she answered.

Gail made a long tone in her throat. "Do I hear resistance?"

Judith moved in close to her. "If I'm going to die," she said, low and tense, "I want it to be in a Galaxy that's maneuvering."

"If there's anything that can be done," Gail said in the same voice, "we're with you."

"You'll know if there is," Darenga replied, all of a sudden drawn down and clear.

"Communications is the one thing Seldoldon still has control of," Gail told her. "You know our call signs. And our crews are loyal."

Darenga sat back in her chair and watched them go out of the room, tall, assured in their manner and bearing, figures that had struck fear and obedience all across the galaxy. No less commanding now.

She turned back to the table. In three years the whole foundation had developed a crack. And she had no doubt that the structure would finally be split wide open. And her first thought was to return to the settlement, take those she loved most to—to where? Where was there in the galaxy a place that would be safe?

Across these dark and impotent thoughts, Seldoldon's voice spoke her name. She looked up.

192

"Are you working up the courage to have breakfast, or are you recovering from it?"

She gestured to a chair. "Sit down," she said. "No, I haven't had breakfast. Are you warning me?"

He gave her an apologetic look. "It provides the proper balance of vitamins and minerals. Look, I traced you here to ask if you want to fly up to Amper with me. I have an appointment with the bishop at eleven o'clock. I'm going to see if I can't straighten out this business in Canigou for you. But if you come we'll get there in plenty of time for a breakfast at Treeko's, and I can guarantee you a meal you've never had before."

"Sounds fine to me," she replied.

"Good!" he said. "Let's go down to the landing strip."

They floated down into Amper, a city of 300,000, cosmopolitan, far removed from the bucolic simplicity of the Gemainshaf. It was a city surrounded and intersected by water, swept clean by steady ocean breezes, its towers and structures glistening with the moisture left by a shredding and lifting bank of clouds that marked the land with sunlight and swift shadow.

A pencil line of vapor outlined the airflow over their wings as Seldoldon settled the craft into a slowly declining flight path into a runway cut off at its end by a broad and dappled bay.

"Amper's grown," Darenga said, noting the geometric expansion toward the ringing hills.

"We've tried to keep it at a minimum, but the municipal laws are being stretched a little further every year—like the galactic laws."

It has gotten away from me, Areia, he had told her as the green and rolling terrain of Ronadjoun had passed below the craft. *The temper of the times has changed. There's no room anymore for the long dream, for the idea of a society equal for all beings.*

He had looked over at her, into the green eyes that held—something. *If you're thinking the old way was better—*

193

No, Andor, that wasn't what I was thinking.

Will you tell me, then?

Yes. I was thinking that there is an unfairness in the nature of life. And I find it . . . incompatible with what seems to be expected from living beings. That there is imposed on us a sense of order, and when we go about trying to keep that order, the penalties against us are too heavy—much too heavy.

If I were a Lambda clone, he had responded after a thoughtful moment, *my answer to that would be that there are no penalties involved, that it's all the random nature of events.*

And how would you answer?

That it is the judgment of God.

Then the cruelty is beyond comprehension, she had replied, and they had both lapsed into silence.

They had breakfast as he had promised and, as he had promised, it was very good. Darenga, long used to the largely raw vegetable diet of the settlement, found the meats and shellfish heavy, so she ate less than Seldoldon obviously hoped she would. But he left the restaurant in good spirits and without sampling any of the wines and liquors that were brought by cart from table to table.

"What do you think you can accomplish with the bishop?" Darenga asked as they stepped out onto the wide, flower-bordered sidewalk.

"He's the head of the Church on Ronadjoun," he answered. "He's the authority that can put a stop to this harassment."

Because he was making a formal visit, Seldoldon had worn his brown brocade tunic and trousers, and his gold chain of office. It made him conspicuous, and all down the street, as in the restaurant, they had been stared at and buzzed over and amiably greeted, until the street had become an obstacle course.

"St. Anne's is just around the corner," he said, smiling over at her apologetically.

They had decided in advance that she would not go in. There was a small art gallery across from the cathedral, and when Seldoldon went up the broad, worn steps, turning once to give her a cheery wave, she crossed the avenue and went into the gallery.

From the window, she could see the first section of the cathedral's interior, an ornate mass which soared abruptly away into darkness. Behind the cathedral was the rectory, and beyond that the bishop's residence. Seldoldon had gone in through the great open doors of the church, but when he returned, over an hour later, it was from the street side of the great stone building.

She saw immediately by his face that it had not gone well. When she started out the door of the gallery to meet him, he made a quick gesture, and she immediately dropped back into the shadow of the room.

"Let's see if there's a back door to this place," he said.

"Back door—?"

He took her arm and they moved past the displays to an exit. Once they were on the sidewalk again, he guided her quickly along, his hand still gripping her arm.

"What the hell is the matter?" she said, matching his long stride and choking down her sudden apprehension.

"I want to get you out of here," he said, and she saw that he was in dead earnest.

"Are we being followed, or what?"

"We may be, I don't know."

"I can keep up with you better if you let go my arm."

"Sorry." He released her, but kept up the pace. "They have a warrant out on you," he said.

"A warrant! A warrant for what? What do they think I've done?"

"Areia, this is the craziest thing I've ever come up against, but there is a law—and he showed it to me—a law that gives the Church jurisdiction over any Ronadjoun citizen who maintains a liaison with a non-human. It has been on the books since the first council meeting after the Time of Exile, one of those bizarre laws that was never expunged because it was never used. But they're acting on its legality now. They've dredged it up and sworn out a warrant on the strength of it." He looked over at her.

"I'm not a Ronadjounian citizen," she said. "They can't arrest me."

"You are a citizen. I gave you sanctuary, remember? And you swore to abide by the laws of the Gemainshaf. The term has narrowed over the years, in the common understanding, but the legal designation includes the entire planet. The warrant is valid."

"And the penalty?"

"The minimum, after a trial by the ecclesiastical court in which there is a conviction, is three years' incarceration in the abbey of the district in which the offense took place. If there is a second offense, the term is fifteen years."

"Can you intervene?" she asked, after they had traveled some distance in silence.

"I don't know," he replied. "We need to get back to the Hall, where we can sit down and plan some strategy."

They had reached the landing port, and slowed down as they went through the terminal.

"Let's cut through here," he told her, and they went through a baggage area onto the strip set aside for small-craft and other minus SOL craft.

They located the smallcraft, and while Seldoldon checked the instruments Darenga cleared them with control. Once they were in the air and drifting away beyond the last pattern of buildings that marked the city, Seldoldon told her, "They were at the settlement looking for you, so M'landan is aware of what's going on."

"Damn them!" she said furiously.

"You're going to need an advocate, Areia; let me represent you."

She put her head in her hands, pressed her fingers hard against her forehead. "You have too many problems now. You don't need something like this, that's sure to be sensationalized."

"Areia, I want to do it. My problems with the Alliance are going to continue no matter what goes on." He gave her a slow smile. "I think I have some ideas for your defense. But the most important thing we need to do, at this point, is to keep you away from the abbey. If you're arrested and given over to abbey authorities it may be a little more difficult. A person under abbey authority can't be released on bond."

"What the hell kind of exemption is that?"

"I would say the original premise was that a prisoner under Church authority would be more easily rehabilitated in an abbey environment. But, whatever the reason, I want to keep you at the Hall."

"Couldn't they arrest me there?"

"I don't think they'd try. That would be an insult to my house, my honor, my name. No, I think they would have to be satisfied that you would be confined in my care."

They had followed the coastline down and were now in sight of the Hall.

Darenga leaned abruptly forward and told him, "Swing off! Swing off!"

"I see them," he answered, already making a backward arc over the ocean and around toward the mountains, where he settled the craft behind a low ridge.

"Those were abbey cars," Darenga said. "And every constable in the district."

"So the presumptuous bastards are going to try and play a game with me."

Darenga sat looking back toward the Hall, which was obscured now by the terrain. "Now what?" she asked.

"Wait a minute, let me think."

She was quiet, her eyes still fixed at a point outside the window, her mind sifting quickly through all the possibilities.

Seldoldon spoke, finally, anger still riding in his voice. "They got this thing worked up pretty damn fast."

Her head came around and she looked at him with a mild expression. "Shall I overpower you and escape?" she asked.

"That would hardly work for you in court. No, we'll go back to the Hall and see what they're trying to do. They'll release you into my custody."

"And if they don't?"

"Don't worry. They're not going to refuse me."

"You didn't think they'd come to the Hall."

"No, but now that I analyze it I can see why they might.

There are questions that could be asked later, questions about why they didn't try. This way they satisfy their obligations, and leave you free—within the Hall."

"I'm not so sure," she replied, glancing down at her hands. She looked back up at him. "You know, if they jail me for three years I'll die."

"It won't happen."

"M'landan is the only one who can keep me alive."

"I understand that, God knows." His gaze drifted away from her face. "I have to move within the law, Areia, just like any other citizen, if what I've worked for all my life is to have any meaning at all. You should understand that more than anybody."

"I do."

"It's going to work out," he said.

"All right, Andor," she replied.

He turned his head away as his hands moved to the controls, and he glanced out the cockpit to judge his clearance. Swiftly, soundlessly, Darenga's fist struck him behind the ear.

His body folded down into his couch, and his head rolled against his chest. Darenga reached across him, flung up the canopy, and jumped to the ground. She came around to his side, pulled him out of the cockpit and lay him in the thick grass. She went back to the craft and set the controls, leaping away as it made a wobbling rise for fifteen yards then tipped and crashed into the ground.

Darenga yanked open the door on the pilot's side, made a swift assessment of the damage, where the metal had buckled, the way the sharp edges of the wreckage were turned. She broke loose a long shard of metal and came back to where Seldoldon lay unconscious.

She crouched down beside him. "We'll try to save your reputation, anyway," she said softly, and made a swift cut through the material of his tunic and into his flesh.

He moaned softly, stirred.

She gave him a quick scrutiny, then took the flat edge of the sheared piece of metal and scraped it down his temple and cheek, removing the first layers of skin. His bright red blood flooded the broad wound, ran down his neck and into his hair.

She turned her head back toward the craft, then glanced up the ridge. She straightened away from Seldoldon's form, dropped the bloody shard inside the cockpit. From an undamaged panel she took a small sleepfloor packet, a box of rations, and from a concealed niche in the deep interior of the compartment a pattern gun.

She laughed drily when she found it, stood staring at it for a few seconds before she shoved it down into the top of her trousers. She glanced at Seldoldon once more, frowning slightly. Then she looked back toward the ridge and started away at once from the scene, moving at an angle that would take her away from the Hall, but southward.

When she had gained a small windgap halfway up the steep slope, she stopped and looked back. Seldoldon had brought himself to a sitting position, and was staring dazedly around him.

"And here we are again, you and I," she whispered, "at opposite ends of the pole." Then, in the Ronadjounian farewell, she added the variation, "A safe journey for us both," and, turning, went through the pass, and in the direction of Canigou.

Chapter 16

It took her twelve days to reach the district. She had travelled only at night, and slept under cover during the day, eating little, keeping far away from the roads and dwellings. She had continually adjusted her line of travel, heading along a southeasterly course. She had seen search craft to the west, but only one had come anywhere near her, and she had remained unobserved.

After the first two days she knew for certain that the search machinery did not include pattern control, or she would have been discovered within hours. Seldoldon, she knew, was the sole person in control of that remnant of the age of the Maintainers, and he apparently wasn't making it available to the searchers. She guessed that it was temporary, that he was using every delay possible under law to give her time. Time for what, she wasn't even sure herself, because there was really nowhere to run. Capture was inevitable.

But she ran anyway, southward, and on the evening of the twelfth day she reached familiar terrain. She had come out halfway up the green flank of the mountain which bordered the fields and the soenderbiest meadow. From the deeply forested slope, she could see the cliffs, the few lighted windows, hanging in the darkness; the dwellings of the human members of the community.

It was quiet and serene. A few drifts of melody came to her, but the meaning was lost in the distance. She didn't have to hear the words, though, to know they were the last drowsy conversations before the night descended and everyone slept. And an immeasurable feeling of peace came over her as she stared down into that melodic twilight.

"You are so close to me," she sang, the notes barely audible. "I feel you here with me."

The constellations of twilight had made their ascent into the midnight sky when Darenga rose from where she had been sitting and began to put together a shelter. Its dimensions were the inflated square of the sleepfloor she had brought with her from the smallcraft, and the sides and roof were constructed from stripped branches of spirion, an evergreen that would keep its natural color and freshness for at least a month. She didn't know if she would need it that long.

It was a blind. A clever bit of camouflaging set between two animal trails. A shelter she could see clearly from, but which only a direct and careful scrutiny would detect. She crawled inside and pulled the hatch closed behind her.

It was fragrant and warm inside, and only the severest rain would penetrate the layers of crosspacked twigs and branches. For the first time in twelve days she felt safe. She burrowed into the eider pocket of the sleepfloor and finally slept.

She awoke to early daylight, shadowed here on this westward slope, the sun not having yet cleared the mountaintop, but its warm, golden light had spread along the uppermost part of the cliffs, and she heard, deep and sweet, the sound of M'landan's voice celebrating the morning with the first prayers.

She lay listening, her fingers covering her lips, her eyes closed, and the tears squeezing out from the thick, pale lashes. When the prayer ended she sat up, sniffed noisily, took a deep breath, and rubbed the tears away roughly with the back of her hands. "Don't be stupid about this!" she said fiercely.

She crept to the small viewing hole and looked down and across the misty fields to where the people were dispersing to their tasks, some to the islands, others to the interior rooms, some to the outbuildings that housed the looms and the laundry. She didn't see M'landan. Later in the day she saw Audane walking with Tlaima in the gardens, to his structured meeting period with some of his brothers and sisters.

The day wore on until the time for mid-afternoon prayers. Darenga had been watching townspeople from Canigou and elsewhere sift in, and she was alarmed at their numbers. And she guessed that there was both loyalty and curiosity involved in that sudden increase. She crouched near the view hole as the people, both M'dian and human, settled to the ground.

There was a sudden stir, a lifting and turning of heads as a Gemainshaf car appeared on the hill, stopped, and two Baaranic guards stepped out and around to the back doors, where they carefully removed a metal box and carried it to where the crowd was seated.

"DHO!" Darenga breathed, as she watched the guards set the box down and then take positions on either side of it. "Well," she said, "the lines are being drawn."

Now the heads turned from the box to the dark entrance of the cliffs. Audane emerged first and took his place at the front edge of the crowd closest to the corridor. He remained standing. Tlaima and Klayon came next, and after them M'landan. The crowd came to its feet. Darenga leaned forward, her chest tight.

The atmosphere of the day, the air pressure, the downward currents of air off the mountain, drove back the sound, but she knew the prayer, his gestures, the responses, and she repeated them softly to herself with his movements, concentrating, focusing down on each detail, memorizing, holding the time steady with both hands and every effort of her will. But it ended. M'landan floated back into the cliffs, the people rose, and the Baaranic guards carried DHO down into the corridor.

Darenga swung away from the hole with a grimace, straightened her cramped legs, and rolled over on her belly. "Is the audience about the gods," she wondered aloud, "or the state of the galaxy?"

On the third day of her encampment Darenga located a small swift-running stream at a distance from her shelter, and washed out all her clothes and set them in the sun to dry while she bathed in a chilling luxury she had not afforded herself since her escape.

It took all afternoon for her clothes to dry, and she padded back to the shelter to wait. This night, she had decided, she was going down to the cliffs.

She started down the slope in the late afternoon, making her way cautiously along the fringes of the old lake bed, taking her time, and staying behind the slow cliffward movement of the farmers. It was when Darenga and the farmers paralleled one another, near the edge of the fields, that a shuttle craft slid over the cliffs and made a declining arc to land on the wide strip separating the islands from the garden slope.

Darenga had dropped to the ground the instant she was aware of the craft, and when the viewing ports had been angled briefly away from her position, as it made its turn, she had leaped for the low brush on the lake bench and buried herself in it, her pattern gun drawn and ready.

It was a moment before the hatch came open, a moment for a slow gathering of M'dians and humans to pause and watch. From this circumspect behavior, Darenga guessed that the arrival of such craft had lately become a frequent and negative experience.

The hatch opened and two crew members in bright blue stepped down, took a stand on either side of the hatchway in a manner that signaled the disembarkation of persons of rank. Seldoldon?

It was first of all the abbot of Mont Clair and two more abbots, and the Bishop of Amper, and with them their retinue of monks, all spreading out around the craft and shifting into groups as they glanced back toward the hatch.

Darenga saw M'landan coming slowly down the pathway from the cliffs, his pace dignified, the bronze hood pulled forward so his face was shadowed. And then she saw a slight hesitation in his step, a movement outward of his arms from his sleeves, a movement arrested. She looked back to the craft to the cause of his sudden agitation.

Her hand gripped the handle of the pattern gun, her fingers automatically searching the first sequence of bar and dial. The figures stepping lightly down from the hatchway were M'dian, a group in the green and black-figured robes of Klada, and three in the pale white robes of Ilanu, changed now, decorated in silver, Trolon first, his chest flashing with linked platelets of engraved silver, Treaden at his side, and another from Ilanu whom she recognized, but whose name she had forgotten.

So it's Trolon. She smiled tightly. *And Laatam. Of course, you would be the prime mover. A Chaeya without her priest. What compensation do you expect for that dishonor?*

The party turned now toward the slope, where M'landan was emerging from the shadows of the silka trees.

"You have come a long distance to satisfy your need for revenge, my brother," he said.

Trolon stepped forward, an imposing figure that held a tension which gave it power.

"I have come a representative chosen by our people," he replied. "And I find that you were not content breaking the law of our gods and our generations, you have also violated the laws of these people and their god in return for the generosity and love they have shown you. You have brought shame and dishonor on us all, first in the private audience of our own world, and now in the public view of all the worlds. You took one to Chaeya who was despised and cast out by her own people. You gratified the filthy lust of your body. You desiccated the source of all life for your city and the ones who called you brother and father.

"If you would make amends for the crimes you have committed on your people and on this people who have given you their love, then honor their just law and give them the one they seek, the one who will be treated with justice and turned from the destructive path she has been forging for herself and for you. Do this, and there will be peace for all of us."

Trolon had been skillful and clever, in the madness that Darenga could perceive, but which was unnoticed by the humans, who were not able to understand even with their translators. It was frightening to Darenga, hugging close to the ground in the rapidly oncoming night. He had struck the perfect note of injury and benevolence, and she knew he was not going to give himself away, not to these humans who would not want to believe it anyway.

M'landan had listened to him silently, his eyes moving now and then to Laatam, who met his gaze steadily, her head up in a quiet posture of dignity.

"I did not realize we were not at peace, my brother," M'landan replied. "Perhaps the peace you mean is not the physical sign of compatibility among people of different species, but the condition of a restless and guilty soul. You come here to add your dissatisfied spirit to the ones who, maneuvering under a cloak of righteous anger, are furthering their own unhappy and ambitious ends. But I will answer you with an honesty you have not afforded this company: the one who was known as my Chaeya asked to be released from her vows to me. And when I consented she left to make her life again among her own people. She is not here, as the many searches of our dwellings have indicated. I do not know where she is. I cannot help you."

It was plain that this was the first anybody knew that the priest's Chaeya had renounced their relationship. Tlaima, who had followed M'landan and stood a few paces behind him, reacted sharply, her hands dropping down from her sleeves to a position at her sides and away from her body. Klayon was less demonstrative, but Darenga recognized that he had seen and understood Tlaima's reaction.

An audible comment ran through the M'dians on the slope, and as well from those near the shuttle. And of that number, Darenga knew Laatam, outwardly cool and sedate, had been rocked by M'landan's announcement.

And as the reactions were still being recorded and felt, but not understood, by the humans, it was at this moment that M'landan's hood turned toward the brush-covered hillside where Darenga lay hidden and motionless. He seemed to look directly at her, the great brilliant eyes seeing everything for that instant, and then the hood turned away.

She released a slow breath.

Trolon, in spite of M'landan's severe response, was undiscouraged. The group with him apparently found nothing in M'landan's words to sway them; his forthrightness had, in fact, made them more adamant. And so the bishop addressed the figure on the slope.

"You call yourself a holy guide, and yet everything you have done in this place denies the name. You've led your people, and the people of my species who have been deceived by your false promises and doctrine, into mortal sin. But your punishment will be determined by a higher power. We most concern ourselves with bringing to justice the woman who has broken our laws. We ask that you give her over to us now."

M'landan was silent. And when they saw he was not going to answer, they slowly filed back into the shuttle. At the last moment, Trolon turned and looked back at M'landan. "I have not said everything."

"I know you have not, my brother," M'landan answered.

Trolon stared toward him as the others moved past and into the craft, until a short phrase from Laatam drew him around, and he followed her through the hatch.

Darenga waited until the shuttle began to rise and turn, and then she made her retreat—low, close to the earth, her eyes on the craft.

The attention of the people on the ground was on the bright blue shuttle, too, all except M'landan, whose dark and brilliant gaze had turned toward the embankment again and the heat pattern he had registered moments before. The time line it traced faded swiftly, but he noted its direction and its speed before he turned around and went back toward the cliffs and his cell.

Darenga closed the shelter door, and dropped belly down on the sleepfloor, and lay with her head on her arms.

Everything was wrong, ugly—misshapen events and short-sighted actions all burning down and scattering debris across an expanse of time that was incomprehensible. The admission had been shameful for M'landan to make, especially in that company, that the one for whom he had altered his life and the lives of everyone dependent on him had forsaken him. It weakened his position, diminished his stature, stretched loyalties to the breaking point, made everything a hazard.

They were flocking together, these birds of a feather, to destroy him. But what he had told them would have to satisfy them for a while—they had obviously searched and researched the entire settlement more than once. She knew that she would have to leave the region right away, perhaps draw the search in another direction.

She turned over on her back and lay staring up at the feathery twigs of spirion that drooped down into the dim space of her shelter.

There was really only the one thing she could do, and that was to get as far away from the settlement as she could before Seldoldon had to give over pattern control to the group who sought her now.

Still, she lay gazing up, inert, enervated.

It had been an old prejudice that had set the religious of Ronadjoun in motion against her. Old hatreds unforgotten, even by those whose chosen life was supposed to embody charity and forgiveness. Not that she had ever believed it did, or expected any more than what she knew to be true of the reactions of Originals to the daily impinging of events on their ideals. They yielded. Untrained, undisciplined, with only the thought of immediate reward, they reached and demanded and struck down what prevented their satisfaction. She'd spent a long—interminably long—lifetime trying to make their lives safe, trying to keep them from killing one another. But they continued to demand, even when all there was left to demand was her small measure of peace. And they would have it. And it would be soon.

She lay very still, with her arms across her face. Then she raised her arms slowly, listening. She had heard a noise. In the few days she had been there she had quickly learned to identify the sounds of the animals that moved quietly along the paths below and above the location of her hut, and the little rooting noises that the scavengers made when they reconnoitered the small territory she had taken for herself. But this was different. Scarcely a sound at all. More the suggestion of a sound.

She came up in a crouch, her fingers poised on the sleepfloor like a runner's. She turned her head slowly, trying to range in, to catch again that subtle passage outside the branches of her shelter.

It was not repeated. She relaxed back on one knee and drew the pattern gun from her belt. She made a swift adjustment to spread the circumference to take in a fifty meter reading in all directions. Nothing but small animals and sleeping birds, insects, and other creatures that were no threat.

She lay the pattern gun to one side and sat back with her hands clasped around her knees. She still had a feeling. . .

And then she heard his call, very close, low, a fragment of song.

"M'landan?" she answered, incredulous. She flung back the hatch and looked out.

He sank down to crouch near her, his face close to hers. "I am glad to see you are safe."

"How . . . did you find me?"

"There was a faint trail. And a glow inside your dwelling."

She closed her eyes briefly. "Of course. I must shine like a lantern. Can you get through here? It is reasonably secure from human eyes."

"I think so."

She moved to one side as he came through the opening with a lithe shift of his body, and the rustle of the cloth of his robe was so familiar and immediate, the faintly sweet warm odor of his body so pervasive, that everything outside that small enclosure was suddenly unimportant.

"This is very comfortable," he said, drawing back his hood and taking everything in. "It feels close . . . and familiar."

"It serves."

Above their heads, the first landward breeze quickened the upper layers of the spirion branches, and through the viewing hole came the scent of oncoming rain.

"Why did you come back?"

"I . . . wanted to see you again. It probably wasn't very smart; I'm putting you all in jeopardy."

"No, you needn't fear that. But your life would have

been in grave danger if you would not have let yourself be led back to me."

"I don't think it's a trap," she replied slowly, trying to understand his meaning. "I could tell by the way they were conducting their search that they hadn't located me. And I'm certain Andor is doing everything possible to keep pattern control out of their hands. That's the only way they could find me."

"Ah, my Chaeya! How one thing so inextricably links itself to another."

It was the way he had said "Chaeya" which had driven out all other meaning in his song. A soft healing word, expressing that their relationship remained unchanged by either her appeal or his agreement.

She touched his robe where it folded over his upright knee. "My vows—"

"—are intact. You took me by surprise that night. I was very confused . . . until later, when I realized your request was the human way of convoluting the present in order to deal with the future."

"Still, you told everyone out there that you had accepted my renunciation."

"Was that not the truth? It is better that they all think so, for their own good. All but Audane. It is necessary for him to know the true situation."

"The true situation," she echoed. "Look at us—crowded down into this one small space they've alloted to us for an undetermined number of minutes." She felt herself sinking into despair, bound by events and irrationalities, and pulled down by her own impotence.

The rain streamed over the hut, poured from the branch tips to the matting of fallen leaves and moss outside. She pushed a woven frame of spirion into the viewing portal, closing out the sporadic gusts of wind and water.

She turned back into the dry, mingled fragrance of spirion and honey and sat against her heels with her hands spread over her knees, looking at the pale outline of his head and the faint light that gathered along his eye.

"It is a space and time precious to me, allotted not by the humans but by the gods and by their instruction."

She looked down at her hands, at last too exhausted in spirit to dispute. The rain was beginning to slacken, not finished yet, but becoming more rhythmic in its fall through the outer foliage. The wind had dropped, and now sighed intermittently through the trees overhead, loosening little falls of water to the ground.

"Any time I can spend with you is precious to me, too," she finally said.

And then, in a voice so gentle she rode on the cradle of its tone before she admitted its meaning, he told her, "We will not meet again after this night, and you must be prepared for this. You must understand perfectly what is to occur and what you must do."

There was a finality in the words he chose and the way he used them. The truth rang in the notes: he believed unreservedly what he had said.

"I am going to put as much distance between me and the settlement as I can before Andor—"

"You will not get any farther than Canigou, my beloved. They will take you there in the streets tomorrow morning."

"This is one of your visions."

"It will happen as I say. But you must understand the rest."

She was worn down, defeated by what she sensed in the air, by the thought of having to run any more, having to leave him. "I'll listen," she replied, remaining as she was, her head heavy and low, her shoulders bowed.

"It's not given to many to know ahead what their contribution will be, but I will give you this knowledge as compensation for what you will feel you have lost."

"I'm not going to lose anything," she said in weak defiance.

"You will spend the next three years in confinement. The first year will be painful and difficult for you, but in the two years following you will be treated well, and you will remember those who were kind to you. At the end of those three years, Audane will be placed in your care. You will be the one who will assure his safety and his visions, once he has reached the age of his priesthood. You must guard him and keep him secluded until he can be brought back before all his people."

"I'll do whatever I can for him," she said, thinking that he wanted reassurance. It was his old concern about succession.

"Yes, I know that it is your will to do so. And it is the will of the gods that Audane have a guardian who can help him understand all the beings he will have under his guidance."

"I'm not sure I can fill that responsibility."

"He will have many wise counselors, Chaeya. The burden will not fall entirely on your shoulders. But you will supply his visions, and he will sustain your life."

"And where is his father in this plan?" she asked, not wanting to say it at all.

"I will train him as I am training him now—to be priest to his people, and to be prepared to be father of his generations."

He moved slightly forward, changing the position of his legs, straightening them so his feet touched the branches that formed the wall. He leaned his weight on his forearm, his face tilted away and palely outlined.

"Then you are one of the wise counselors."

"No. I am the father who must prepare the way for the next."

There was no use for her to say anything to this, so she let it pass quietly, this annunciation of his life's purpose. And she reminded herself: Well, you have seen him now. You have sat beside him, and you have seen that he was well and unharmed by all this madness. Now you will be content. Now you will leave. And you will be thankful that there is nothing they can do to him now that they have made their public stand. They said it was you they wanted, and that's who they will get. Only it will be many miles from this warm and beautiful moment, this touching of hand and tongue, this gentle, slow, and loving exploration, this renewal—

"My most precious and most loved, the gods have granted me this last time with you. I have their approval, if I have your consent."

It seemed so poignant, this request. And it was apparent, then, that this was the first time he had approached her without a sense of guilt.

"My loving friend," she answered, putting her hands close about his face, "you have my consent . . . you have my consent."

The release of laanva was slow at first. He was severely controlling it. He said, his voice as well controlled, "Lie back, Chaeya. Rest your hands against the floor."

And she did as he asked, slowly, so her hands were not pulled away from the shields, so the ooze of liquid was not interrupted, nor the pain abated. It was only when she looked into his face, felt the weight of his body distributed into his arms and pressing down on her palms, heard the sudden long and falling tone that was his cry for compassion, that she knew what he was going to do.

"Please," she said, too weak, too absorbed in the unyielding and exquisite pain to struggle. "Oh, please don't do this to yourself! Please!"

"You . . . must . . . be . . . sustained. You must live!"

"Don't let him do this!" she cried out to the rain, to the forest, to the heavens. "M'landan, don't do this!"

"It . . . must . . . be done," he answered.

Chapter 17

"Her competency to stand trial has never been in question, although the high ambassador has tried to make it an issue. She is completely rational—brain scans have shown her to have a normal brain wave pattern, and her behavior is what we could expect from anyone in this grave situation —she is subdued. There can hardly be any doubt, your Excellency, that we have illustrated—and she has admitted —her violation of a law honored by men and demanded by God and nature."

She had been aware for several days that there was a persistence to her hallucinations; not a repetition, but a similarity of place and scene, and she had thought, *Is this really happening? Am I really where I seem to be? In this place, being judged by these men?* And she had watched Andor Seldoldon quietly build his case in her defense, skillful and persuasive, the smooth ebb and flow of the Ronadjounian language used to the best advantage by a master. She had sensed in a tunnel-visioned way that members of the audience in the high and echoing stone chamber were swayed. But she perceived, from the activity along the L-shaped wooden bench that held the brown-clothed judges, that the number concerned with reason and fairness were few. And so the trial had finally ended.

Seldoldon had been admitted to this small room that she had seen shift from a soft fragrant lace of branches and solidify into stone, and now he sat on the one chair, a large wood and leather piece with beautifully executed religious scenes carved on the sides and top. He was bent forward with his forearms resting on the thick brocade of his trousers, the fingers of his hands moving in a thoughtful, parallel motion, as he stared at the stone floor.

This smooth and steady motion had been fascinating

215

her, and she had been watching it as if there were a great revelation about to be made to her in the rhythm of his hands. But now his dejection was beginning to be apparent to her, and she floated up from where she had been sitting on the edge of a bed which, with the small table next to it and the chair where Seldoldon sat lost in thought, was the only furniture in the space. She came up beside him, lay her arm across his shoulders, and pressed her cheek against his hair.

"It wouldn't have made any difference what you tried," she told him.

He lifted his head in surprise, and she stroked the soft chestnut hair away from his temples. "Nothing would have changed their verdict."

"I realize that," he said, staring up at her. "You seem . . . alert."

"I think I am. At least there's a clarity now to everything —to all the things I've been watching happen over the past weeks."

She straightened away from him and went back over to the bed. She sat down with her hands braced on her knees, and arched her head with a tired motion. She sighed. "This isn't such a bad place. It has all I need. And the bed's comfortable." She spread her hands over the coverlet. "Don't abuse yourself over this, please," she told him. "Will you be able to visit me? They won't bar my advocate, will they?"

"I don't think they'll want to try holding you incommunicado. It's only too apparent now to everyone that their reason for pressing this trial in the first place was to stop a rival in this district. There can be men of the crudest motives in the highest occupations. Not all the Church agrees with this—Roenay has just managed to work up support. Geoffrey was trying to dissuade the judges, but with both the bishop and Roenay . . . I only wish you could have been sent to Rouyn Abbey while I'm working on your appeal."

"Who is there to appeal to?" she replied with a little laugh.

"The cardinals, for one. The patriarch, if I have to."

"No."

He stared at her. "You don't mean that."

"Yes I do. If you try to appeal, I'll have you dismissed as my advocate."

"You aren't serious. This is three years of your life you're talking about."

"Don't oppose my wishes, Andor. Don't try to do what I ask you not to do."

"Then tell me why! Why do you want to stay locked up in this place?"

"What difference does the prison make if I can't be with my people?" She looked away. "Freedom might make resolutions easier to break. No, I'll stay here."

He studied the stone floor again, then raised his head to look at her. "I'll want to know if they're not treating you well."

She smiled. "I'll let you know."

He stood up. "I'll be back in a week." He called out to the monk who stood down the corridor, then turned back to her, hesitated. Then he bowed slightly. "In one week," he repeated, and went through the heavy door. It closed behind him with a deep and solid tone.

He did come once a week after that, for three months. He had a scribe unit brought to her and, from his own collection, a case of books—real books—on every subject she could name.

"The scientific information is a little outdated," he had told her, "but the literature is Earth's finest."

Because the ITU in her brain translated language through sound waves, it was useless for the written languages. So she read aloud to herself those languages she was unlearned in.

Seldoldon had become more introspective with each visit —more preoccupied. "I'm not going to be able to come down here quite as often for a while," he told her one day.

"Of course," she replied immediately.

"Things are getting tense at the Hall," he explained, although she had asked for no explanations. "The Arkdikhs and Arcustans have been creating little skirmishes all over our quandrant. Nothing overtly done, as you can guess, but they're behind it. Every time I'm away for a few hours, they call a session and try to get some of their resolutions passed. Tren and DHO can't pull it alone."

"Why have you been coming down here if this has been going on? Please—stay at the Hall, where you're needed."

He gave her a wry grin. "I thought maybe I was needed here," he replied.

"You know I enjoy your visits, Andor. But, as you can see, I have everything essential to survival, and you've brought me the tools to keep my mind active. So you can rest assured that I'm comfortable and cared for."

He stood with one hand braced against the stones, the other on his hip, his head tilted down so that his hair swayed from his shoulders in a loose wave.

"I'll be back at the end of the month no matter what—"

"It's not necessary, Andor."

"I'll be here—even if the whole galaxy is falling apart." He leaned toward the screened slot in the door and called the monk. "I was at the settlement earlier today," he told her as they stood waiting.

"How is everything?"

"The islands are flourishing."

She waited, her hands gripping her wrists inside the sleeves of the loose and coarsely woven garment she had been given to wear.

"They are all well." It was all he could say within the injunction against giving her any information about M'lan-dan, and she asked him no questions.

"Do you want me to bring some more books when I come?"

She smiled at him. "I think I have enough.

The door swung open.

"Goodbye, Areia."

"Be careful, Andor," she replied.

When the end of the month came and went, Darenga supposed that the pressures of the Alliance problems had kept Seldoldon at the Hall. Still, she was uneasy enough to ask the monk, "Did Lord Andor send a message to me?" when he appeared at the view slot for his periodic check on her. But he made no response.

Darenga spent most of the afternoon at the window, looking down toward the abbey gateyard, which she could see from her vantage point. No one came but a few tradespeople from the town. In the sky above the ocean inlet near the abbey she saw a brief swift trail that identified an LS 4.

She finally turned away from her vigil when she heard the food bin open. Before the monk could have gotten very far down the corridor, she called out again for information about Seldoldon. Again, the only answer she got was silence.

When more than a week had passed she began to feel alarmed. It was not like Seldoldon, no matter how pressing the circumstances, to make a commitment and then not honor it—at least not without some explanation.

What she could see of the surrounding countryside from her window seemed peaceful. And all was peaceful in the direction of the settlement. People came and went from the abbey as they always did. But she remained uneasy—an uneasiness that grew over the second week.

She had been noticing an increasing activity in the sky. More LS 4s, on maneuvers, it seemed to her, and, of late, in groups. She was determined now to get an answer. When the monk came to the screen, she was waiting.

"If you can't speak to me, dammit, get someone here who can! I want to know what's happened to Lord Andor. Do you hear me? Now! Get someone here now!" She had said it in Standard Maintainer, and he had started back, his eyes widening, and then swung about and traveled quickly back down the hallway.

She waited for over three hours. All down the long stone corridor to the bend, where the light was streaming in from a window she couldn't see from the angle of the small screen, to the first downward step of the stairway she couldn't see, there was silence. She looked at the fine circulation of dust through the bands of light at the end of the hall, listened to the close chirping of the birds under the abbey's sloping roof, and then she yelled, "Someone come here! Come here, damn you! Come up here!"

And when there was no answer, she began a long insistent tone in Songspeech, a tone that rose and fell to the upper and lower extents of her voice range. She continued it for over two hours, until she heard a double set of footsteps coming in a measured pace down the corridor. She rose from the bed, still warbling the endless tone, and went to the screen.

It was the prior and, behind him, the day monk.

"You can stop that now," he said.

"Are you going to give me some answers?"

"What is it you want to know?"

"Where is Lord Andor?"

"At the Hall, I presume. Where his responsibilities keep him."

"He was going to come back two weeks ago. What's happened to him?"

"As far as I know, nothing has happened to him."

"Then he must have sent a message—"

"There has been no message."

She stared through the screen at the face beyond. It was immobile, disinterested. She began the tone again.

"You're not making things easy for yourself," he said tightly, and swept away up the corridor again, the day monk at his heels.

She continued her assault through the next day, spacing her vocal periods carefully, so her keepers would be uneasy and so her throat would hold out. No one came around. No one made hourly checks. No food was brought to her. She timed herself so that as soon as the monks' voices faded, with the tolling of the offices, her voice would begin. In between times, she slept or read.

On the third day, there were several footsteps in the corridor, and the face appearing at the screen this time was Abbot Roenay's.

"What do you think to gain with this?" he asked.

"An answer. Where is Lord Andor?"

"At the Hall."

"Why hasn't he been here?"

"I have no idea. Does that answer your question?"

"No! Call him. Find out why he hasn't been down here or sent a message—if indeed he hasn't."

"You ask me to presume to demand from the high ambassador why he has not set aside his business to visit you? You are arrogant beyond my · understanding, Captain Darenga."

"And you tax me to the very end of my patience, Abbot Roenay. If you really aren't holding any information from me, then at least satisfy yourself that no harm has come to him. Surely you're aware, even here, of the state of the Alliance."

"The Alliance is in perfect health, Captain."

"You're an idiot—sir," she replied.

The abbot backed away from the screen with an expression of disgust. He waved his hand toward the night monk. "Feed her," he said.

She laughed. "Raw vegetables and fruit!" She called out to his back. "I'll leave the meat for pious men!"

But she was hungry, and when the food came through the bin door she was quite willing to accept it. It was a thick soup of vegetables and she spooned it up eagerly. And it wasn't until she had eaten half of it, and the sequence of minutes was blending with the order of visual sensations, the order of chair and bed and books with the flow of time itself, that she shoved the bowl away and staggered up.

"You're so stupid . . . it's such an old trick. . . ."

And she felt the anger that she would have felt if she had still been a Maintainer, still fleet captain, still some power in a system that had been ripped open, turned inside out, and left shuddering in the grip of a multiplicity of hands that could only destroy.

She made it to the bed before the drug overcame her.

She had to give the abbot credit for wanting to prevent injury to his monks, for if they would have tried to take her, conscious, from her cell, she would have resisted violently; she was that removed now from the kindness and gentle love that had restrained her in the recent past.

This room she now occupied was long and narrow, as if a hallway had been converted into a cell. The toilet facilities were open—a seat and a sink, that was all. For a window there was a single slit some two and a half inches wide and fifteen inches high. Her bed was a coarse blanket folded on the stone floor. The books had been taken away. And that filled her with rage. They had taken away that one remnant of the outside world that had been left to her.

She had awakened groggy and sick, but aware of a face at the door grill, watching her as she managed to reach the toilet and then hung clinging to its sides as she vomited.

"You son of a bitch!" she said as soon as she was able. "You son of a bitch," and then a long and virulent string of Arcustan profanity that drove the face away. At the far end of a corridor, she heard a metal door draw closed with a muffled clang.

She thought at first that it was to be a temporary arrangement—the abbot exercising his authority and bringing quiet back to the routine of the abbey. She had no doubt that, in a few days, once he had been satisfied that she was not going to try the same tactic again—and she had decided she wouldn't—that he would order her returned to the surface again, up from the dark and silent room that faced out toward a wall that a few thin pale weeds leaned against.

The sun shone down into the narrow slit for about two hours a day, the light moving steadily across the stone blocks of the floor and providing her with a clock of sorts. She knew when her keeper—there was only one now, a sullen young man who seemed to particularly dislike his task—was coming with her one meal. That was when the bar of sunlight first appeared on the stones. He came back for the plate and to make his check when the light slowly dimmed and then faded away. There were variations on this schedule as the sun slowly shifted its narrow path in the Ronadjounian heavens.

She had finally realized that this was not a temporary arrangement, after all. Whatever had detained Seldoldon continued to occupy him to the extent that the abbot felt safe in treating her as he was doing. She could only conjecture about a situation that would result in the neglect she was now suffering, and it scared her, because as long as Seldoldon had been coming she knew everything was all right at the settlement. She had no way of knowing anything now. Anything but the short track of the sun across her floor and the sound of the rain every evening.

She exercised her body—the long, narrow room enabled her to make three running strides, do a leaping turn against either wall and return. She could do one fierce cartwheel, and two flip-overs. If she had been an animal, those first months, she would have gnawed at the grill.

Her exercising gradually became less strenuous, more methodical, and executed with a weary determination that kept her muscles toned but did nothing for her spirits. She did long strings of calculations in her head, scratching the answers in stone, as if it mattered, with a fragment of wire she had found in a crack in the floor. And she watched the progress of the weeds that stretched up the wall outside. It occurred to her that, like the weeds, her own body would suffer if she were not to receive any sunlight. So she determined to take advantage of the brief light and, after her meal was brought, took off the garment she wore and placed it on the floor, and then lay face down on it. The bar travelled over her skin, its shallow warmth finally ending at the back of her knees before it disappeared. Whether it was mentally induced or actual fact, she felt better once she began this daily routine and could see her skin regaining its healthy color.

One afternoon she lay in a half dream, with the sun bar warming a strip across her navel, when she became suddenly alert, aroused by something at the threshold of her consciousness. She opened her eyes slightly, the only movement of her body, the heavy, pale lashes barely lifting as she surveyed the room. Abruptly she came up in a quick twisting turn and looked toward the door.

The young monk's face was close to the screen, his fingers pressed against the metal until it had made white furrows in the flesh.

She leaped up with a cry of rage and hurled her clothing

at the door. *"Cochon!"* she yelled in Ronadjounian as she heard his footsteps hurrying down the corridor. "You pig!"

The metal door slammed shut behind him.

For some nights she had been watching the sky, the brightening haze above the wall outside the window slit, the slow upward casting of L'Epervier. And now the first hazy catch of stars cleared the dark stone barrier, and with it came the faint and drifting perfume of jimasette.

A harvest would be beginning this night, and she saw quite clearly the serene face inclined, the circular blossom tilted up, everything frozen in the white glow that streamed out from priest and flower alike.

She turned away from the window slot and began to pace the room, fast at times, more slowly at others, pacing, pacing, until L'Epervier's light was replaced by the sun and all traces of jimasette had vanished. Then she lay down and slept.

She had stopped taking sun baths for a while after the monk had seen her, not out of modesty, but because she resented his encroachment on the small privacy she had. But she resumed after a few days had lapsed, and then it became a contest between them that she would hear him soon enough to pull the blanket over her. She invariably won.

But he came early with her meal one day, stood silently outside the door as she looked at him through the grill. He held the plate toward her.

She stared back at him, long ago having given up trying to hold a conversation with a monk.

He lowered the plate and stared back at her, boldly, without the usual casting down of his glance that was the appropriate behavior. He made a motion toward her with the plate again, then drew it back, pointing with one hand into the room. She turned slightly to follow his direction. The bar of sunlight lay steady and golden on the floor. She brought her head slowly back around, her eyes brittle green.

"You'll break every vow but your vow of silence, is that it? Well, Brother Peeper, keep your food. Keep it from now on. But you're going to have a hell of a hard time explaining why I died of starvation."

They both turned resolutely away from the window. She dropped cross-legged to her blanket as the door at the end of the corridor firmly closed.

She didn't eat for over a week. When he came to the window with his silent bargain she ignored him, sitting quietly with her back bared to the sun, her arms around her legs, her forehead resting against her knees.

Finally, fearing he might be found out, she reasoned, the monk put her food in the bin and left. It didn't seem important anymore. She sipped a few spoonfuls of the liquid, ate nothing of the vegetables and meat. She simply had no appetite.

The perfume of jimasette had kept her awake and pacing at night, and she slept little in the day. She began to have a terrible and overwhelming feeling of impending doom. And she began to wonder if anything in the world existed outside this narrow band of her experience. At night, now, in the grip of this horror, she would call out his name, a sad trilling measure that she repeated again and again, as a penitent might say her beads.

The monk was becoming alarmed now, because he had found her plate untouched for several weeks, and he had gone so far as to finally speak.

"Please eat," he said, his mouth close to the screen.

She opened her eyes to look up at the ceiling. "Now," she whispered, "you've broken all your vows."

It may have been hours later—or days, she didn't know, and she didn't care. She had been walking among the islands of L'M'dia, and she could see the great, golden globes with their black tracery nodding above her, and she could hear, quite plainly, the soft drumming of the empty bud tips of the fan-like branches. And she could hear M'landan's baritone, without lyrics, just a deep and lovely melody that she concentrated on, wanting to remember it. But there were other voices, outside in the corridor, echoing against the stone, and she started up from the blanket and looked toward the door. Miraculously, it opened, and there were several figures in the doorway.

"She had been unruly," Roenay was saying to Geoffrey of Rouyn. The comment was ignored.

"Can you walk, Captain Darenga?" Geoffrey asked her.

"I can walk," she replied, her voice convincing enough, although she wasn't really sure. But she knew that she was leaving, that she was being taken above ground to somewhere away. Her first year was over.

Chapter 18

There were restrictions on her at Rouyn: she was not allowed to go beyond the abbey grounds, although she could freely move about as long as she obeyed the rules of the community as any other lay person was expected to do.

Rouyn was a dual monastery, with buildings for nuns and monks side by side. The duties of the monasteries, which Geoffrey ruled over, were shared equally, whether it was work in the fields and orchards, the infirmary, whether it was domestic tasks or administrative, all was shared by both houses.

All activities of the abbey were conducted around the offices of the day, as they were in any monastery, but the feeling of pleasure in this order was tangible. All tasks were carried out lovingly and with patience. Except for certain silent periods honored in both houses, conversation was both allowed and encouraged, although frivolous conversation was never approved.

It was an environment that drew Darenga steadily back into balance. She was given a comfortable and sunny room that looked out over the orchards, and for the first few days she had stayed in that room, more at ease there than in the bright and sunny air beyond the windows. No one urged her to do anything else, although they made it apparent that she was welcome to try. So she began to take her meals with the community in the refectory, a room of vast ceiling and heavy wooden tables and benches and a great fireplace that could have stabled a soenderbiest. Meals were eaten without conversation, as passages were read from their old and sacred texts. It was not unlike the life of the M'dians in its routine and simplicity, and Darenga fell into it willingly and with relief.

She had been given a summary of events leading from Seldoldon's final visit, and found them a combination of the many possibilities she had considered.

"Lord Andor did send messages; they were not passed on."

Geoffrey would say no more, and Darenga respected his reluctance and did not ask any questions about it. Seldoldon, she found out, was on a Galaxy outside the Triad, and had been there ever since a building series of incidents in the Council had split the Alliance asunder, sending half of the members out into space with the Arcustans and Arkdikhs, the others into the Alliance fleet. They hovered in the giant ships, cruising the troubled space between Arcus and the Triad, patrolling into the atmosphere of those uneasy planets that requested it. The Alliance mechanism now supported the Loyalists, led by Seldoldon. The Secessionists had scattered into their newly assembled craft and their pirated Galaxies, and were carrying on hit and run raids and sometimes engaging the Alliance LS 4's in small conflicts at the same time that negotiations were being conducted between both powers.

Seldoldon had not forgotten his self-imposed responsibility to Darenga, Geoffrey informed her. He had been pressing his aides to move the governmental and ecclesiastical machinery of Ronadjoun to have her taken from Mont Clair Abbey and placed at Rouyn, a maneuver that had taken almost a year and which was the only thing he could do for her since she had forbidden him to appeal through the courts.

"I regret that these matters took so long to complete," Geoffrey told her. "There were questions of jurisdiction and responsibility."

And pride, thought Darenga, remembering the face of Roenay when she had been taken from her cell. But she did not voice it, and Geoffrey turned his attention to the role of host that he had assumed with her. She was actually no longer a prisoner in the usual sense, except that she was forbidden to have any contact with M'landan, or discuss him, ever.

From time to time, however, word of the M'dians would reach the abbey, and it would be pure chance that she would hear it, since that information was usually filtered away from her. Geoffrey was a kind and generous man, but he took his legal and moral obligations seriously.

Darenga wore the plain brown one-piece garment which the community wore, securing her hair back with a scarf-like headpiece, as the nuns did when they were working outside. So when the group of travelers had come in from the coast on their way further inland, and had been afforded the hospitality of the abbey for the night, the people had no way of knowing that Darenga was not a member of the convent.

"The rains have been heavy this year," one of the women said to her as they walked through the inner courtyard. "Have you gotten much rain here?"

"No more than usual," Darenga answered.

"The settlement has been practically inundated," she went on, speaking of the M'dian colony as a native of Canigou might, although Darenga knew it was an affectation; the woman was from Amper. But she did use the non-hostile terminology.

Darenga tried to honor the restriction Geoffrey had imposed on her, but the woman went on before she could speak.

"I saw L'Hlaadin," she said, glancing over at her. "He is certainly a magnetic being. He spoke to our group—sang, I mean—his voice is marvelous. I could see immediately why he has such a following—"

"I'm sorry," Darenga said abruptly, "I can't talk with you about this," and she left the woman and went through the cloister and into the church and sank down on one of the benches. She was shaking all over. She clasped her hands together hard and pressed them between her thighs, huddling down into her body. "Oh, God," she said, and began to cry.

"You have a visitor." The monk stood at her open door, and Darenga could see the mild excitement that lay behind his eyes.

She rose from the small desk where she had been reading. "A visitor? Who?"

"Do you want it to be a surprise?"

"I can see you expect it to be a pleasant one."

"I'm certain it will be."

"Is it Lord Andor?"

"Yes!"

"Where is he?" She was already going swiftly down the hallway, with the monk straining his instructions to always proceed in a calm and moderate manner. Darenga slowed.

"With Father Geoffrey," he answered, and went as far with her as the door.

"Thank you," she said, receiving his warm smile, acknowledging in her voice his excitement for her.

She knocked on the door and Geoffrey called for her to come in.

Seldoldon was rising from a chair as she opened the door, and she saw immediately how drawn his face was, how his clothes hung from his body. And she realized from his expression that her own appearance was a shock to him.

"This is a surprise," she said, coming up to him with a glance at Geoffrey, who stood quietly behind him. "But I am pleased."

"Father has just told me about Mont Clair. I am so deeply sorry."

The tears came rushing into his eyes as he spoke, and it upset her. She made a little turn away. "It was a year ago. It's all faded now." She looked at Geoffrey and found him an anchor. "The kindness I've been shown here more than makes up for it."

Seldoldon, never abashed by his own emotion, put his arms around her. "You look so thin," he told her, half-crying, his fingers cupped around her head and holding it as he looked into her face.

"You do, too," she replied, caught up in his emotion. "And so tired."

"God knows I am," he said, and held her then as if he might never let go.

Discreetly, Geoffrey had gone into an adjoining room and sat down by the fire that had been lit when the first gusts of the evening rain began. In a few moments, Darenga and Seldoldon came through the doorway, Seldoldon with his arm about her shoulders, Darenga with her hands gathered into her sleeves.

He released her into a chair across from Geoffrey and took up a position on the hearth where, with one elbow resting on the mantel and his fingers linked loosely together, he could face them both.

"I'm here for an hour or so, and then I have to go back to the Hall and from there up to the 152," he said in answer to Darenga's question of how long he could stay.

"Can you say anything about the status of things?"

"It's shaky," he answered. "Shaky. We're still negotiating; that's about the only bright element in this whole fiasco. But the raids continue. They're trying to drain us."

"Is there a chance the fighting will be brought into our atmosphere?" Geoffrey asked.

"I won't try to gloss over the danger, Father; there's always a chance. That's why I'm trying to keep at least a thin cover of fighters in the Triad. I don't want to leave the planet open for them to drop in here."

"So," Darenga told him, following what he wasn't saying as well as what he was, "the larger craft are fairly evenly distributed, but the LS 4 class and whatever modified craft they've managed to assemble on Arcus outnumber yours."

He looked up from his study of the flames. "That's a good, succinct estimate. What would be your solution to the problem?"

It was her turn to gaze into the fire.

"If I were commander," she finally said with reluctance, "I would draw them into combat. Not head on, but through some device that would make the Arcustans look —inept. The purpose, of course, would be to make them angry. Once you've made an Arcustan mad, she'll make her own mistakes, and you'll have the advantage you need."

"For instance?"

"You have to think like an Arcustan. Assume their

boundless arrogance. They have been making fools of you, you know."

"There's not a whole hell of a lot we can do except come after them when they strike," Seldoldon replied a little stiffly.

"Have you run their raiding pattern through the computers? Although their plan should be obvious enough without going through that procedure."

"No."

"Who's your captain?"

"Wiley."

"Have you consulted with her?"

He admitted that, aside from the basic operations of the ship, he hadn't.

"She's your best source of information, Andor. Let her give you the benefit of her skill. Let her do what her lifetime of training has prepared her for. She can tell you exactly the things I can, only she's on the scene and I'm not. She can make the same kinds of decisions I can, and when her conditioning and genetics prevent her from giving the commands that will have to be made, then you can give them for her. Work with her, Andor, or you may have nothing left to work with at all."

Geoffrey had been listening to her quiet admonition to Seldoldon with a grave expression. "I have a tendency to forget who you are," he said to her.

Her eyes turned on him, clear and thoughtful. "I have never been able to forget," she answered.

As Seldoldon talked, the more he revealed of the situation, the more Darenga realized just how tenuous the peace was. In the course of the hour, Seldoldon had moved from fireplace to chair, only to come to his feet again in a constrained restlessness that told Darenga the extent of the burden he carried. She guessed that his journey to the abbey was in part a desire for alleviation, but, from his tightly controlled gestures and speech, she knew he had not found it.

Now he announced that he had to leave, and both she and Geoffrey rose and walked with him into the corridor.

"Before I go, Father——"

"Of course, Andor," Geoffrey replied, anticipating. He turned aside into the church.

"Please wait for me," Seldoldon told Darenga.

She nodded, stood watching, as he followed Geoffrey up the far aisle of benches, where the abbot turned and sat down. The high ambassador knelt beside him. The acoustics of the room were perfect, and Darenga heard his low voice begin, "Bless me father, for I have sinned——"

She turned away and continued down the corridor to the main doors, and stood gazing out into the rain-drenched evening, wondering if the weight he carried now and the weight that would surely be added in the days to come could be eased by anything or anyone.

But the Ronadjounian summer passed without any disturbing news traveling along the road leading from the main arterial connecting the interior with Canigou and the Hall and, over the coast route, Amper.

The hillsides had begun to change color with the short Ronadjounian autumn, and the quiet and pleasant fruit harvest was going on. Darenga was in the orchard nearest the abbey walls, leveling the dark purple fruit that was being poured from baskets into the loading bin, when a craft came plunging out of the brilliantly clear and cloudless sky on a low screaming trajectory that took it so close above the trees that the sockets of the laser-stroke were clearly visible for that instant it passed overhead, whipping the upper branches of the fruit trees and hurling the fruit, like shrapnel, through leaves and ladders to the ground.

Darenga flung herself under the metal bin, her arms covering her head, her face against the freshly turned earth. Everyone else instinctively ducked to the ground or clung, crouching, to the ladders.

The explosion, as the LS 4 buried itself in the sloping ground beyond the cultivated fields, was tremendous. She yelled, "Keep down!" just as the metal fragments came bursting into the orchard. Her whole body crawled with the fear that a projectile would bury itself in her back. She heard a scream, but did not dare move until everything had stopped falling.

She raised her head, heard a moan and a short supplication. She scrambled out from under the bin and made a quick survey. Some of the trees had been sheared off, and there were leaves and branches and fruit scattered all over the ground. To the east of the grain fields beyond the orchard, a plume of smoke located the wreckage.

The scream had come from one of the monks, who sat white-faced on the ground, holding his arm, but there appeared to be no other injuries.

A group from the infirmary had come out of the gate and was running toward them. Darenga held her arms up in the air. "Stop!" she called out, Standard Maintainer, "Go back!"

They hesitated, but when she repeated her command they retreated. She swung around to the people in the orchard. "Hurry," she told them, "Go into the abbey! Hurry!"

She brought her weight up under the injured monk, and another monk quickly supported him from the other side. "There may be more coming," she explained to the group that crowded around indecisively. That moved them all into action, and they ran for the wall, Darenga and the aiding monk half-carrying the injured man through the gate and into the safety of the building.

Geoffrey had been at the gate when they came through and had seen the injured monk to the infirmary. Now he returned to the courtyard, where Darenga was collecting the stragglers and directing them into the abbey. "Does this mean we're going to be attacked?" he asked her, looking at the empty sky and then toward the plume that lay close to the ground.

"I don't know."

"Could someone have lived through that?"

"No one of your faith, Father. But I'm going out there to check. Everyone should stay inside the buildings until we can determine who is going to follow this craft in."

"Shouldn't there have been someone investigating by now?"

"Yes," she answered. "And I can't figure out why they haven't."

Geoffrey walked with her to the gate and then, at her urging, returned to the security of the abbey.

She stood in the overhang of the gatehouse and scanned the sky from horizon to horizon. Nothing was visible in the clear air except the flights of the small birds that inhabited the eaves and crevices of the monastery roofs.

She crossed into the first orchard and examined the damage there, picking up pieces of the wreckage and trying to identify them. Then she moved cautiously out of the cover of the orchard and into the grain field. The disintegration of the craft had spread engine parts and debris into the field, and whole sections of it had been leveled as neatly as if a scythe had passed over it. The wreckage would have been easily spotted from the air, and she wondered at the total absence of either accompanying craft or pursuit craft, if that had been the situation.

There was very little of the fuselage left, but she was able to discern from what remained of the altered controls that the craft had been in use by an Arcustan. There was no trace of the pilot. Which could have indicated a reconnaissance craft in trouble and an ejected pilot coming to earth far from the site. There might be time, after all.

She turned around and ran back to the abbey, and was met by an alarmed Geoffrey. "What have you found?"

"I think we've had some incredible luck," she answered. "I think we're going to be able to get rid of this mess without anyone ever knowing there was a crash here. And, Father, remaining secluded and unnoticed may be our only chance for survival."

With the entire community set to work, all the parts of the craft that could be found, and what was intact of the fuselage, were buried in a deep pit dug by the abbey tractor, and covered over and the mound camouflaged with hastily replanted native vegetation. The area of the fields that had been damaged by the flying debris was harvested, and the equipment left poised at the end of the strip, as if ready to begin the next day.

The orchard was cleaned up to the extent it was possible to do so. Darenga, judging it all with a critical eye and her knowledge of how their reconstruction would appear from

235

the air, pronounced it done just as the first showers of the evening rain fell on a tired but jubilant community.

They were all sitting at the evening meal when, over the quiet voice of the chantress, came a high and whining sound. Everyone glanced up, except Darenga, who looked toward Geoffrey and, receiving a nod, got up from the table and went to the main door.

The last glow of the sun reached into the western quadrant of the sky and struck the metal of a group of LS 4s, which was completing a wide exploratory curve. Darenga watched them level out and, finding nothing in the terrain below to keep their attention, take a 30° turn from the abbey and begin a trajectory that would hoist them straight out of the atmosphere.

Darenga returned to the quiet dining room. She looked toward Geoffrey and gave him a discreet nod.

"*Gratias agamus Domino Deo nostro,*" Geoffrey said, and there was a fervent and echoing, "*Deo gratias.*"

Chapter 19

The weather was wetter than usual that spring, and the abbey planting got off to a late start. And it was when the orchards were being trimmed, in preparation for the new growth, that there began an increasing amount of traffic on the main highway that lay about a mile down from the monasteries.

Darenga watched it with growing apprehension. She went back into the abbey and, after a brief search, found Geoffrey in the kitchen.

"Why is there so much traffic on the road?"

He walked out the rear door with her and into the courtyard, where they could see over the walls and down the mountainside to the highway. He stared down at the road, his blue eyes narrowed to the distance. The early thermals that moved the air up the slope from the wide canyon where the highway wound through the shadows lifted and curled the pale ends of his hair, giving his face a delicate, sculptured look. "There may have been flooding along the coast," he finally answered.

"If that were true, wouldn't they simply move to higher ground? Why are they coming so far inland?"

"They have belongings," he observed, not answering her question.

They stood looking down on the steady, light traffic, mostly people on foot carrying bundles, now and then an electric car piled with boxes and baskets. She glanced over at him. "May I have permission to go down there and talk to them?"

He looked up at her and then back down toward the scene below. "There is a group turning off on our road," he said. "Perhaps they can tell us what's happening on the coast."

It took over a half hour for the figures to climb the narrow track to the monasteries, but when they appeared on the bend in the road leading to the gate the word was passed to Geoffrey, and he came down to meet them, a man of unassuming appearance, undistinguishable from the rest of the monks except for a strength and directness in his manner that singled him out. It was recognized by the visitors, as he greeted them and offered the hospitality of the abbey. All this was custom, and Darenga went back into the building to wait until the formalities were over, the gestures of humility and love completed before she quietly joined the group in Geoffrey's quarters.

"I have people in the interior—Renaud—my sister and her husband," a man was saying. "I didn't see any point in waiting until the axe fell to get out of Amper."

"They've been flying over every day, so low and fast every window in my house was broken," a woman added. "Where's the Alliance support? Why are the Secessionists getting away with this? So I got my family out of there now—before the shooting starts."

"We wonder where the Alliance force is," another man continued. "Nobody knows anything. Not even at the Hall, when we stopped there. Lord Andor's aides wouldn't tell us anything, and believe me, I wasn't going to stand around and listen to their excuses, not when the lives of my family are at stake in their game, whatever it is. I don't even think they know what it is."

It was the general feeling of these refugees that they were being abandoned for some nebulous and undefinable greater interest. Darenga listened to their complaints for a while and then left.

Over the next few days the traffic along the road doubled, and the abbey received more visitors, although not the amount Darenga expected.

"They're rushing to the interior," Geoffrey told her when she mentioned it. "They think it will be safe there. Can you feel the evil hanging in the air? That's why they run. Why do you think Lord Andor isn't sending in his force?"

"He may be trying to keep the fighting away from

Ronadjounian ground level." That was not all she thought, but she saw no reason to make him even more uneasy. She sensed that it was the major deception that she had suggested to Seldoldon. That he was gambling on the Arcustans and Arkdikhs becoming overconfident if he drew back from his own planet. She suspected that the Secessionists had laid a cover skirmish that was meant to engage the Alliance forces. And she guessed that Seldoldon had accommodated them. Certainly, if he had listened to the advice of his Lambda captain, that's exactly what he should have done. It was a question now of holding patience.

In the line of refugees, she had watched to see if there were any M'dians. There were many people she recognized as residents of Canigou; apparently the panic had finally reached that town. But she saw no one from the Settlement. She could ask no questions, but she became more concerned as each day passed.

The LS 4s of the Secessionists had flown over the region, high, leaving a circular stream of vapor dissipating in the atmosphere as they made their turns and accelerated northward. All traffic on the road had come to a stop each time they had circled, only to restart again with an increased pace.

That same evening, in a driving rain, three aides from the Hall were admitted into the abbey. They sank, wet and exhausted, to the stone bench near the doors, not even rising when the abbot appeared before them.

"What is wrong?" he asked.

"They have attacked, Father," one said, his face contorting. "The Gemainshaf is in ruins." He dropped his head down and began to sob.

The man next to him put his arm around his shoulder and pulled him against his body.

The third man stared up into Geoffrey's face. "They came in under the rain, straight off the ocean; we didn't even know they were coming."

"How did you get here?" Darenga said from where she

had entered the hallway. All three turned their heads at the sound of Standard Maintainer and slowly came to their feet.

"A smallcraft, Captain Darenga," the senior aide told her. "We landed it about three miles from here and covered it up. Lord Andor had given orders that the abbey was to remain clean."

"Did the attacking craft land?"

"No, they didn't. They just . . . blew us in and left. But there were already reports coming in from Amper. We weren't looking in the right direction when the craft came in."

"They attacked Amper?" Geoffrey asked, dismayed.

"The outskirts. They had attacked the outskirts when the communications went down."

"What was the last report from Lord Andor?" Darenga's gaze was concentrated on the senior aide's face.

"All the Galaxies were grouped inside the Vregan solar system—there had been an earlier attack there. . . ."

Darenga did a swift calculation. The SOL fighters of the Alliance stationed with the Galaxies were approximately ten hours from Ronadjoun. If there had been a plan, they should have been in an intercept position at the beginning of the Secessionists' first run. Now a slow fear began to surface.

She had let Geoffrey continue the questioning, and nodded when he indicated he wished to see the men, staggering already from shock and exhaustion, fed and allowed to rest.

Darenga met him at the door to his room when he returned. Her face was composed, her eyes steady as they met his from inside the brown hood of the jacket she had put on over her abbey clothing. "I must speak with you, Father," she said.

"And I was about to call for you," he answered in his mild voice as he directed her into the room.

She turned and found him looking at her, his hands relaxed in front of him, one over the other, his whole manner calm and decisive.

240

"Under the law, you are in my custody," he told her. "And although you still have part of the sentence remaining, I see no purpose in holding you for that time, not in these dangerous and uncertain days. I have a duty to remind you that if the offense for which you were convicted is repeated, if you are found in association with L'Hlaadin again, you will be imprisoned for fifteen years."

It was the first time he had spoken the name, and it gave the presence that had moved like a shadow between them sudden reality. M'landan's bright image was as close to her now as the time it would take for her to reach the settlement.

"I understand your warning," she replied.

"It is given to you in love," he told her.

"Yes, I know."

"Are you leaving now?"

"There are things I must do."

He looked at her for a long moment before he said, "If you decide to return, you will always be welcome here."

"You've been . . . very kind to me, Father."

"Your life has been more difficult than most," he replied, and then added gently, "God go with you."

She lowered her head briefly, then looked at his pleasant face once more. Silently, she left.

The highway was crowded now, and the people on foot were traveling faster than the few vehicles that were inching along in the press. The rain had stopped, and the clouds were clearing away from the bright stars. The wind blowing inland from the coast was brisk and cold against Darenga's face as she walked quickly along, staying close to the shoulder of the road and out of the main stream of pedestrians.

There was not much conversation being made along the route; the people seemed preoccupied, conserving their energy to maintain the pace that was being set from behind them.

There were many small children, some being pushed in carts along with the baggage of their parents, others being

241

alternately carried by members of the immediate group around them, the small and bewildered burdens being shared in this time of terrible emergency. There were the injured, too, survivors from Amper and the Gemainshaf, but she recognized no one.

"You're heading in the wrong direction, Sister," someone called to her.

She glanced over her shoulder, but the voice had been unfamiliar and the figure lost in the darkness and the crowd. But it brought a fact into perspective. She had kept her silence regarding M'landan for so long that she had forgotten she was no longer held to that restriction.

She surveyed the oncoming crowd that welled toward her out of the darkness until she recognized someone wearing the clothing particular to Canigou. She caught the woman's arm. "Excuse me, but do you know anything about the situation of the M'dians?"

The woman pulled free with an angry distracted look. "What the hell do I care about them!" she answered, and whirled away.

Darenga stared after her.

"I can tell you something about them, Sister."

Darenga swung back to find another woman standing beside her. She was holding a sleeping baby in one arm, and had just set a large case on the ground.

"Her food," she said, with a nervous attempt at laughter that signaled hysteria. "She has to have a special kind; they may be out of it in Trudeau." She looked down at the case. "But it's heavy," she said dully.

"Do you have some news of the M'dians?" Darenga gently prodded.

The woman looked up at her and shifted the baby to her other arm. "The only thing I can tell you, Sister, is that my uncle went up there to warn them to go while they could. But, you see, L'Hlaadin is dying, and they won't leave him."

"Dying?" Even as she repeated the word, it made no sense.

The woman glanced around at the people hurrying past her and leaned over to pick up the case. "Yes. My uncle said they won't leave, none of them, not even all the humans that live there, and there was no way he could persuade them to, as long as L'Hlaadin is still alive. But my uncle thought it wouldn't be very long. L'Hlaadin is pretty bad off, I guess."

She hoisted the baby a little higher on her arm. "I'd better go," she said. The woman smiled fleetingly, then started away, the case striking against her legs.

"Wait!" Darenga called.

The woman stopped abruptly and turned as Darenga came up to her in a swift stride. She waited, as she had been told, staring up at this tall nun who spoke in the old language of the Maintainers, and who was standing now with her eyes closed as if it were difficult for her to speak further. And then the eyes were open, clear and green and fringed with thick, pale lashes that in the indistinct light seemed white.

"You're tired," Darenga told her. "You can't go much farther trying to carry your child and that case. Stop at the abbey. They'll have a place for you and your baby where you'll be safe. Tell the abbot that Areia sent you."

"Sister Areia?"

"Just Areia," she replied, and turned back through the crowd.

Where there was a clear space, she ran, and where there wasn't room for running, she walked in a fast, long stride that was, nevertheless, frequently hampered by the flow against her. But she continued without stopping, hoping to find the highway less-traveled as she drew nearer to Canigou. And then, when the lights of the town were in sight, there came shrieking down out of the darkness an LS 4 that leveled out above the highway, skimming meters above the people, who began running and screaming with terror under the sudden blaze from the landing lights.

In seconds the craft had swept away, and they could see its lights burning along ahead until the curve of the terrain obscured it. Darenga picked herself up from the ditch at the side of the road and helped the person next to her to his feet.

"They didn't shoot at us," he said in a shaky voice.

"Not this time," she answered. "Are you all right?"

"I . . . I think so."

Darenga turned abruptly and began running, again, down the center of the roadway that was cleared of people for these few minutes. But the road through Canigou remained clear, the people still reluctant to come out of cover, and she ran unimpeded past the outskirts and into the forested area beyond. She slowed as a pain struck her side, but she still pushed herself forward, head down, breath coming in noisy gasps as she tried to urge recovery from her body. About a mile past the town she turned off the highway onto the road that led up the long hill to the settlement. Now she slowed to a walk, knowing she couldn't keep up her pace along that distance and stay conscious. And it was then that she heard the LS 4 sweeping back. And she knew that this time they were using laser-stroke.

She hugged the embankment of the road, afraid to look up, afraid in some crazy way that, if she did, the pilot would detect her cowering against the wet slope and return to burn out her life before she could reach the settlement.

When the craft had disappeared, she turned away from what she could hear on the highway below her, and started again at a labored trot up the hill. She expected the LS 4 to return, to renew its assault on the refugees, only the next strike, she knew, would bring more than one. She reached the top of the hill in the panic of this thought, and ran along the upper path toward the cliffs beyond the gardens and the silka trees that showered raindrops and pale blossoms on her as she ran beneath them.

At first she thought it a trick of her pounding heart and rushing blood, that low and terrible tone which slowly rose along an unresolved and infinite scale that was the sound of death itself. A light and the sound came from deep within the structure of the cliffs, and she followed them past the gathering of humans, whose numbers seemed endless, past the lines of M'dians who saw and recognized her, but made no comment. Her legs would not answer to the command to hurry, to outrun what rushed ahead of her down that corridor, but there seemed no connection any more between her brain and the body that contained it. It was a separate and unwilling entity carried forward by an automaton.

It was like moving through deep water, this travel through the M'dian sound of grief. But she reached the doorway and stepped into the light. She came forward to the pallet where he rested, his arms folded into the sleeves of his robe, his bronze hood drawn about his face. Figures drew back as she approached, making way, allowing her to sink down to the pallet. She lay her hand on his arms and looked down into the face that even in age and death still held its serene beauty. And in the instant when her own welling grief would have found its voice, the voices of the M'dians went abruptly still. It was a warning, but she did not want to think about what it meant. She had come to the end of the vision, and she wanted to go no farther than that. She belonged here—here beside this still figure. But even as grief bent her forward, the thought came clearly: *this shell. He is gone.*

From the other side of M'landan's body, a figure rose, and Darenga saw M'landan's face in the hood. A face that was brilliantly lit by a flash of light that bleached the room and was as suddenly extinguished even as her name rang in the darkness: *"Mia'iana."*

It drew her to her feet and away from the grief that had threatened to submerge her. She leaped for the doorway.

"Come forward!" she called out in Songspeech. "Shield your eyes! Don't look back!"

She ran past the oncoming figures toward the entrance. There was another flash of light, and a slow fall of rubble from above. She saw the streaks of light that marked the incoming and pursuing Alliance craft. They came in like avenging angels, wheeling across the sky after the Arcustans and Arkdikhs, hurling their thunderbolts in a cold and determined revenge that Darenga understood. And she knew that Seldoldon, rankled and savage over the delay that had caused so much destruction, now was at the head of the attacking force, a retaliation so unexpected that this wing of the Secessionists faltered in their response and recovered too late.

But she had been too long alive, too long an observer of the peoples of the Alliance, too astute a commander to believe that there would be a decisive victory. It was only a battle. And between battles, there was only relative safety.

She looked around to see Audane, his arms outspread to gather in the few remaining M'dians and humans and send them into the safety of the inner rooms. She helped him, moving them away from the entrance, pushing them back from the bursts of destructive light and sound.

"Are they landing?" He was outwardly calm, speaking to her in Ronadjounian across the cloaked figures that moved between them. But she sensed the urgency in his question.

"No," she answered, looking toward the opening. There were humans at the entrance, men and women, crowding into the corridor. Darenga drew against the cool sandstone to avoid being pressed back into the interior. In the crowd was a large group of men from the Mont Clair abbey, some injured and stumbling, being supported by the others. And at their head, Roenay himself, badly burned across his bare shoulder and arm where the brown cloth had been scorched away.

The pressure of the crowd heaved him forward and directly in front of Darenga. He halted, maintaining his balance with difficulty, but holding her eyes with bitter hatred. His glance shifted; she followed it, and found Audane beside her, recognizing now that it had been he who had drawn her back against the wall. The three stood motionless. And then Roenay was shoved ahead, staggering slightly, regaining his footing, no course for him but straight ahead, yet staring back at them with a wild rage, until he was swept out of sight.

"We must leave immediately," Audane said.

She looked up into his face, a young face reminiscent of the father, but unique in itself.

"I'll go."

"Mia'iana." His voice stopped her as she swung away, the notes vibrating. "The danger is to us both."

246

"Yes. You're right. Tell them you're leaving. Audane—"

He turned to look at her. "Why are you afraid? Didn't my father prepare us both for this?"

She brought her hands together, less a gesture of supplication than control. "*Your* fear isn't hidden from me. Go on, tell them. Audane—let them know you'll come back . . . when it's time."

She watched him walk away, graceful, swift, shimmering down the darkness of the corridor. *His father's grace,* she thought.

From outside came a different sound, now. She went over to the entrance and looked up, seeing only a great blur in the sky. A trick of her eyes and her disbelief, for the blur became a lowering shape filling half the sky, a great ringed ship descending, visible for miles. She watched in amazement. The rings were fire, the outer particles burning off in the slow friction of the atmosphere, the kilometers-long flagella whipping in silver arcs as the Galaxy continued its slow, fantastic descent. Seldoldon's dangerous symbol of victory. In all her experience, she had never heard of this being done, an orbital ship brought deep into the atmosphere. A gamble of desperate necessity—and a Lambda at the controls. Was it Gail? She felt a sense of deep, unquenchable pride as she watched the giant ship hold its position, glowing, trailing streamers of fire to the ground far below, only an instant tethered, its Alliance insignia brilliantly visible. Then, slowly at first and then faster, it began to rise away until it disappeared, a bright star behind the mountains.

Daring, dangerous, the symbol to draw the spirit of the Ronadjounian people together for the reconstruction. For this moment. And in this moment of fire and glory for Seldoldon and his bright dream, she and Audane would make their escape, for the true peace was to come from another direction. And it would not come with fire and symbolism, but would arrive unobtrusively and would endure.

"I am ready, Mia'iana. Where will we go?"

"I don't know, Audane." She pulled her hood around her face. "Wherever we are led."

His hands reached out to hold her face up to his. Delicately, his tongue coiled down and briefly touched her eyelids. "Then let us begin our journey," he sang. He lowered his hands into his sleeves and, moving past her, started down the path that opened through the fields.

THE FALL OF WORLDS TRILOGY
BY FRANCINE MEZO

The FALL OF WORLDS trilogy follows the daring galactic adventures of Captain Areia Darenga, a beautiful starship commander bred for limitless courage as a clone, but destined to discover love as a human.

THE FALL OF WORLDS   75564 $2.50

Captain Areia Darenga is brave, beautiful, intelligent and without passion. She is no ordinary human but part of a special race bred for a higher purpose—to protect the universe from those who would destroy it. For without the blinding shackles of human emotions, Areia can guard her world without earthly temptations. But when she leads a battle against a foe, Areia finds her invisible control shattered—her shocking transformation can only lead to one thing—love.

UNLESS SHE BURN   76968 $2.25

A tragic battle in space has transformed Captain Areia Darenga into a human and leads her to a death she would have never known. Exiled to the hostile planet of M'dia she lives in the desolate reaches of a desert, struggling for a bleak survival. But then she is rescued by M'landan, a handsome alien priest who awakens in her a disturbing passion and mystical visions of a new and tempting world.

NO EARTHLY SHORE   77347 $2.50
(Coming in March 1981)

Captain Areia Darenga has found life-giving passions in the arms of M'landan, high priest for the M'dia people. Forced from their planet, M'landan and his people are threatened by an alien race who seek their total destruction. As they are mercilessly tracked across the universe by their enemies, Captain Areia, M'landan and his people search for a world where the race may be reborn.

Available wherever paperbacks are sold, or directly from the publisher. Include 50¢ per copy for postage and handling: allow 4-6 weeks for delivery. Avon Books, Mail Order Dept., 224 West 57th St., N.Y., N.Y. 10019

AVON Paperback   2812-4-A
5-20
C

Mezo 1-81